Text Book Of

ORGANISATIONAL BEHAVIOUR

For

BBA Semester - II

As Per the New Syllabus

Sunil Lalla
B.A., M.B.A., M.M.M.,
D.P.L. (Diploma in Taxation Laws)

Dr Praveen Prasad
M.Com., Ph.D. and
D.H.E. (Diploma in Higher Education)

Neha Shukla
MBA
ISB&M College of Commerce, Pune

NIRALI PRAKASHAN™
ADVANCEMENT OF KNOWLEDGE

N3753

Organisational Behaviour   ISBN 978-93-5164-978-6

First Edition : January 2016

© : Authors

Published By :

NIRALI PRAKASHAN

Abhyudaya Pragati, 1312, Shivaji Nagar,
Off J.M. Road, PUNE – 411005
Tel - (020) 25512336/37/39, Fax - (020) 25511379
Email : niralipune@pragationline.com

☞ DISTRIBUTION CENTRES

PUNE

Nirali Prakashan : 119, Budhwar Peth, Jogeshwari Mandir Lane, Pune 411002, Maharashtra
Tel : (020) 2445 2044, 66022708, Fax : (020) 2445 1538
Email : bookorder@pragationline.com, niralilocal@pragationline.com

Nirali Prakashan : S. No. 28/27, Dhyari, Near Pari Company, Pune 411041
Tel : (020) 24690204 Fax : (020) 24690316
Email : dhyari@pragationline.com, bookorder@pragationline.com

MUMBAI

Nirali Prakashan : 385, S.V.P. Road, Rasdhara Co-op. Hsg. Society Ltd.,
Girgaum, Mumbai 400004, Maharashtra
Tel : (022) 2385 6339 / 2386 9976, Fax : (022) 2386 9976
Email : niralimumbai@pragationline.com

☞ DISTRIBUTION BRANCHES

JALGAON

Nirali Prakashan : 34, V. V. Golani Market, Navi Peth, Jalgaon 425001,
Maharashtra, Tel : (0257) 222 0395, Mob : 94234 91860

KOLHAPUR

Nirali Prakashan : New Mahadvar Road, Kedar Plaza, 1st Floor Opp. IDBI Bank
Kolhapur 416 012, Maharashtra. Mob : 9850046155

NAGPUR

Pratibha Book Distributors : Above Maratha Mandir, Shop No. 3, First Floor,
Rani Jhanshi Square, Sitabuldi, Nagpur 440012, Maharashtra
Tel : (0712) 254 7129

DELHI

Nirali Prakashan : 4593/21, Basement, Aggarwal Lane 15, Ansari Road, Daryaganj
Near Times of India Building, New Delhi 110002
Mob : 08505972553

BENGALURU

Pragati Book House : House No. 1, Sanjeevappa Lane, Avenue Road Cross,
Opp. Rice Church, Bengaluru – 560002.
Tel : (080) 64513344, 64513355,Mob : 9880582331, 9845021552
Email:bharatsavla@yahoo.com

CHENNAI

Pragati Books : 9/1, Montieth Road, Behind Taas Mahal, Egmore,
Chennai 600008 Tamil Nadu, Tel : (044) 6518 3535,
Mob : 94440 01782 / 98450 21552 / 98805 82331,
Email : bharatsavla@yahoo.com

niralipune@pragationline.com | www.pragationline.com

Also find us on www.facebook.com/niralibooks

Preface ...

People are the most integral part of an organisation. Success and failure of any organisation depends not only on the way the organisation functions or the technology used, but how effective an organisation is in attracting, developing, training, retaining, motivating its employees in an ethical manner.

It's the human factor which leads to the functioning of the entire organisation, be it process, technology, coping up with upcoming challenges and so on. Organisational behaviour is concerned with the nature and behaviour of people within the organisation.

The book is aimed at informing students about the importance of understanding people's behaviour in the organisation in order to achieve growth, success and also to inculcate changes arising due to the internal and external environmental factors of the organisation.

Care has been taken to keep the language simple and adhere to the syllabus designed. The latest facts and simple diagrams that have been presented in the book shall certainly make learning easy for the students.

All the topics have been arranged to maintain a logical flow and have been duly numbered.

We are grateful to all the authors whose books have been referred to make this book comprehensive.

We would take this opportunity to show our gratitude to our publishers Shri. Dineshbhai Furia and Shri. Jignesh Furia for the confidence reposed in me and for giving us this opportunity to reach out to the students of management studies.

We are grateful to those who have been supportive in our effort by providing us with valuable inputs and inspiration.

We would also like to acknowledge the contributions of Mrs. Supriya Singh, Mr. Malik Shaikh, Mr. Nirmal Kumar and Mrs. Anjali Muley and the entire team of Nirali Prakashan for their valuable and much needed contribution to the publishing of the book.

We would welcome feedback and suggestions for the improvement and development of the content. While efforts have been made to make the book expansive, any suggestions or views to improve this book would be most welcomed.

Any suggestions or comments towards the enhancement of the content of this book are most welcome at niralipune@pragationline.com.

Authors

Syllabus ...

(1) Introduction
- (a) Definition of O.B,
- (b) Key elements of O.B.
- (c) Nature and Scope of O.B.
- (d) Disciplines contributing to O.B.

(2) Individual Perspective
- (a) Personality: Concept, Determinants and Types, How Personality influences O.B
- (b) Attitudes: Types, Components and Functions, Attitudes and O.B.
- (c) Concept of Job Satisfaction
- (d) Perception: Definition, Basic Elements, Factors Influencing Perception, Attribution.
- (e) Learning: Meaning and determinants.

(3) Interpersonal Relationship
- (a) Developing interpersonal relations
- (b) Conflict: Meaning, Sources, Types.
- (c) Intrapersonal Conflict: Role Identity, Role Perception, Role Expectation, Role Conflict.
- (d) Interpersonal Conflict (Transactional Analysis and Johari Window)
- (e) Aspects of Conflict (Functional and Dysfunctional)
- (f) Conflict Management

(4) Group Dynamics
- (a) Groups in Organization, Nature, Membership, Process of Group Development, Types of Groups, Group structure
- (b) Group Norms, Group Conformity, Group Cohesion, Group Size, Group Think, Group Shift.
- (c) Group dynamics and Inter-group dynamics

(5) Motivation and Leadership
- (a) Meaning
- (b) Types of Motives
- (c) Theories of Motivation
  - (5.c.i)   Hierarchy of needs Theory
  - (5.c.ii) Theory X and Theory Y
  - (5.c.iii) Motivation-Hygiene Two Factor theory
  - (5.c.iv) Goal Setting Theory
- (d) Motivation applied - Financial and non-Financial motivators
- (e) Meaning, Functions, Styles, Traits of Leadership
- (f) Fielders Leadership Contingency theory
- (g) Path Goal Theory
- (h) Charismatic Leadership Theory
- (i) Ohio State Leadership Quadrants and Management Grids

(6) Change management and Development
- (a) Why organisation changes? Planned change, Resistance to change, Managing resistance to change
- (b) Meaning of Organisation development, Characteristics, Objectives
- (c) Work Stress: Meaning of stress, Nature and sources of stress, consequences of stress, coping strategies for the stress, stress and task performance

***

Contents ...

***

Chapter **1**...

Introduction

Contents ...

Learning Objectives ...

- ➢ To understand the meaning and definition of organisational behaviour
- ➢ To know the key elements of organisational behaviour
- ➢ To study the importance of organisational behaviour
- ➢ To understand the nature and scope of organisational behaviour
- ➢ To study the organisational behaviour models
- ➢ To know the evolution of organisational behaviour
- ➢ To understand the framework of organisational behaviour
- ➢ To study the various disciplines contributing to organisational behaviour

1.1 Organisational Behaviour

1.1.1 Meaning and Definitions of Organisational Behaviour

Organisational behaviour is a field of study that analyses the impact that individuals, groups and structures have on behaviour within organisations, so that such knowledge can be used for improving the organisation's effectiveness.

People often come together to form groups as human nature is gregarious. These groups are formed by people to collectively perform activities of common interest. Organisational behaviour (OB) is the area of study which focuses on human beings and their interaction with other groups and individuals within the organisation. It deals with the study of how people interact within groups, the attitudes of people and groups towards each other and towards the organisation as a whole and its effect on the organisation's functioning and performance. Normally this study is applied to create more efficient business organisations. The central idea of the study of organisational behaviour is to provide a scientific approach to the management of workers.

Organisational behaviour is the multidisciplinary field that seeks knowledge of behaviour in organisational settings by systematically studying individual, group and organisational processes. This knowledge is used both by scientists interested in understanding human behaviour and managers interested in enhancing individual well- being.

Definitions of Organisational Behaviour

1.   **Fred Luthans:** *"Organisational behaviour is directly concerned with the understanding, predicting and controlling of human behaviour in organisations."*

2.   **Stephen Robbins:** *"Organisational behaviour is a systematic study of the actions and attitudes that people exhibit within organisations."*

3.   **L. M. Prasad:** *"The study and application of knowledge about human behaviour related to other elements of an organisation such as structure, technology and social systems."*

1.1.2 Key Elements of Organisational Behaviour

In organisational behaviour, the key elements are people, structure, technology and the external elements under which the organisation operates. When people come together in an organisation, in order to accomplish an objective, some basic kind of infrastructure is needed. People also make use of technology in order to get the job done, so that there is a mutual interaction of structure, people and technology. Moreover, these elements are influenced by the external environment and thus they influence it.

We will consider each of the four elements of organisational behaviour in brief, as below:

1.   **People**

People are considered as the internal social system of the organisation. These people consist of individuals and groups, and small groups as well as the large ones. They exist in order to achieve their objectives and organisations exist to serve people. Thus, people do not exist to serve the organisation.

Work force is considered as one of the critical resources that need proper management. In managing human resources, managers have to deal with the following concerns:

(i) Individual employee who are expected to perform the tasks allotted to them.

(ii) Dyadic relationships such as superior-subordinate interactions.

(iii) Groups who work as teams and have the responsibility for getting the job done.

(iv) People outside the organisation system such as customers and government officials.

2. Structure

Structure helps in defining the official relationships of people in an organisation. Various jobs are needed in order to accomplish the entire organisational activities. An organisation works smoothly with the services rendered by employees, managers, accountants and assemblers. All these people are required to work in a structural way so that their work can be highly effective. Power and duties are the main structures. For example, one person has the power and authority to make decisions that affects the work of other people.

Following are the key concepts of an organisation structure:

(a) **Hierarchy of Authority:** This explains the distribution of authority amongst various organisational positions and this authority grants certain rights to the position holder which also includes the rights to give direction to others as well as the right to punish and reward.

(b) **Division of Labour:** This explains the distribution of various responsibilities and the method in which these activities are divided up and assigned to all the members of the organisation, thus considering it to be an element of the social structure.

(c) **Span of Control:** This explains the manager's span of authority over the total number of subordinates.

(d) **Specialisation:** This explains the count of specialities being performed within an organisation.

(e) **Standardisation:** This explains the existence of various procedures for monitoring the regularly recurring activities or events.

(f) **Formalisation:** This explains the extent to which the procedures, rules and communications are written down.

(g) **Centralisation:** This explains the concentration of authority in order to make decisions.

(h) **Complexity:** This area refers to both, the horizontal differentiation as well as the vertical differentiation. Horizontal differentiation highlights the number of units within the organisation and vertical differentiation highlights the number of hierarchical levels of the organisation.

We can structure the organisation either as relatively rigid, formalised systems or as relatively loose, flexible systems. Thus, the organisational structure can vary on a continuum of high rigidity to high flexibility.

3.   Technology

Organisations have various technologies for transforming the inputs and outputs. These technologies consists of activities, process, physical objects and knowledge, all of which are boiled down together to bear on labour, raw materials and capital inputs during a transformation process. The core technology is that set of productive components which are most directly associated with the transformation process, for example, assembly line or production in a manufacturing firm.

Technology helps in providing the economic and physical resources with which the people work. They won't be able to accomplish much with their bare hands, thus they make buildings and design machines in order to assemble resources and work processes. The outcome of this technology makes a significant influence on working relationships. A steel mill does not have the same working conditions like that of a hospital and an assembly line is not the same like that of a research laboratory. The biggest advantage of technology is that it allows people to do better and more work; however, it also restricts people in many ways. It comes with its own benefits and costs.

Classification of Technology:

Thomson classified technology into three categories: Long-linked technology, Mediating Technology and Intensive Technology.

(i)   **Long-linked Technology:** In this type of technology, tasks are divided and sub-divided into a number of interdependent and sequential steps, wherein the outputs of one unit becomes the inputs of the next unit, for example assembly line. This helps in facilitating high volume of efficiency and output. This type of technology requires mechanic structures with high levels of standardisation, specialisation and formalisation.

(ii) **Mediating Technology:** This technology creates a link between various parties that are supposed to be brought together in a direct or indirect way, for example, banks making use of mediating technology in order to lend money to borrowers by taking money from depositors.

(iii) **Intensive Technology:** This type of technology is used to bring a group of specialists together in order to solve complex problems by using a variety of technologies, for example, hospital where patients are treated with the help of experts brought together from different fields of specialisation. In this system, co-ordination of different activities is achieved through mutual adjustment amongst those specialists engaged in solving the problem in different units. Thus, organic structures would fit in this system by making use of intensive technology.

4. Environment

All organisations operate within a set of external environment. A single organisation cannot exist alone on its own. It forms a part of the larger system that contains several other elements. All these elements mutually influence each other in a complex manner that thus becomes the life style of the people.

Individual organisation like school or factory cannot escape from being influenced by this external environment.

It affects the working conditions, influences the attitudes of people and provides competition for power and resources. Every organisation interacts with the other members of its environment.

This interaction allows the organisation to hire employees, acquire raw materials, obtain knowledge, secure the capital, and lease, build or buy equipments and facilities. Since the organisation provides a service or product for consumption by the environment, it also interacts with its customers. Other environmental actions that regulates or over sees these exchanges, interacts with the organisation as well, for example, advertising agencies, distributors, trade associations and government of the counties in which the business is conducted.

Two Distinct Sets of Environment:

(i) **Specific Environment:** This consists of the customers, suppliers, government's agencies, competitors, unions, employees, political parties, etc.

(ii) **General Environment:** This consists of the political, economical, cultural, social and technological factors within which the organisation embeds.

Organisation is embedded in an environment within which it operates. Some of the external factors like social, cultural, economical or governmental aspects may be completely out of the organisational control to change them. However, various other factors like stocking up and buffering supplies during high demands, being in tune with the technological changes taking place, sizing up the market or being a step ahead of the competition are all very well within the organisational control. In order to manage these situations effectively, it requires adaptability to changes, close and constant vigilance, and also being able to manage problematical situations through good decisions making. Organisations that are proactive (which means watchful and takes actions before the crisis occur) and can manage their external environment have proved to be more effective as compared to those that are reactive (which means, caught off guard and wakeup after the crises occur) and are not able to cope up effectively.

Fit between Environment and Structure:

Firms facing a turbulent or a fast changing external environment were proved to be highly effective when they had more organic structures which helps in providing flexibility for quick changes to be made within the internal environment of the organisation. Likewise, firms that operate in a relatively stable external environment were proved to be highly effective when they had more of mechanistic structures. This mechanistic structure thus allows the system to operate in a predictable manner since responsibility, authority; rules and procedures were clearly specified.

1.1.3 Nature of Organisational Behaviour

1. Organisational behaviour is multidisciplinary in nature

The field is multidisciplinary in nature. It draws heavily from a variety of social science disciplines.

The study of organisational behaviour considers the orientation of psychology to understand the human mind, that is, behaviour and sociology, to understand the role of an individual in an organisation, as a member of the organisation group, its diversity of ideas, culture, food, language, its ideas, and values.

2. Organisational behaviour attempts to improve organisational effectiveness and the quality of life at work

In earlier times, the people as employees in companies were assumed and considered to be lazy who disliked work, and if given the choice would not like to work. Such a theory was propounded by a researcher called McGregor and this theory was called Theory X.

Today if you ask officials, they are very optimistic of the people in an organisation as employees and believe that if they are given the right opportunities and are adequately trained, then people as employees love to work and enjoy the challenges that work provides.

The approach that assumes that people are not inherently lazy is called Theory Y, and it assumes that people have a psychological need to be recognised and enjoy a high self-esteem by seeking to achieve good performances and so, enjoy a higher social status in society. The Theory Y perspective prevails within the field of organisational behaviour today.

3. Organisational behaviour recognises the dynamic nature of organisations

Organisational behaviour scientists recognise that organisations are not static, but dynamic and ever changing. They recognise that organisations are open systems, that is, self sustaining systems that are constantly in the process of processing input into output.

For example, as a human resources function, organisations take skilled manpower from society, train them and make them capable of creating products and services that the organisation specialises in. These are further sold back in the society and community. When people buy these products or services, in turn organisational employees make more and the cycle continues.

4. Organisational behaviour assumes that there is no one best approach

What is the best leadership style to be adopted? What motivates people to bring out the best in them? Should important decisions be made by groups or individuals? There is no one best answer for all these points.

This means that organisational behaviour uses a contingency approach; an orientation that recognises that behaviour in work settings is the complex result of many interacting factors.

1.1.4 Scope of Organisational Behaviour

Organisational behaviour is a field of study that investigates the impact that individuals, groups and structures have on behaviour within an organisation for the purpose of applying such knowledge towards improving an organisation's effectiveness.

It is an interdisciplinary field that includes sociology, psychology, communication, and management; and it complements the academic studies of organisational theory (which is focused on organisational and intra-organisational topics) and human resource studies (which are more applied and business-oriented). It may also be referred to as organisational studies or organisational science. The field has its roots in industrial and organisational psychology.

Organisational studies encompass the study of organisations from multiple viewpoints, methods, and levels of analysis. For instance, one textbook divides these multiple viewpoints into three perspectives: modern, symbolic, and postmodern.

Organisational behaviour helps to understand different activities and actions of people in the organisation. It also helps to motivate them. People, environment, technology and structure are the main four elements of organisational behaviour.

The study of organisational behaviour is useful in understanding and influencing human behaviour for better achievement of organisational goals. Individual performance forms the foundation of organisational performance. It is critical for effective managers to understand individual behaviour. Let us look at the scope of organisational behaviour.

1. **Individual Behavioural Processes:** Organisational behaviour provides the knowledge base for understanding behaviour within the organisation. It incorporates techniques from various disciplines and equips the students with tools to effectively manage individuals and groups/teams within organisations and have a better understanding of organisational culture. The many areas where organisational behaviour is applied are individual characteristics, perception and attitude, emotions, personality, values and performance. By gathering a deeper understanding of relationships between performance, managers can develop or draw a clear approach towards working with their subordinates and becoming effective themselves.

2. **Individual Motivation:** The theories of motivation, attempt to explain and predict how desirable individual behaviour can be aroused and sustained and how undesirable behaviour can be stopped. The performance of employees is determined by the interaction of their motivation and their ability to work, and managers must understand these aspects.

3. **Rewards:** The organisation's reward system has a profound influence on the individual's performance. Rewards can be used effectively by managers to increase

performance and can also be used to attract skilled employees to join the organisation. Employees can get especially motivated, if their work performance leads to a sense of personal responsibility, a feeling of autonomy and meaningfulness towards contributing to the organisation's goals.

4. **Stress and Conflict Management:** An important result of the interaction between the job and the individual is the stress that an individual undergoes. Stress is a state of imbalance within an individual that often manifests itself in symptoms such as hypertension, excessive perspiration, nervousness and irritability. Depending upon the tolerance level of individuals, stress may be perceived as either positive or negative. Some respond positively through increased motivation and commitment and finish the job, while others may turn to alcohol or drug abuse. Organisations are funding and implementing wellness programmes for their employees so as to reduce the negative effects of stress.

5. **Behaviour of Individuals in Groups and Teams:** Group behaviour and expectations have a strong impact on individual's behaviour and interpersonal influence. Groups are formed either by the management to carry out the assigned tasks (formal groups), or they are formed as a result of common interests and friendship (informal groups). Depending on the intention of the group members, the effect of the group can be either positive or negative. Managers understand the influence of the groups and the resulting cohesiveness, roles, norms and processes that develop within and between groups. Sometimes, competition between groups may lead to benefits of the organisation and sometimes it may lead to intergroup conflicts.

6. **Power and Politics:** Managers derive power from organisational and individual sources. Power is the ability to get someone to do something that one wants to be done or to make things happen in the way one wants them to happen. Formal power, as a result of the organisational hierarchy, translates into performance evaluation and salary increase recommendations. The respect and admiration that a manager draws from others is a result of the power exercised due to expertise and abilities.

7. **Organisational Processes:** Some processes of organisations like communication, decision-making and leadership are covered within the scope of organisational behaviour. Let us now discuss these processes.

8. **Communication:** The process of communication links people within the organisation and integrates the activities of the organisation with the demands of the environment as also the internal activities.

9. **Decision-making Process:** Organisations rely on individual decisions as well as on decisions taken by groups of people. The decisions made will be effective if proper goals and the means of achieving them are identified. Managers exercise power while taking decisions about the welfare of employees, designing and implementing rules and policies and distributing organisational resources.

10. **Leadership Processes:** Leadership qualities for individual, group and organisational performance can be made more effective by focusing on traits and behaviours for achieving the desired results.

1.1.5 Need of Organisational Behaviour

The main reason for studying organisational behaviour is that most of us work in organisations so we need to understand, predict and influence the behaviour of others in an organisational setting. All of us need organisational behaviour knowledge to address the peoples issue when trying to apply other ideas.

The study of organisational behaviour is needed for the following:

1. Helps to improve skills (ability of employees and use of knowledge to become more efficient).

2. It is also an important part to improve marketing process by understanding consumer (buying) behaviour.

3. It helps to understand basis of motivation and different ways to motivate employees properly.

4. Understanding of personnel/employee nature is important to manage them properly and to understand the framework.

5. The scientific study of behaviour helps to understand and predict organisational events.

6. Helps to increase efficiency and effectiveness of organisation.

7. It helps to create healthy, ethical and smooth environment in organisation.

8. Improves managers as well as employees work skills.

Ultimately, organisational behaviour helps to increase efficiency and productivity, that is, the profit of the organisation.

1.1.6 Importance of Organisational Behaviour

1. **Controlling and Directing Behaviour:** After knowing about the mechanism of human behaviour, managers are needed to control and direct the behaviour so that it complies with the standards needed for attaining the organisational goals. Thus, managers are needed to control and direct the behaviour at all levels of individual communication. Therefore, organisational behaviour helps the managers to control and direct in different areas such as use of power and sanction, leadership, communication and building an organisational climate favourable for better communication.

2. **Use of Power and Sanction:** The behaviours can be controlled and directed by the use of power and sanction, which is officially defined by the organisation. Power can be defined as the capacity of an individual to take specific actions and maybe utilise them in many ways. Organisational behaviour explains how different means of power and sanction can be used so that both organisational and individual goals are attained at the same time.

3. **Leadership:** Organisational behaviour brings new insights and understanding to the practice and theory of leadership. It recognises different leadership styles that are available to a manager and considers which style is more suitable in a given situation. Therefore, managers can take up styles keeping in view the different sizes of organisations, people and situations.

4. **Communication:** Communication helps people in keeping contact with each other. To attain organisational goals, the communication must be efficient. The communication process and its work in inter-personal dynamics have been assessed by organisational behaviour.

5. **Organisational Climate:** Organisational climate refers to the total organisational situations that have an effect on the human behaviour. Organisational climate takes a system point of view that have an effect on human behaviour. Besides improving the satisfactory working conditions and sufficient compensation, organisational climate comprises creation of an atmosphere of effective management; the chance to realise personal goals, congenial associations with others at the work place and a sense of achievement.

6. **Organisational Adaptation:** Organisations, as dynamic entities are characterised by pervasive changes. Hence, organisations have to accept the environmental changes by making appropriate internal plans such as persuading employees who generally tend to resist any changes.

1.1.7 Limitations of Organisational Behaviour

Some of the limitations of organisational behaviour are:

1. Organisational behaviour cannot remove conflict and frustration but can decrease them. It is a way to progress but not an answer to the problems.

2. It is only one of the several systems that operate within a big social system.

3. People who have less knowledge about things may develop a 'behavioural basis', which gives them a narrow perspective, that is, a tunnel vision that stresses on satisfying employee experiences while ignoring the broader system of an organisation related to all its public.

4. The law of diminishing returns also works in the case of organisational behaviour. It defines that at some point, increase of a desirable practice begins to generate declining returns and at times, negative returns.

5. The idea means that for any situation there is an optimum amount of a desirable practice. When that point is exceeded, the returns are rejected. For example, too much security may cause a less employee initiative and expansion. This connection shows that organisational effectiveness is attained not by maximising one human variable but by operating all the system variables together in a balanced way.

6. A major concern about organisational behaviour is that its information and methods could be used to influence people without regard for human welfare. People who do not have ethical values could use people in unethical ways.

Although organisational behaviour does have limitations, these limitations should not blind us to the tremendous potential that organisational behaviour can contribute to the advancement of civilisation. It has provided and will provide much improvement in the human environment.

By building a better climate for people, organisational behaviour will release their creative potential to help solve major social problems. In this way, organisational behaviour may contribute to social improvements that stretch far beyond the confines of any one organisation. A better climate may help some person to achieve a major breakthrough in solar energy, health, or education.

Improved organisational behaviour is not simple to apply. But the chances are there. It must generate a higher quality of life in which there is improved harmony within each individual, among people, and among the organisations of the future.

1.1.8 Evolution of Organisational Behaviour

In the early days, people worked from dawn until dusk under intolerable conditions of disease, filth, danger and scarcity of resources.

During the period of Industrial Revolution (1800) **Robert Owen**, a young factory owner first emphasised the human needs of employees. He refused to employ young children. He taught his workers cleanliness, and improved their working conditions. He was called 'The Heal Father' of personnel administration.

Andrew Ure published his work "The Philosophy of Manufactures" in 1935. In this work he recognised the value of the human factor in manufacturing. He facilitated the provision of tea, medical treatment, sickness payments and ventilation to workers.

Fredrick W. Taylor is called the father of scientific management. His work led to improved recognition and productivity for industrial workers.

In 1914 **William Gilbreth** published his work "The Psychology of Management" which gave emphasis to the human side of work.

In the 1920s and 1930s, **Mayo** studied human behaviour at work at Harvard University. The study was conducted at the Western Electric Company, Hawthorne Plant. This study showed that the worker is not a simple tool but a complex personality interacting in a group situation. Mayo is recognised as the father of 'human relations.'

In the 1940s and 1950s, major research projects were developed in the University of Michigan, and Ohio State University. An age of human relations had begun. In 1957 **Douglas McGregor** presented Theory X and Theory Y, in which alternative assumptions about employees were formulated. According to these theories, management's personnel practices, decision-making, operating practices, and even the organisational design flow form assumptions about human behaviour.

Theory X assumes that most people dislike work and will try to avoid work, so that the management is forced to coerce, control and threaten employees to obtain satisfactory performance. Theory Y assumes that employees will exercise self-direction and self-control if the management provides an appropriate environment. Thus, historical background supports that organisational behaviour is a maturing field, and has a bright future.

1.1.9 Organisational Behaviour Models

There are different models of organisational behaviour. Some of them are in practice while others have become outdated. Within an organisation, there may be more than one model being practiced by different departments. Different managers may adopt different models according to their personal preferences.

The various organisational behaviour models are discussed below in detail:

1. **The Autocratic Model:** This model lays emphasis on power. It believes that the persons in commanding position must have the power to demand from their subordinates and an employee who does not follow orders will be penalised. The autocratic management believes that in order to get the desired output, employees must be directed, persuaded and pushed into performance. Thus, the management's approach is authoritative, formal and official. Employees are submissive to their managers, but out of apprehension rather than respect. This affects employees' morale adversely as they are over-dependent on their managers and have a feeling of discontent and insecurity towards management.

2. **The Custodial Model:** This model lays emphasis on money rather than power and leads to employees' over-dependence on an organisation. The custodial management tries to satisfy the security needs of employees and use it as a motivating force. It provides its employees with several economic rewards and benefits which make them well-maintained and satisfied. However, organisations not having sufficient wealth to provide pensions and other benefits cannot follow a custodial approach. The disadvantage of this approach is that it makes the employees over-contented and results in poor performance and low levels of motivation and co-operation.

3. **The Supportive Model:** Unlike the previous two models, this model lays emphasis on leadership rather than power or money. Supportive management tries to create an environment that encourages employees to grow and accomplish what they are capable of. Management's approach is to support the employee's job performance rather than to simply support employee benefit payments. It believes that workers are not passive or resistant to work by nature and they will come forward to take responsibility and contribute, if management provides them a chance.

   This model brings in a feeling of belongingness and participation among the employees towards the organisation. Thus, this model is beneficial as compared to autocratic and custodial models since employees are more strongly motivated as their status and recognition needs are met in a better manner.

4. **The Collegial Model:** The term "collegial" refers to people working together as a group. This model is an extension of the supportive mode and lays emphasis on creating a sense of partnership with employees. Managers are seen as joint contributors rather than as bosses.

The management's approach is supporting teamwork and being the employees' coach. As a result employees get the sense of self-discipline, responsibility and obligation to uphold quality standards that will bring credit to their jobs and company. Another advantage of this approach is that in this kind of environment employees normally feel some degree of fulfilment, worthwhile contribution, and self-actualisation, even though the employee benefits may be modest. Employees feel that managers are also contributing towards their success; they are easily accepted and respected by them.

5. **The System Model:** This model lays emphasis on building a relationship with employees based on trust. Management's approach is to demonstrate a sense of care and being sensitive to the needs of a diverse workforce with rapidly changing needs and complex personal and family needs. As a result, employees get self-motivated and perform better as they are committed to organisational goals. Thus, employees develop a feeling of ownership for the organisation and its product and services.

The following table summarises these five models.

Table 1.1: Models of Organisational Behaviour

	Autocratic	Custodial	Supportive	Collegial	System
Basis of Model	Power	Economic resources	Leadership	Partnership	Trust, community meaning
	Authority	Money	Support	Teamwork	Caring compassion
	Obedience	Security and benefit	Job performance	Responsible behaviour	Psychological ownership
	Dependence on the boss	Dependence on the organisation	Participation	Self-discipline	Self-motivation
	Subsistence	Security	Status and recognition	Self-actualisation	Wide range
	Minimum	Basic co-operation	Awakened drive	Moderate co-operation	Commitment to organisational rules

1.1.10 Framework for Organisational Behaviour

Organisational behaviour is the study and application of knowledge about how people as individuals and as groups act within organisations. It can be defined as the understanding, prediction and management of human behaviour in organisations. Organisational behaviour is related to other disciplines like organisation theory, organisation development and personnel/human resources management.

Managers need certain skills and competencies to successfully achieve their goals. The most significant management skills are the technical, human and conceptual skills.

People develop generalisations by observing, sensing, asking and listening to various people around them. They use these generalisations to explain or predict the behaviour of others.

A systematic approach to the study of behaviour will bring to light important facts and relationships that provide the basis for more accurate understanding, prediction and control of behaviour.

It is important to know how a person perceives a situation to predict his behaviour. There are differences as well as consistencies that can be seen in people's behaviour.

An overall model of organisational behaviour can be developed on the basis of three theoretical frameworks. They are:

- Cognitive
- Behaviouristic, and
- Social learning

1. The Cognitive Framework

The cognitive approach gives more credit to people than the other approaches and is based on the expectancy, demand and incentive concepts.

Cognitive Theories

- **Expectancy Theory**

  It describes internal processes of choice among different behaviours.

- **Equity Theory**

  It describes how and why people react when they feel unfairly treated.

- **Goal-setting Theory**

  It focuses on how to set goals for people to reach.

2. The Behaviouristic Framework

A group, made up of different people and several relationships among those people are even more difficult. In the fact of this engulfing complexity, organisational behaviour must be dealt with.

In the end, the work of organisations gets completed through the behaviour of people, by oneself or collectively, on their own or in partnership with technology. Thus, central to the management task is the management of organisational behaviour.

"To do this, there must be the capacity to *understand* the patterns of behaviour at individual, group, and organisation levels, to *predict* what behaviour responses will be elicited by different managerial actions, and finally to use this understanding and prediction to achieve *control*".

Organisational behaviour scientists study four primary areas of behavioural science:

- Individual behaviour
- Group behaviour
- Organisational structure, and
- Organisational processes

They examine many aspects of these areas like personality and awareness, attitudes and job satisfaction, group dynamics, politics and the role of leadership in the organisation, job design, the impact of stress on work, decision-making processes, the communications chain, and company cultures and climates.

They use various methods and approaches to assess each of these elements and its effect on the people, groups, and organisational effectiveness.

In their work, *Organisations: Behaviour, Structure, Processes,* **Gibson**, **Ivancevich**, and **Donnelly** stated, "The behaviour sciences have provided the basic framework and principles for the field of organisation behaviour."

Each behavioural science discipline provides a slightly different focus, analytical framework, and a theme for helping managers, answer questions about themselves, non-managers, and environmental forces."

Regarding individuals and groups, researchers try to decide why people behave the way they do. They have developed various models that are designed to describe the individuals' behaviour. They examine the factors that influence personality development, including genetic, situational, environmental, cultural, and social factors.

Researchers also inspect different types of personality and their effect on business and other establishments. One of the main tools used by organisational behaviour researchers in these and other parts of study is the job satisfaction study.

These equipments are used not only to determine job satisfaction in such tangible areas as pay, benefits, promotional opportunities, and working conditions, but also to guess how a person and group behaviour patterns control corporate culture, both in a positive and negative way.

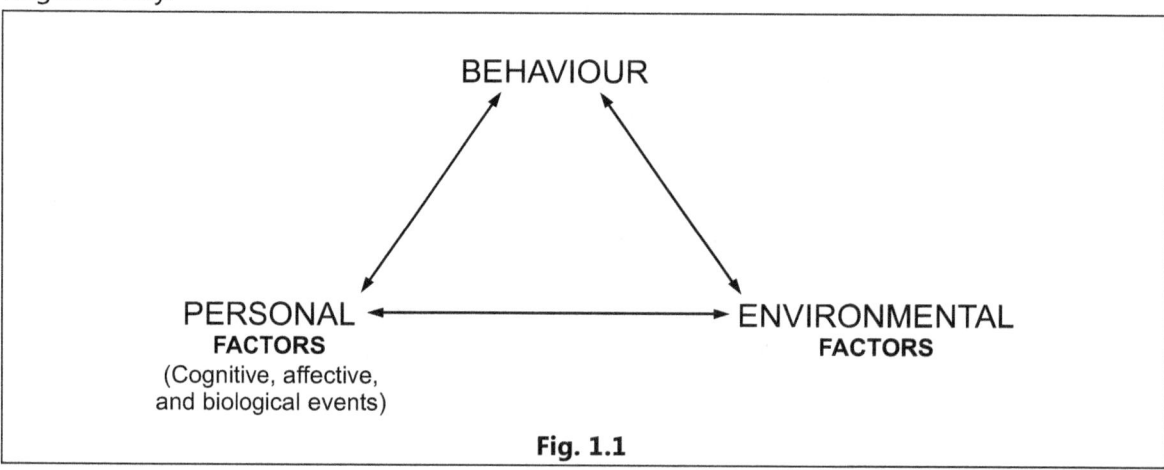

Fig. 1.1

3.   The Social Cognitive Framework

Social cognitive theory, used in psychology, education, and communication, points that portions of an individual's knowledge acquisition can be directly related to observing others within the context of social interactions, experiences, and outside media influences.

In other words, people do not learn new behaviours solely by trying them and either succeeding or failing, but rather, the survival of humanity is dependent upon the replication of the actions of others.

Depending on whether people are rewarded or punished for their behaviour and the outcome of the behaviour, that behaviour may be modelled. Further, media provide models for a vast array of people in many different environmental settings.

Social cognitive theory is a learning theory based on the concepts that people learn by watching what others do and will not do; these procedures are important to understand one's personality.

While social cognitists agree that there is a good amount of influence on development produced by the behaviour that is learnt and displayed in the environment in which one grows up, they think that the individual is just as significant in determining moral development.

People learn by observing others, with the environment, behaviour, and cognition.

These three factors are not static or independent components; rather, they control each other in a process of triadic reciprocal determinism. For example, the behaviour observed can change an individual's way of thinking (cognition).

In the same way, the environment one is raised in may influence later behaviours, just as a father's state of mind will decide the environment in which his children are brought up in.

It is important to note that learning can occur without a change in behaviour. According to **J. E. Ormrod's** general principles of social learning, while a visible change in behaviour is the most common proof of learning, it is not absolutely necessary.

Social learning theorists say that because people can learn through observation alone, their learning might not of necessity be shown in their performance.

Social cognitive theory is used today in several different areas. Mass media, public health, education, and marketing are just a few. An example of this is the use of celebrities to promote and launch numerous products to certain demographics.

1.1.11 Disciplines Contributing to Organisational Behaviour

Organisational behaviour is built on the contributions from a number of behavioural sciences such as Psychology, Sociology, Anthropology and Political Science.

1. **Psychology:** Psychology is the scientific study of human and animal behaviour with the object of understanding why living beings behave in a certain way. It deals with the study of individual behaviour and its reasons. It includes topics like learning, perception, personality, training, leadership effectiveness, needs and motivational forces etc.

2. **Social Psychology:** It is the study of relations between people and groups. It has made significant contributions in the areas of measuring, understanding and changing attitudes, communication patterns etc.

3. **Sociology:** It is the study of society. It is a social science that studies how humans behave in a society. It has contributed to organisational behaviour through the study of group dynamics, work groups, organisational cultures, organisational theory and structure, power, conflicts and intergroup behaviour.

4. **Anthropology:** It is the study of different societies. It helps in gaining understanding of organisational culture, organisational environments and differences between cultures.

5. **Political Science:** It is the social science that deals with the study of behaviour of individuals and groups within a political environment. It predicts the behaviour of people in organisations by looking at it through a political perspective.

1.1.12 Challenges and Opportunities for Organisational Behaviour

Organisational behaviour offers a number of challenges and opportunities for managers. It can help in improving the quality and productivity of organisations. This can be done by ways listed below:

1. By giving its employees opportunities to participate in planning and bringing about changes within the organisations.

2. Organisational behaviour through its vast study areas helps a manager to improve people skills by being a good listener and giving proper feedback.

3. Organisational behaviour recognises the fact that two persons are not the same. Work force diversity, if managed properly, can increase creativity and improve decision-making by bringing about diverse perspectives into view.

4. It provides guidelines for understanding differences between national cultures which may also result in change in management practices.

Organisational behaviour has led to putting more confidence in the employees. Managers learn how to give up control and employees learn how to take responsibility of their work and take correct decisions. Thus empowerment is an outcome of organisational behaviour. It is a challenge for managers to enhance employee creativity and acceptability for change so that organisations can maintain flexibility and remain successful.

Points to Remember

- Organisational behaviour is the area of study which focuses on human beings and their interaction with other groups and individuals within the organisation.

- Organisational behaviour is directly concerned with the understanding, predicting and controlling of human behaviour in organisations.

- The key elements in organisational behaviour are people, structure, technology and the external elements in which the organisation operates.

- There are different models of organisational behaviour. Some of them are in practice while others have become outdated. Within an organisation there may be more than one model being practiced by different departments. Different managers may adopt different models according to their personal preferences.

- Managers need certain skills and competencies to successfully achieve their goals. The most significant management skills are the technical, human and conceptual skills.

- Organisational behaviour is built on the contributions from a number of behavioural sciences such as Psychology, Sociology, Anthropology and Political Science.

- The organisational behaviour models are:

  1. Autocratic model
  2. Custodial model
  3. Supportive model
  4. Collegial model
  5. System model.

Questions for Discussion

1. Define organisational behaviour.
2. Describe the key elements of organisational behaviour.
3. Discuss the need and importance of organisational behaviour.
4. Discuss the models and approaches of organisational behaviour.
4. What are the challenges and opportunities that managers face in today's workplace?
5. Write short notes on:
   (i) Nature of organisational behaviour.
   (ii) Scope of organisational behaviour.
   (iii) Autocratic model.
   (iv) Cognitive framework of OB.

Chapter 2...

Individual Perspective

Contents ...

Learning Objectives ...

➢   To define personality, and explain the factors that determine an individual's personality

➢   To identify the key traits in the Big Five Personality Model

➢   To contrast the three components of an attitude

➢   To explain the formation of attitude

➢   To summarise the relationship between attitude and behaviour

➢   To describe the importance of perception on work behaviour

➢   To explain the factors that influence perception

➢   To define learning and outline the three major theories of learning

➢   To explain the types and process of learning

2.1 Personality

2.1.1 Concept

Our personalities shape our behaviours. If we want to understand the behaviour of someone in the organisation, it helps to know something about their personality. When psychologists talk about personality, they don't mean that a person has charm, a positive attitude towards life, a smiling face, nor is a contestant in a beauty pageant. They mean a dynamic concept describing the growth and development of a person's whole psychological system.

Personality looks at the aggregate whole, rather than looking at parts of a person. The aggregate whole is greater than the sum of the parts.

Personality plays a vital role in organisational behaviour as it affects the way people think, feel, and behave which in turn affects the workplace. People's personalities influence their behaviour and attitudes towards a given situation and also the way they make decisions. Interpersonal skills hugely affect the way people act and react to things during work. At the workplace, personality also affects things as motivation, leadership, performance, and conflict. The more the manager understands how personality in organisational behaviour works, the better equipped they are to be effective and accomplish their goals.

2.1.2 Definitions of Personality

A brief definition of personality would be that personality is made up of the characteristic set of thoughts, feelings, and behaviours that make a person unique. In addition to this, personality arises from within the individual and remains fairly consistent throughout life.

Gordon Allport gave the most frequently used definition of personality nearly 70 years ago. He said personality is, "the dynamic organisation within the individual of those psychophysical systems that determine his unique adjustments to his environment".

J. B. Kolasa defines personality as, "Personality is a broad, amorphous designation relating to fundamental approaches of persons to others and themselves. To most psychologists and students of behaviour, this term refers to the study of the characteristic traits of an individual, relationships between these traits and the way in which a person adjusts to other people and situations".

2.1.3 Determinants of Personality

Several factors influence the shaping of our personality. Major among these are
1.   Heredity,
2.   Culture,
3.   Family Background,
4.   Our Experiences through Life,
5.   The People we interact with.

1.   Heredity

Genetic factors play a vital role in what we tend to become. Whether we are tall or short, experience good health or ill health, quickly irritable or patient, characteristics can, in many cases, be traced to heredity. How we react to people's reactions and criticism can also influence how our personality is shaped.

2.   Culture

The culture and the values we are raised in, significantly tend to shape our personal values and inclination. Thus, people born in different cultures tend to develop different types of personalities which in turn influence our behaviours. India being a vast country with a rich diversity of cultural backgrounds provides a good study on this. For example, we have seen that people in Gujarat are more enterprising than people from other states; Punjabis are more diligent and hardworking; people from Bengal are more creative and with an intellectual bend of mind.

3. Family Background

The socio-economic status of the family, the number of children in the family and birth order, and the background and education of the parents and extended members of the family such as uncles and aunts, influence the shaping of personality to a considerable extent. Usually the first born have different experiences, during their growing years than those born later. Family members mould the character of all children, almost from birth, in several ways through role-modelling, and through various reinforcement strategies such as rewards and punishments which are judiciously dispensed.

4. Experiences in Life

Whether one is miserly or generous, trusts or mistrusts others, have high or low self-esteem and the like, is partially related to the past experiences the individual has had. For example, if someone came to you and pleaded with you to lend him ₹ 100 rupees which he promises to return in a week's time and you give it to him even though it was the last note you had in your pocket to cover the expenses for the rest of that month. Suppose the individual never again showed his face to you and you have not been able to get hold of him for the past three months. Also, suppose three such incidents happened to you with three different individuals in the past few months. What is the probability that you would trust another person who comes and asks you for a loan tomorrow? Rather low, one would think. Thus, certain personality characteristics are moulded by frequently occurring positive or negative experiences in life.

5. People We Interact With

"A person is known by the company he or she keeps" is a common saying. The implication is that people persuade each other and tend to associate with members who are more like them in their attitudes and values. Beginning from the childhood, the people we interact with influence us. Initially, our parents and siblings, then our teachers and class-mates, later our friends and colleagues, and so on. The influence of these various individuals and groups helps in shaping our personality. Thus, our personality becomes shaped throughout our lives by at least some of the people and groups we interact with. In summary, our personality is a function of both heredity and other external factors that shapes it. It is important to know what specific personality predispositions influence work behaviours.

2.1.4 Types of Personality

The Big Five Personality types are as follows:

1. **Openness to experience:** This trait involves people who are innovative, curious, appreciative of a variety of experience along with being more consistent and cautious. The candidate has excellent creative skills and is very well-trained.

2. **Conscientiousness:** This trait has people who are hardworking, organised and dependable. It has people who are efficient, easy-going and carefree. They show self-discipline and aim for high achievement; planned rather than spontaneous behaviour. These individuals are motivated, very dedicated and flexible when handling overwhelming tasks.

3. **Extraversion:** This trait includes people who are gregarious, assertive and sociable. They look at predispositions towards being outgoing and energetic. People with this trait are very satisfied in their careers and receive promotions very easily .Their assertive traits help them in being very talented managers.

4. **Agreeableness:** This trait has people who are friendly, compassionate and co-operative rather than cold, unkind, suspicious towards others. "Agreeable" individuals tend to be trustworthy, co-operative, helpful, and generally caring in regards to others. This personality trait is especially important in careers and situations that require gaining the confidence of others.

5. **Neuroticism:** This trait involves people who face nervousness, sensitivity and negative thoughts (a tendency to experience unpleasant emotions like anger, anxiety or depression easily). Neuroticism has a slightly different connotation in organisational behaviour. People who are highly "neurotic" in the psychological context often have a drive to improve themselves.

2.1.5 Theories of Personality

1. Traits Theory

The traditional approach of understanding personality was to identify and describe personality in terms of traits. In other words, it viewed personality as revolving around attempts to identify and label permanent characteristics that describe an individual's behaviour. Popular characteristics or traits include shyness, aggressiveness, submissiveness, laziness, ambition, loyalty, and timidity. This distinctiveness, when they are exhibited in a large number of situations, is called personality traits. The more consistent the characteristic and the more frequently it occurs in diverse situations, the more important that trait is in describing the individual.

Early Search for Primary Traits

Efforts to isolate traits have been stuck because there are so many of them. In one study, as many as 17,953 individual traits were identified. It is virtually impossible to predict behaviour when such a large number of traits must be taken into account. As a result, attention has been directed toward reducing these thousands to a more manageable number. One researcher isolated 171 traits but concluded that they were superficial and lacking in descriptive power. What he sought was a reduced set of traits that would identify underlying patterns. The result was the identification of 16 personality factors by **Raymond Cattell**, which he called the source, or primary traits. These 16 traits have been found to be generally steady and constant sources of behaviour, allowing prediction of an individual's behaviour in specific situations by weighing the characteristics for their situational relevance. Based on the answers individuals gave, they have been classified on the basis of the answers given to the test. They are classified as:

(a) Extroverted or Introverted.

(b) Sensing or Intuitive.

(c) Thinking or Feeling.

(d) Perceiving or Judging.

2. Thematic Apperception Test (TAT)

It is a projective test that offers more validity. The TAT consists of drawings or photographs of real-life situations. People taking the test are instructed to construct stories based on these images, and trained professionals then score the recorded stories for predefined themes. Psychologists assume that the stories people tell reflect the unconscious.

The Thematic Apperception Test, or TAT, is a projective measure intended to evaluate a person's patterns of thought, attitudes, observational capacity, and emotional responses to ambiguous test materials. In the case of the TAT, the ambiguous materials consist of a set of cards that portray human figures in a variety of settings and situations. The subject is asked to tell the examiner a story about each card that includes the following elements: the event shown in the picture; what has led up to it; what the characters in the picture are feeling and thinking; and the outcome of the event.

Because the TAT is an example of a projective instrument— that is, it asks the subject to project his or her habitual patterns of thought and emotional responses onto the pictures on the cards— many psychologists prefer not to call it a "test," because it implies that there are "right" and "wrong" answers to the questions. They consider the term "technique" to be a more accurate description of the TAT and other projective assessments.

3. The Myers-Briggs Type Indicator (MBIT)

MBTI assessment is a psychometric questionnaire designed to measure psychological preferences in how people perceive the world and make decisions.

Fundamental to the Myers-Briggs Type Indicator is the theory of psychological type as originally developed by Carl Jung. Jung proposed the existence of two dichotomous pairs of cognitive functions:

The "rational" (judging) functions: thinking and feeling

The "irrational" (perceiving) functions: sensation and intuition

Four Dichotomies

Extraversion (E)	(I) Introversion
Sensing (S)	(N) Intuition
Thinking (T)	(F) Feeling
Judging (J)	(P) Perception

Note that the terms used for each dichotomy have specific technical meanings relating to the MBTI which differ from their everyday usage. For example, people who prefer judgement over perception are not necessarily more judgmental or less perceptive. Nor does the MBTI instrument measure aptitude; it simply indicates preference for one over another.

Someone reporting a high score for extraversion over introversion cannot be correctly described as more extraverted: they simply have a clear preference.

Point scores on each of the dichotomies can vary considerably from person to person, even among those with the same type. However, Isabel Myers considered the direction of the preference (for example, E vs. I) to be more important than the degree of the preference (for example, very clear vs. Slightly clear). The expression of a person's psychological type is more than the sum of the four individual preferences. The preferences interact through type dynamics and type development.

(a) Extraversion/Introversion (E/I)

Myers-Briggs literature uses the terms extraversion and introversion as Jung first used them. Extraversion means "outward-turning" and introversion means "inward-turning". These specific definitions vary somewhat from the popular usage of the words.

The preferences for extraversion and introversion are often called "attitudes". Briggs and Myers recognised that each of the cognitive functions can operate in the external world of behaviour, action, people, and things ("extraverted attitude") or the internal world of ideas and reflection ("introverted attitude"). The MBTI assessment sorts for an overall preference for one or the other.

People who prefer extraversion draw energy from action: they tend to act, then reflect, then act further. If they are inactive, their motivation tends to decline. To rebuild their energy, extraverts need breaks from time spent in reflection. Conversely, those who prefer introversion "expend" energy through action: they prefer to reflect, then act, then reflect again. To rebuild their energy, introverts need quiet time alone, away from activity.

The extravert's flow is directed outward towards people and objects, and the introvert's is directed inward towards concepts and ideas. Contrasting characteristics between extraverts and introverts include the following:

- Extraverts are "action" oriented, while introverts are "thought" oriented.
- Extraverts seek "breadth" of knowledge and influence, while introverts seek "depth" of knowledge and influence.
- Extraverts often prefer more "frequent" interaction, while introverts prefer more "substantial" interaction.
- Extraverts recharge and get their energy from spending time with people, while introverts recharge and get their energy from spending time alone.

(b) Sensing and Intuition

Sensing and intuition are the information-gathering (perceiving) functions. They describe how new information is understood and interpreted. Individuals who prefer sensing are more likely to trust information that is in the present, tangible, and concrete: that is, information that can be understood by the **five senses**. They tend to distrust hunches, which seem to come "out of nowhere". They prefer to look for details and facts. For them, the meaning is in the data. On the other hand, those who prefer intuition tend to trust information that is more abstract or theoretical, that can be associated with other information (either remembered or discovered by seeking a wider context or pattern). They may be more interested in future possibilities. For them, the meaning is in the underlying theory and principles which are manifested in the data.

(c) Thinking and Feeling

Thinking and feeling are the decision-making (judging) functions. The thinking and feeling functions are both used to make rational decisions, based on the data received from their information-gathering functions (sensing or intuition). Those who prefer thinking tend to decide things from a more detached standpoint, measuring the decision by what seems reasonable, logical, casual, consistent, and matching to a given set of rules. Those who prefer feeling tend to come to decisions by associating or empathising with the situation, looking at it 'from the inside' and weighing the situation to achieve the balance of the greatest harmony, consensus and fit, considering the needs of the people involved. Thinkers usually have trouble interacting with people who are inconsistent or illogical, and tend to give very direct feedback to others. They are concerned with the truth and view it as more important than being tactful.

As noted already, people who prefer thinking do not necessarily, in the everyday sense, "think better" than their feeling counterparts; the opposite preference is considered an equally rational way of coming to decisions (and, in any case, the MBTI assessment is a measure of preference, not ability). Similarly, those who prefer feeling do not necessarily have "better" emotional reactions than their thinking counterparts.

(d) Dominant Function

According to Myers and Briggs, people use all four cognitive functions. However, one function is generally used in a more conscious and confident way. This dominant function is supported by the secondary (auxiliary) function, and to a lesser degree the tertiary (third) function. The fourth and least conscious function is always the opposite of the dominant function. Myers called this inferior function the shadow.

The four functions operate in conjunction with the attitudes (extraversion and introversion). Each function is used in either an extraverted or introverted way. A person whose dominant function is extraverted intuition, for example, uses intuition very differently from someone whose dominant function is introverted intuition.

2.1.6 How Personality Influences Organisational Behaviour

People's personality plays a very vital role in organisational behaviour because the way that people feel, think and behave affects various aspects of the workplace. Personalities influence a person's behaviour in groups, his attitude and the way he makes decisions.

Interpersonal skills create a huge affect on how people act and react to things while at work. At workplace, personality also affects other disciples like leadership, motivation, conflict and performance of the employees. If the managers understand deeply about how personality in organisational behaviour works, they will be better equipped to be affective and thus accomplish their goals.

People have various views about the world which indirectly affects their personalities. A person will handle any situation or crises as per his personal beliefs, values and personality traits. These so called personality traits are developed throughout a person's lifetime which cannot be changed easily and thus it is more important for the managers to understand this concept rather than to fight it.

Various personality traits like emotional stability, openness and agreeableness helps in predicting that an employee will work better in teams, have less conflict and thus have positive attitudes about his work. People with this kind of personality should be placed in situations wherein they would be leading others or working in a team. People who lack these personality traits will have lesser motivation comparatively and will react more negatively when placed in these similar situations.

A positive interpersonal skill is one such personality trait that highly affects the workplace. A person exhibiting this trait apparently enjoys working in team and he has the empathy and sensitivity that helps him to get along well with their team members. People which such personality trait are usually placed in situations where they manage employees, work with customers or mediate problems.

Personality of a person greatly affects his independence and decision-making. Personality traits like conscientiousness, self-efficacy and pro-activity helps in good-decision making under pressure and independence, whereas traits like neuroticism does not allow the same as mentioned above. Individuals with such personality traits can be placed in appropriate positions in order to give their best.

When individuals are placed with particular characteristics in jobs that suits them the best, it automatically raises their levels of motivation. It also affects their overall performance at work because they are happy personalities on a daily basis. This helps in achieving overall and better productivity at work as more is getting accomplished due to happier employees and better attitudes.

2.2 Attitude

2.2.1 Introduction

When someone says "I like your dress," she is expressing her attitude towards your dress.

Attitudes are evaluative statements about objects, people, or events. These statements may be either favourable or unfavourable.

Many organisations are concerned with the attitudes of their employees, as attitudes are linked to behaviour. Employees' satisfaction or dissatisfaction with their jobs affects the workplace. Attitudes are complex; to understand them better we need to break them up into their fundamental properties or components.

2.2.2 Definition of Attitude

Attitude can be defined as, "a complex mental state involving beliefs and feelings and values and dispositions to act in certain ways."

For example, if someone says that "I like my job". This statement expresses his attitude towards his job.

2.2.3 Characteristics of Attitude

1. An attitude is the predisposition of the person to assess some objects into a favourable or an unfavourable manner.

2. The most recurring phenomenon is "attitude". People at their place of work have attitudes about lots of subjects that are connected to them. These attitudes are firmly set in a complex psychological structure of principles.

3. Attitudes are different from values. Values are the principles, whereas attitudes are our feelings, thoughts and behavioural tendencies toward a certain thing or situation.

4. Attitude is a tendency to respond to a specific set of facts.

5. Attitudes are evaluative statements that are either favourable or unfavourable regarding the objects and people at events.

An attitude is "a mental state of readiness, organised through experience, exerting a specific influence upon person's response to people, objects and situations with which it is related". Attitudes therefore state one's tendencies towards a given part of the universe. They also provide an emotional basis for one's interpersonal tendencies and identification with others. Managers in organisations are required to understand employees' attitudes in order to manage efficiently. Attitudes do influence the behaviour of people and their performance in organisations.

2.2.4 Types of Job Attitude

A *job attitude* is a set of evaluations of one's job that constitute one's feelings toward beliefs about, and attachment to one's job.

Employees evaluate their advancement opportunities by observing their job, their occupation, and their employer. A job attitude is a set of evaluations of one's job that constitute one's feelings toward, beliefs about, and attachment to one's job.

1. **Job Involvement:** Identifying with one's job and actively participating in it, and considering performance, and important to self-worth. Employees with high level of job involvement strongly identify with and care about the kind of work they do. High levels of job involvement have been found to be related with fewer absences and low resignation rates.

2. **Organisational Commitment:** Identifying with a particular organisation and its goals, and wishing to maintain membership in the organisation.

3. **Perceived Organisational Support (POS):** The degree to which employees feel the organisation cares about their well-being.

4. **Employee Engagement:** An individual's involvement with, satisfaction with, and enthusiasm for the organisation.

5. **Job Satisfaction:** Satisfaction results when a job makes the achievement of individual values and standards possible, and displeasure occurs when the job is seen as obstructing such achievement. This attitude has received a lot of attention by researchers and practitioners because at one time it was thought to be the cause of improved job performance. The term "job satisfaction" refers to a person's general attitude toward his or her job. An individual with a high level of job satisfaction holds positive attitudes toward the job; a person who is unhappy with his or her job holds negative attitudes about the job. Now, because managers are concerned for creating a high performance place of work, researchers continue looking for definite answers about the causes and results of job satisfaction.

2.2.5 Components of Attitude

The definition of attitude indicates that they have three components: cognitive, affective, and behavioural. Sometimes, our cognitions may influence our feelings, which may, in turn, influence our behavioural tendencies. However, it is important to recognise that different people with the same beliefs may develop different feelings, and that different people with the same feelings may develop different behavioural intentions. Also, we will see there may even be cases, in which our beliefs will be influenced by our feelings, or even by our actual behaviours.

There are three components of attitude:

- Cognitive component
- Affective component
- Behavioural component

(1) Cognitive Component

It refers to that part of attitude which is related in general knowledge of a person. For example, he says, "smoking is injurious to health". Such type of idea of a person is called cognitive component of attitude.

The cognitive component of attitudes is our cognitions or beliefs about the facts pertaining to the attitude object. For example, we may believe that salespersons in our firm receive high pay or that our firm is the oldest in the industry. These beliefs may be correct or incorrect.

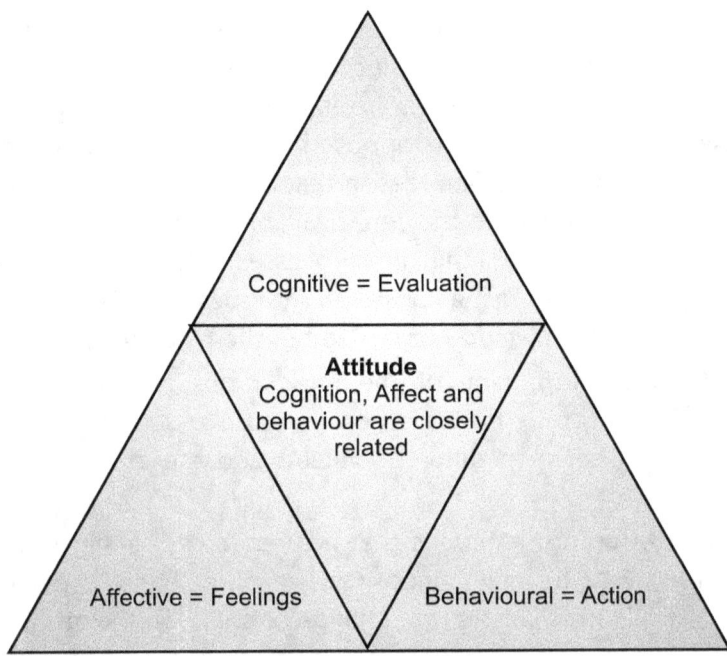

Fig. 2.1: Components of Attitude

(2) Affective Component

The second component, the affective component is made up of our feelings toward the attitude object. It involves evaluation and emotion. For instance, we may think favourably or unfavourably about another employee or think a particular rule is good or bad.

This part of attitude is related to the statement which affects another person. For example, in an organisation a personal report is given to the general manager, in the report he points out that the sale staff is not performing their due responsibilities.

(3) Behavioural Component

The third component, the behavioural tendency component is the way we intend to behave toward the attitude object. We may, for example, intend to tell off the boss or ask for a raise or outperform a co-worker.

It's generally agreed that attitudes form only one determinant of behaviour. They represent predispositions to behave in particular ways, but how we actually act in a particular situation will depend on the immediate consequences of our behaviour, how we think others will evaluate our actions, and habitual ways of behaving in those kinds of situations.

2.2.6 Formation of Attitude

Attitudes are learned. People acquire attitudes from many sources but the point that is to be emphasised is that attitudes are acquired and not inborn. Our responses to people and issues eventually change. The two main influences on attitudes are direct experience and social learning.

1. **Direct Experience:** Attitudes can develop from a personal good or bad experience with an object. Direct experience with an object or person is a great influence on attitudes. Research has indicated that attitudes that are obtained from direct experience are stronger, are held more assertively and are more opposed to change than are attitudes that are created through indirect experience. One reason that attitudes that are obtained from direct experience are so powerful is because they are available. This implies that the attitudes are simply accessed and are active in our thinking processes. When attitudes are available, they are recalled into consciousness, as fast as possible. Attitudes that are not learned from direct experience do not exist, and thus we do not remember them easily.

(a) **Classical Conditioning:** One of the basic processes that are fundamental for attitude formation can be described on the basis of learning principles. Individuals develop relations between different objects and the emotional reactions that go with them.

(b) **Operant Conditioning:** Attitudes that are reinforced, either orally or nonverbally, have a tendency to be maintained. On the other hand, a person's attitude that brings out ridicule from others may change or abandon the attitude.

(c) **Vicarious Learning:** In which an individual learns something through observing others can also account for a development in attitude especially when that person has no direct experience with the object about which the attitude is assumed. It is through vicarious teaming procedures that children pick up the prejudices of their parents.

2. **Social Learning:** In social learning, the family, peer groups and culture form a person's attitude in an indirect way. Substantial social learning happens through modelling, in which people acquire attitudes by just observing others. For a person to learn from observing a model, four processes must occur.

(a) The learner must concentrate on the model, the attitudes, values and work ethics.

(b) The learner must retain what was observed from the model.

(c) Behavioural reproduction must take place; that is, the learner must practise the behaviour.

(d) The learner should be encouraged to learn from the model.

Social learning can take place through the following ways.

(a) **The Family:** A person learns various attitudes through imitating his/her parents. If the parents behave positively towards an object and the child has a high regard for his parents, he will probably accept a similar attitude, even without being told about the object, and even without having a direct experience. Children also learn to accept specific attitudes by the reinforcement they are given by their parents when they show certain behaviours that reflect a suitable attitude.

(b) Peer Groups: Peer pressure shapes attitudes through group acceptance of people who express attitudes that are well-liked, such as exclusion from the group, placed on people who promote attitudes that are not well-liked.

(c) Modelling: A considerable amount of social learning happens through modelling, in which people acquire attitudes by just observing others. The observer overhears other people conveying something or watches them getting involved in a behaviour that reflects an attitude, and the observer accepts this attitude.

2.2.7 Measurement of Attitude

It is supposed that one can measure an individual's attitudes by asking certain questions about thoughts, feelings and possible actions towards an attitude object. Attitudes can be determined by sensitive and intuitive regulations based on the action and remarks of individual employees and their observed behaviour. Another technique is to analyse the data from specific factors like turnover rates, absenteeism and production levels. Thus, inference and prediction from behaviour data and interviews that are carried out with a structured questionnaire and proper rating scale are the general tools for attitudinal measurement. The techniques of measuring attitudes that are well-liked are

1. Self-reports
2. Existing Data (Daily contacts)
3. Direct Observation Techniques
4. Physiological Reaction Techniques

1. Self-reports

The most ordinary technique is the self-report method, which is used in most organisations to determine the attitudes of workers. This is generally in the form of questionnaire that is to be completed by the employees who are dealing with their feelings about their work and related matters. These self-reports are generally called "attitude surveys". An attitude survey includes a set of statements or questions each having a scale that is allotted to the answers. Based on the answers to each of the statements, results are acquired that give the information needed by the management. There are three main types of attitude scaling methods and these are

(a) Equal Appearing Interval Scale – L. L. Thurston Scale

(b) Summated Rating Scale – Rensis Likert Scale

(c) Semantic Differential Scale – C. E. Osgood Scale

(a) Equal Appearing Interval Scale: L. L. Thurston's Equal Appearing Scale is the procedure of measurement of attitude that is used most widely. This technique includes a questionnaire which is completed by the employees. It is an easy scale as it requires only one judgement for each item or for each statement. The statements range from the two extremes of "most favourable" to the "most unfavourable". The entire statements are categorised under 7, 9, or 11 options each and the responses of the employees are then summarised and presented for analysis and action.

(b) Summated Rating Scale: The Summated Rating Scale was developed by **Likert** and is even easier than the Thurston Scale. Each statement has five likely degrees of approval and the respondent has to check one of the five degrees always, often, sometimes, seldom and never. The answer to each statement shows how much one does agree or disagree with the statements. The summation of the points shows the individual's attitude. This scale is preferred because it is easy and is used widely.

(c) Semantic Differential Scale: This scale devised by **C. E. Osgood**, concentrates on the meaning given to a word or a concept by an individual. Most words have two meanings.

    (i)   Semantic or dictionary meaning

    (ii)   Connotative meaning (what a word suggests apart from the thing it explicitly denotes or names.)

The semantic differential scale contains many pairs of opposite choices that have a scale value in between the extremes. The respondent marks the score along the scale for his attitude about the specified object. The scores that are allotted to each statement are then summarised. A high score reflects a more favourable attitude whereas a low score indicates a less favourable attitude.

2. Existing Data

In most organisations, numerous employee records in different types are already available which can give a measurable data and determine the general level of satisfaction among the workers. Some of the data can be retrieved from

    (a)   Employee's personal records

    (b)   Performance reports

    (c)   Waste and scrap reports

    (d)   Quality records

    (e)   Absenteeism reports

    (f)   Accident reports

    (g)   Training records

    (h)   Medical reports

    (i)   Exit interviews

Employee reactions and behaviour pattern is a good direction to evaluate the attitude of people. In the same way, applying good working practices and employees who follow standard working process also give an important insight into the level of satisfaction perceived by them.

3. Direct Observation Techniques

Through daily contact with workers, managers have access to information that is related to absences and complaints. Recommendations given by employees and feedback given from employees to counsellors also give clues about behavioural indicators and indirect clues about how happy the employees are. These can be used to plan further interventions and to develop positive attitudes.

4.   Physiological Reaction Techniques

Some physiological reactions like heart beat rate, pupil dilation and skin sensitivity are indicative techniques which compare responses of the member in front of a natural object and in front of an attitude object.

Due to the ease of administering the Thurston, the Likert and the Osgood scales, the other techniques of attitude measurement are not much favoured. Most of them use a great deal of time and are subjected to the evaluator's judgement and so are not used widely. Though, in most cases, the direct observation technique and the current information give indications for the work that needs to be completed in the area of attitude building.

2.2.8 Functions of Attitudes

An attitude is known to serve four major functions of an individual: 1. the adjustments function, 2. the ego defensive function, 3. the value expressive function and, 4. the knowledge function. Ultimately these functions help in serving people's needs which protects and enhance the image they hold about themselves. In simpler terms, these functions acts as the motivational bases which reinforces and shapes positive attitudes towards goal objects which are perceived as negative attitudes or need satisfying towards other objects perceived as threatening or punishing. These situations are diagrammed in figure below. The function itself helps us to understand why people hold such attitude which they do towards psychological objects.

1.   Adjustment Function

The adjustment function helps in directing people towards rewarding and pleasurable objects and thus pulls them away for the undesirable and unpleasant ones. It thus serves the utilitarian concept of minimising punishment and maximising reward. Due to this, the consumer's attitudes largely depend on their perceptions of what is punishing and what is satisfying the need. As we all know that consumers perceive products, services and stores as satisfying need or unsatisfying experiences, we should thus expect their attitudes to vary towards these objects in relation to the experiences that have been occurred.

2.   Ego Defensive Function

Attitudes meant to protect the self image and ego against threats helps in fulfilling the ego defensive function. Moreover, many outward expressions of such attitudes reflect the opposite of what a person perceives him to be. For example, a consumer making a poor investment or a poor purchase decision will staunchly defend his poor decision as being correct at that time or as being a result of poor advice from some third person. Such ego defensive attitude helps in protecting our self image and often we are not aware of them.

3.   Value expression function

As ego defensive attitudes are formed for protecting one's self image, value expressive attitudes enables the expression of the person's centrally held values. Thus, consumer's adopt certain attitudes in an effort for translating their values into something more tangible and easily expressible. Therefore, a conservative person is likely to develop an unfavourable attitude towards bright clothing and instead might get attracted towards pin striped, dark suits.

Marketers should actually develop an understanding about what values a customer wishes to express about himself and then they should design products and promotional campaigns accordingly to allow these self expressions. However, not all products lend themselves to this form of market segmentation. Products with highest potential for value expressive segmentation are the ones with high social visibility. For example, Saks Fifth Avenue clothes, cross pens, Bang & Children stereo systems and Ferrari automobiles.

4. Knowledge function

We humans need an orderly and structured world, and thus we seek stability, consistency and understanding. These needs lead to development of attitudes towards acquiring knowledge. Moreover, it also specifies the needs which are to be known. For example, a person who does not play snooker nor wishes to learn the sport is unlikely to seek knowledge or an understanding of this particular game. Thus, it will influence the amount of information search devoted to this area. Therefore, due to our needs to know forms attitudes about what we believe we need or not need to understand.

Moreover, attitudes enable the customers to simplify the complexity of the real world. This means, the real world is so highly complex for us to cope with, that we start developing mechanisms in order to simplify situations. This entire process involves sensory thresholds, selective attention and attitudes. Attitudes lead to categorising or grouping of objects as a method of knowing about them. Therefore, whenever a new object is experienced, we tend to categorise it into some group which we know something about. In this method, we can share our reactions for other objects in the same category. This proves to be efficient as we do not have to put in much effort in reacting to each new object as a completely unique situation. Consequently we often come across customers reacting in similar manner to various advertisements like limited time offers, going out of business sales, American made goods, etc. However, there is surely some risk of error for not looking at the new information or unique aspects about objects, but for better or worse, our attitudes play a major role about how we feel and react to new examples of these situations.

2.2.9 Attitude and Organisational Behaviour

It's generally agreed that attitudes form only one determinant of behaviour. They represent predispositions to behave in particular ways, but how we actually act in a particular situation will depend on the immediate consequences of our behaviour, how we think others will evaluate our actions, and habitual ways of behaving in those kinds of situations. In addition, there may be specific situational factors influencing behaviour. Sometimes we experience a conflict of attitudes, and behaviour may represent a compromise between them.

Compatibility between Attitudes and Behaviour

The same attitude may be expressed in a variety of ways. For example, having a positive attitude towards a political party doesn't necessarily mean that you actually become a member, or that you attend public meetings. But if you don't vote for this political party in a general election, people may question your attitude. In other words, an attitude should predict behaviour to some extent, even if this is extremely limited and specific.

> ***Every single instance of behaviour involves four specific elements:***
> 1. *A specific action.*
> 2. *Performed with respect to a given target.*
> 3. *In a given context.*
> 4. *At a given point in/of time.*

Attitudes can predict behaviour, provided that both are assessed at the same level of generality. There needs to be a high degree of compatibility (or correspondence) between them.

Attitudes can predict behaviour if you ask the right questions.

According to the principle of compatibility, measures of attitude and behaviour are compatible to the extent that the target, action, context and time element are assessed at identical levels of generality or specificity.

For example, a person's attitude towards a 'healthy lifestyle' only specifies the target, leaving the other three unspecified. A behavioural measure that would be compatible with this global attitude would have to aggregate a wide range of health behaviour across different contexts and times.

The Strength of Attitudes

Most modern theories agree that attitudes are represented in memory, and that an attitude's accessibility can exert a strong influence on behaviour. By definition, strong attitudes exert more influence over behaviour, because they can be automatically activated. One factor that seems to be important is direct experience.

> ***The components of an organisation's attitude include strategy, posture and culture.***

Successful organisations like Apple, Coca-Cola, the Red Cross and Ritz-Carlton all have a distinct attitude. For example, Apple leads its competitors in designing innovative products. Winning attitudes do not emerge by chance. Leaders aligning their organisation's strategy, posture and culture create them.

2.3 JOB SATISFACTION

2.3.1 Concept of Job Satisfaction

If people were asked on how they feel about their jobs, we would most likely find that they have strong emotional reactions regarding their jobs. This is not unexpected considering that employees spend about one third of their lives at work.

Job satisfaction has been regarded both as a general attitude as well as a satisfaction with specific dimensions of the job such as pay, the work itself, promotional opportunities, supervision, colleagues and so forth. These may communicate in different ways to create the feeling of satisfaction with the job. The degree of satisfaction may differ with how well the results satisfy or go beyond the expectations. **Mumford (1991)** analysed job satisfaction in two ways. First, in terms of the fit between what the organisation needs and what the employee is looking for and second, in terms of the fit between what the employee is looking for and what he/she is really getting.

Since an average employee spends half of his/her life in the organisation, there are some concerns that have to be addressed especially in the context of job satisfaction. These have to do with steadiness of satisfaction, work context, and supervisory behaviour. In an interesting research' by **Straw and Ross (1985)**, it was established that job satisfaction is relatively a steady arrangement, and does not change over time. In their survey of over 5000 men who changed jobs between 1969 and 1971, it was established that the expressions of job satisfaction were very stable. Although they had different kind of jobs, employees who were happy or unhappy in 1969 felt equally happy or unhappy in 1971 too. Although some researchers have defined the disposition of stability of job satisfaction, follow-up researches have, however, encouraged it.

Job satisfaction can be defined as a person's general positive attitude towards his or her job. It is a positive state resulting from the appraisal of one's job or job experience. It is observed both as a general attitude as well as a satisfaction with particular dimensions of the job such as pay, the work itself, promotion opportunities, supervision, colleagues, etc. The extent of satisfaction may differ with how well the results satisfy or go beyond the expectations.

Job satisfaction is the level of contentment an individual feels concerning his or her job. This feeling is mostly based on a person's knowledge of satisfaction. Job satisfaction can be influenced by a person's capacity to finish the required tasks, the level of communication in an organisation, and the manner in which the management treats the employees. Job satisfaction falls into two levels - affective job satisfaction and cognitive job satisfaction. Affective job satisfaction is an individual's emotional feeling about the job as a whole. Cognitive job satisfaction is how satisfied employees feel regarding some part of their job, such as pay, hours, or benefits.

2.3.2 Definitions of Job Satisfaction

Job satisfaction is the result of a number of variables. It is difficult to define exactly, considering (or covering) the number of elements contributing to job satisfaction. Let us examine some definitions of job satisfaction.

E. A. Locke in his article on 'Causes of Job Satisfaction' defines, "Job satisfaction is a pleasurable or positive emotional state resulting from the appraisal of one's job or job experience".

Stephen Robbins and **Seema Sandhi define as**, "Job satisfaction is a collection of feelings that an individual holds towards his or her job".

Job satisfaction implies a person's attitude towards the job. Many factors can form one's job satisfaction. In this reference, the term can be defined as; job satisfaction is an employee's positive attitude towards job situation and is mainly determined by contents of job, pay, promotion, supervisor, co-workers, and working conditions. High job satisfaction is reflected in form of better performance, co-operation, decreased turnover and absenteeism, and high commitment towards overall organisation.

2.3.3 Determinants of Job Satisfaction

Many factors have an effect on job satisfaction they are also known as determinants, dement or influences. **Fred Luthans** considers following (first) six factors that affect one's level or degree of job satisfaction.

1. **The Work Itself:** The work that an employee carries out is the main source of motivation and satisfaction. Job/work contents are the basic inputs in job satisfaction. Job characteristics including nature, timing, variety, job requirement, responsibility and challenges, autonomy, degree of complexity, etc., have differing effects on an individual's job satisfaction and the impact of these features is mediated by personality characteristics.

2. **Pay:** Money is the main reason why people work. Money (wage, salary, or income) helps people in achieving their basic requirements. It is also a source of fulfilling secondary requirements like affiliation, power, esteem, etc. If the employee feels that he earns more than what he contributes, he tends to be happy.

3. **Promotion:** Promotion has differing degrees of effect on job satisfaction and it is based on different considerations, like seniority, performance, extra contribution, extra achievements, promotion with/without transfers, and promotion with unrelated tasks. Promotion brings about positive effects on pay, status, relations, and authority and responsibility. When promotion opportunities match with one's expectations, then it can be a source of job satisfaction.

4. **Supervision:** The type and nature of supervision is a significant source of job - satisfaction. Supervisor's style, attitudes and approach, assistance, co-operation, etc., can have an effect on job satisfaction. A frank and helpful supervisor can add to job satisfaction. The participative climate that is created by the supervisor is another important issue in this context. Participative climate has a positive effect on job satisfaction.

5. **Work Group:** Normally, one has to perform his work with a group. Individual performance, time and again, relies on group performance. Therefore, a group or team can moderate the impact action. Friendly, co-operative, and honest work group creates a healthy atmosphere, makes the job an enjoyable place. The team members encourage, comfort, advice, assist, etc. have positive effect on job satisfaction.

6. **Working Conditions:** Overall working conditions affect job satisfaction. Proper working condition can allow an employee to perform his work easily. Cleanliness, attractive surroundings, temperature, ventilation, facilities, or amenities, etc., can extend job satisfaction. In all, organisation climate and culture changes one's attitude of job satisfaction.

7. **Other Factors:** Apart from those six factors, there are many factors that have an effect on the level of job satisfaction, such as

   (a) Level of job: Higher level job is connected with high pay, high status, and more autonomy, and, thus, it gives more satisfaction.

   (b) Personality Characteristics: To what extent particular job offers satisfaction is decided by the interchange of personality characteristics of people. All jobs do not give equal job satisfaction to all.

   (c) Personal Factors: Age, sex, education, training, etc., are accountable for the level of satisfaction and dissatisfaction.

2.3.4 Measurements of Job Satisfaction

Measuring job satisfaction has been a challenging, process to racial scientists as it cannot be directly observed nor correctly inferred. However many useful methods have been developed to measure job satisfaction. These measures are of great importance to employers as they provide important information regarding what is and is not being done correctly at the workplace. Reactions to work have been evaluated in the following ways.

1. **Paper Pencil Test:** This is the most frequently used approach. Scales which are standardised and tested with norms are used to gather data. The norms give information for particular groups or industries to make comparisons. One of the extensively used measures is the JDI or Job Descriptive Index.

2. **The Critical incident Method:** In this approach the people are requested to remember incidents that for the most part are pleasing or unpleasing to them. The replies are then checked to make out underlying themes.

3. **Interview:** This is significant as it allows in-depth questioning to know the causes and nature of satisfaction or dissatisfaction.

4. **Confrontation Meeting:** In this, small groups of employees are brought together and motivated to share their feelings honestly concerning their jobs. The assumption is that in a group surrounding occasionally, people feel free to talk about things they may hesitate to talk about, if they are interviewed alone.

Another approach of measurement has been to evaluate general or global job satisfaction. This is determined with numerous statements that directly measure job satisfaction. Statements like, "I am satisfied with my job," "I have to come to my job everyday' and "If I start my career again, I would choose the present job," are presented and the respondents are asked to talk with them on a five or six point scale. Another more well-liked approach has been the summation score. Employees are asked to report feelings about certain parts of their job. These dimensions are rated on any standardised scale and then added up to create an overall job satisfaction score. Yet another effort taken to calculate job satisfaction has been through the Need Satisfaction Scale (**Porter, 1961**), which measures the present, ideal, and the significance of satisfaction on 13 items developed after Maslow's Need Hierarchy Theory. A rather unique way of measuring job satisfaction was recommended by **Kunin (1955)**. His technique included faces with expressions ranging from deep scowl to broad smile. The respondents are given statements that are connected to job satisfaction and are asked to recognise their responses with the suitable face. This way the respondents are able to recognise their feelings rather than just putting them in scale values.

Another way to measure job satisfaction is operationalising important responses to dissatisfaction and evaluating their absence or presence amongst the respondents. **Farrell (1993)** has pointed out that employees may show their dissatisfaction in several ways. He has recommended four important responses based on the dimensions of constructive-destructive and active-passive.

1. **Exit (active-destructive) behaviour** directed towards leaving the organisation, looking for new position, resigning.

2. **Voice (active-constructive) behaviour** that tries to improve conditions, like making suggestions, and talking about the problems with the supervisors.

3. **Loyal (passive-constructive) behaviour** that is characterised by wait and watch, hoping that the circumstances would improve. In the face of external criticism, they raise their voice for the organisation, trusting that the organisation/management would do something about it.

4. **Neglect (passive-destructive) behaviour** that passively allows the situations to get worse; decrease in effort, increase in error ratio, absenteeism, late coming and so on.

2.3.5 Influence of Job Satisfaction on Behaviour

As job satisfaction is a very significant attitude, it will be discussed in detail here. The results of a positive work attitude are organisational citizenship behaviours. These are also called OCBs and are reflected in the employee's predisposition attributes to be co-operative, useful, caring and conscientious. It is said that the people who show OCBs, perform better and get higher rewards.

From a managerial and organisational effectiveness point of view, it is significant to understand how satisfaction connects to the desired outcome variables. If job satisfaction is high, will the employees perform better and the organisation will become more effective? If job satisfaction is low, will there be performance problems and ineffectiveness? We will now talk about the impact of job satisfaction on these major parts:

1. Job satisfaction and performance.
2. Job satisfaction and turnover.
3. Job satisfaction and absenteeism.
4. Job satisfaction and workplace theft, violence and bending of rules
5. Job satisfaction and stress.

1. Job Satisfaction and Performance

Job satisfaction can have an effect on numerous job performance variables and research has been done on the assumptions that

(a) Job satisfaction leads to improved job performance.

(b)   Job performance leads to improved job satisfaction.

(c)   Job satisfaction and job performance exist in a relationship which is moderated by other variables such as rewards and salary.

However, some results which have emerged are that a happy employee is not necessarily a high performer and the efforts taken by the management to make everyone happy will not necessarily yield high levels of productivity. Similarly, the assumption that a high performing employee will probably be happy is also not supported by research. The last assumption concentrates on rewards as positively influencing the performance and this outlook implies that the rewards that a person gets as a result of good performance and the extent to which these rewards are perceived as sensible or equitable, have an effect on both the extent to which the circumstance results from the performance and the extent to which the performance is affected by satisfaction. This means that if an employee is rewarded for good performance and if the reward is considered as fair by the employee, job satisfaction will increase and this consecutively will affect the performance positively, leading to other rewards and continued higher levels of job satisfaction.

However, satisfaction will necessarily not improve a person's performance but it will improve either the departmental or the organisational level. When employees are involved and found to have higher levels of satisfaction with their jobs, there is a rise in productivity, customer satisfaction and even profits in the organisation.

Better performance normally, leads to higher economic, sociological and psychological rewards. If these rewards are regarded as fair and reasonable, then there is an improvement in satisfaction because employees feel that they are receiving rewards that are consistent with their performance. However, if rewards are seen as insufficient for the level of performance, dissatisfaction tends to rise. In either of the cases, the level of satisfaction either causes a higher level or a lower level of commitment, which then has an effect on the effort and the performance again. This results in a continuously operating performance-satisfaction-loop. The implication here is that management must dedicate its efforts to help increase employee performance, which will provide satisfaction and commitment as a by-product.

In case the employees have a low performance, they do not get the rewards that they were aiming for and so they become unhappy. On being unhappy, they might start showing negative behaviours like increased absenteeism, higher turnover, tardiness, theft, and even poor organisational citizenship behaviour.

2.   **Job Satisfaction and Turnover**

The relationships of job satisfaction and turnover are:

(a)   When the organisation's attitude towards the employee is negative and the employee's attitude towards the organisation is also negative, the employee leaves the organisation by mutual agreement.

(b)   In cases, where the organisation's attitude towards the employee is negative but the employee's attitude toward the organisation is positive, the employee is laid-off.

(c)   At times, the organisations attitude towards the employee is positive but the employee has a negative attitude towards the organisation, in such cases, the employee leaves the organisation willingly.

(d)   In circumstances where the organisation and the employee have a positive attitude towards each other, the employee stays with the organisation.

High job satisfaction does not keep low turnover, but it does help out to an extent. However, if there is more job dissatisfaction, there will probably be high turnover. Employees who have lower satisfaction generally have higher rates of turnover. Such employees are not satisfied, they get very little appreciation while performing their jobs or they clash with their peers or supervisors and are more ready to seek attractive alternatives of employment and leave their organisation.

Although a state of no turnover is not advantageous to an organisation, a low turnover rate is generally attractive. This is due to the considerable cost incurred by the organisation in the form of training and the disadvantages of inexperience of the new employee who is employed, along with the cost of well defined knowledge that the person who has left, has taken with him.

Voluntary turnover has been studied in depth by **Mobley** and the process followed is given below. It is directly connected to job satisfaction.

(a)   After experiencing job dissatisfaction for a while, an employee may start thinking about whether he would like to quit.

(b)   The possible positive and negative facets of leaving the job are then studied.

(c)   If the positive aspects are found to be more attractive, the employee begins to look for alternative jobs.

(d)   As soon as the substitutes are found, they are then analysed regarding each other and regarding the current job.

(e)   A decision concerning the intention to stay or leave is then taken and the following action is then acted upon.

This multistage process does allow managers to consider the cues given by the employees and intervene before it is too late. There are many negative impacts of turnover felt by the organisation, which include costs that are connected to separation, with continuing a vacancy, with replacement by new employees, with training of new employees; with cost or low moral for example, loss of friendships with valued colleagues and concerns about personal job losses by others.

However, there are some positive functional aspects of turnover such as

(a)   Increased opportunities for internal promotion.

(b)   Voluntary removal of disruptive employees.

(c)   Infusion of expertise from the newly hired employees.

The important question which managers are required to answer for each employee who leaves is "Are the right people staying and are the right people departing?"

3. Job Satisfaction and Absenteeism

It is significant to remember that although high job satisfactions will not essentially result in low absenteeism, but low job satisfaction will probably bring about absenteeism. It has also been found that employees who consider that their work is significant in the organisation, display lower absenteeism rates than those employees who feel that their jobs are not significant.

When employees are unhappy with their jobs, they may psychologically and physically withdraw themselves or they may act aggressively and retaliate for the wrong intentions presumed.

Another way in which employees may show their dissatisfaction with their job situations is by being tardy. This is a short period of absenteeism and the employee will come to work but will turn up late. Such an employee does not actively involve itself in the organisation. This may disrupt productive relations and also affect the timely completion of work. Another phenomenon called full attendance happens when employees come to work even when they don't feel like, for example when they are not well and are suffering from migraine, flu, lower back pain or arthritis, etc. This tends to decrease the employee's productivity. Sensitive managers are required to be empathetic and yet assertive enough to motivate employees to stay away from work on such times and they must push for a sensible absenteeism rate.

It is significant to keep in mind that although high job satisfaction will not necessarily result in low absenteeism, even then, low job satisfaction will probably cause an increase in absenteeism. It has also been found that employees, who believe that their work is significant to the organisation, show lower absenteeism rates than those employees who feel that their jobs are not significant.

4. Job Satisfaction and Workplace Theft, Violence and Bending of the Rules

A high level of dissatisfaction within the organisation can even lead to behaviours such as stealing, using the firm's services/property without permission or committing some frauds. These acts represent theft or the unauthorised removal or usage of company resources.

Such kind of behaviour is seen because these employees feel they are overburdened, exploited or that they get impersonal treatment from their organisation and this might be their means of "getting back" or taking revenge for being mistreated.

Dissatisfied employees may also tend to bend the rules to get a sense of equity in their own minds or do it for getting personal gains.

When dissatisfaction is at the highest level, one of the extreme results can be in the form of aggression or verbal or physical assault at work. Other reasons like stress may also be the reason why employees face violence and managers must take adequate steps to prevent it.

5. Job Satisfaction and Stress

It is found that employees that are happy with their jobs tend to have better physical health; they learn new things at work more easily and have fewer grievances. By building-up the job satisfaction, perceived stress may really decrease in employees.

Job satisfaction is just one part of life satisfaction. A person's level of satisfaction directly or indirectly influences his feelings about other parts. This spill over-effect happens in both directions and managers are required to be attentive to subtle clues about the employee's satisfaction.

In addition, as employees grow older, they tend to become happy with their jobs. Individuals that have higher-level occupations also tend to be happy with their jobs, as they have better working conditions, are better paid and have more important jobs. Research also suggests that employees which work in small organisations have a higher level of job satisfaction as compared to those in larger organisations. This is related to the direct and personal contact of employer with the employees.

2.3.6 Theories of Job Satisfaction

1. Maslow's Theory

This theory is based on the following hierarchy of needs to be satisfied.

1. Physiological requirements like food, clothing, and shelter may be primarily satisfied at work by salary/wages.

2. Safety/security requirements like safe working conditions, job security may be satisfied at work and benefits are granted.

3. Social requirements like sense of belonging, acceptance and appreciation may be mainly satisfied at work by harmonious teams.

4. Esteem requirements for status/power may be mainly satisfied at work by promotion and respect for position/expertise.

5. Self-actualisation needs like need for fulfilment may be mainly satisfied at work by challenging work which realises an individual's potential.

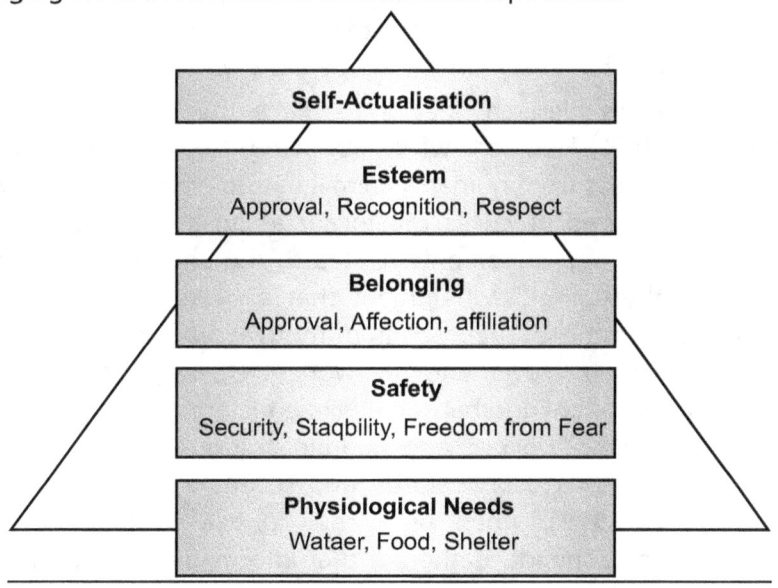

Fig. 2.2: Maslow's Hierarchy of Needs

Maslow's needs hierarchy was developed to describe human motivation in general. Although, it's main tenants is applied to the work setting, and is used to explain job satisfaction. Within an organisation, financial compensation and healthcare are some of the benefits which help an employee in meeting their basic physiological requirements. Safety needs can display itself through employees feeling physically protected in their work climate, as well as job security or have appropriate company structures and policies. When this is fulfilled, the employee's can concentrate on feeling as though they belong to the company. This can come in the form of positive relationships with co-workers and supervisors in the company, and whether or not they feel they are a part of their team/ organisation. Once they are happy, the employee will try to feel important and appreciated by their colleagues and their organisation. The final step is where the employee seeks to self-actualise; where they need to grow and develop so as to become everything they want to become. Though it is seen as separate, the progressions from one step to the next all contribute to the process of self-actualisation. Thus, organisations that want to improve employee job satisfaction should try to meet the basic requirements of employees before progressing to address higher-order requirements.

2. Herzberg's Theory

Frederick Herzberg conducted extensive surveys to find out what made people happy at work. Two sets of factors emerged which affected behaviours.

The first set avoided dissatisfaction. They avoided high labour turnover absenteeism and industrial dispute. He called these **hygiene factors** as they avoided an organisation from becoming unhealthy. The second set was those which actively encouraged people to give it committed performance. He called these **motivators**.

Herzberg emphasised that both sets of factors are significant. If hygiene factors were missing, people felt that that they are being treated unjustly, and this brought about revenge in psychology. He proposed that every job should be a growth experience.

Herzberg used Maslow's hierarchy needs to make the motivator/hygiene theory of employee motivation. In 1968, Herzberg wrote about the two different needs of man. The first need is the one that comes from human's animal nature or the inbuilt drive to avoid pain from the setting or the learned practices that occur as an answer to the basic biological requirements. The other set of requirements relates to the unique features of humans, the capacity to attain. It is through this attainment that a person experiences psychological growth. Herzberg also gave a theory that growth or motivation factors intrinsic to the job are: achievement, recognition for achievement, the work itself, responsibility, and growth for advancement. He also gave the theory that the hygiene factors or those factors that generate dissatisfaction are company policy and administration, supervision, interpersonal relationships, working conditions, salary, status, and security. Herzberg's two-factor theory was tested by **Schmidt (1976)**, when he carried out a study using 74 educational administrators in Chicago. Schmidt gathered the information using a modification of Herzberg's interview method and a questionnaire on the features of the job. Each principal was asked to think of an incident that made him feel extremely good or extremely bad about his job as an administrator, either in his current position or in previous administrative positions.

3. Affect Theory

Edwin A. Locke's Range of Affect Theory (1976) is the most popular job satisfaction model. The main principle of this theory is that satisfaction is determined by an inconsistency between what one needs in a job and what one has in a job. Additionally, the theory defines that how much one values a given aspect of work (e.g. the degree of autonomy in a position) moderates or how satisfied/dissatisfied one becomes when expectations are or are not met. When an individual values a specific aspect of a job, his satisfaction is more greatly impacted both positively and negatively, compared to one who doesn't value that aspect. To demonstrate, if employee A values autonomy in the company and employee B is uninterested about autonomy, then employee A would be more happy in a position that provides a high level of autonomy and less happy in a position with little or no autonomy compared to employee B.

4. Equity Theory

Adams equity theory also includes a social constituent in which the person compares his inputs and results to those of others. It argues that a major input into job performance and satisfaction is the degree of equity or inequity that people observe in their work condition.

Equity theory was influenced by **James Adams** and was created in1965. Equity theory was based upon three main assumptions.

First, that people develop principles about what forms a fair and reasonable return for their contributions to their jobs.

Secondly, equity theory supposes that people have a tendency to compare what they observe to be the exchange they have with their employers to that which they see the co-workers have with their employers.

Thirdly, equity theory holds that when people consider that their own treatment is not fair, relative to the exchange they observe others to be making, and they will be encouraged to do something about the inequity.

For example, one employee believes that another employee makes twice as much as they do. Whether that faith results in dissatisfaction depends on their beliefs about the value of contributions they make as compared to their colleague. People can stand seeing others getting more money and earn benefits if they do think that others are contributing more in the way of inputs. One main criticism of equity theory is that issues of fairness and justice can be a matter of "the eye of the beholder". There is always the possibility that what one considers is not matching with what is actually occurring. Another restriction to this theory is that it can be difficult to compare one organisation to another, thus this theory is made locally for the person.

2.4 Perception

2.4.1 Introduction

The world as it is perceived, is the world that is, behaviourally important. People's behaviour is based on their perception of what reality is, not on reality itself. What we perceive can be substantially different from objective reality. For example, employees at Google may view it as a great place to work – excellent benefits, favourable working conditions, interesting job assignments, good pay, understanding and responsible management – but it is very unusual to find such agreement amongst all employees.

Perception is the organisation, identification, and interpretation of sensory information in order to represent and understand the environment.

All perception involves signals in the nervous system, which in turn result from physical stimulation of the sense organs. For example, vision involves light striking the retinas of the eyes, smell is mediated by odour molecules and hearing involves pressure waves.

Perception is not the passive receipt of these signals, but can be shaped by learning, memory, and expectation. Perception involves these "top-down" effects as well as the "bottom-up" process of processing sensory input. The "bottom-up" processing is basically low-level information that's used to build up higher-level information (that is, shapes for object recognition).

The "top-down" processing refers to a person's concept and expectations (knowledge) that influence perception. Perception depends on complex functions of the nervous system, but subjectively seems mostly effortless because this processing happens outside conscious awareness.

2.4.2 Definitions of Perception

* *"Perception can be defined as the process of receiving, selecting, organising, interpreting, checking, and reacting to sensory stimuli or data".*   **– Udai Pareek**

* *"Perception may be defined as a process by which individuals organise and interpret their sensory impressions in order to give meaning to their environment".*   **– S. P. Robbins**

2.4.3 Importance of Perception

The manager in an organisation will only be successful if the pre-determined objectives have been obtained easily. Without doubt, it can be said that the attainment of objectives depends on the behaviour of the employees and that behaviour is influenced by observation. The reason for this is that people do as they understand. Thus, if the manager wants to know about and control the behaviour of his subordinates he must have the knowledge of perception. He must be careful of the fact when people make a wrong perception of the true facts and when people make a right perception of the facts. Making a true perception is helpful in all the managerial functions but a right perception has great significance in the following fields.

1.   **Performance Appraisal:** The reason for performance appraisal is to assess the work of the employees. The career of an employee relies on the performance appraisal and the performance appraisal is influenced by perception. If a manager assesses the work of his subordinates with a positive perception, then his assessment/appraisal will be of high order or if a manager assesses the work of the subordinates with a negative perception, then his appraisal will be of low order. Generally, there are two bases of assessing the work of the employees – objective and subjective. In case of objective assessment, the assessment is done on the basis of facts. For example, suppose the objective of a sales executive is set at rupees ten crores and the original sale is that of rupees eight crores; without doubt, the evaluation of the employee will be on a lower level. There is no particular place for any type of perception. Conversely, in case of subjective evaluation the appraisal is based on an individual's interest rather than facts. For example, a sales executive has been given the target of good sales. Now, the sales attained by him are good or not in the eyes of his boss, depend on the general impression of the boss about the sales executive. Thus, when the appraisal is completed subjectively, perception has an important role to play.

2.   **Selection:** Perception has an important role in selecting the employees. Employees can be selected either by conducting the interviews or without the same; however, when the selection of the candidate is done without conducting the interview, then the entire process depends completely on the perception. In other words, a perception about the candidate that he has the required abilities is created by first looking at the candidate. Perception thus formed is generally wrong. Then again, even if the selection of the candidate is finished through interview   still then the perception controls the selection. Every individual interviewing the candidate makes a separate perception of the candidate. Thus, which candidate will be selected or not depends on the perception.

3.   **Assessing Level of Efforts:** In some organisations the employees are assessed not because of work-performance but because of level of efforts put into it. In other words, if the efforts made have been good, the employee is assessed with a high rating regardless of the results. The assessment made on the basis of level of efforts is subjective. This completely depends on perception. If the boss gets the impression that his subordinate is really trying hard, his assessment would be high. At times, it has been seen that the employees are thrown out of the firm just because the amount of efforts that has been put in has been less. In short, it can be said that while assessing on the basis of level of efforts, perception has an important role to play.

4.   **Interpersonal Relations:** Every organisation is a group of different individuals. In order to run the organisation easily, the employees set up interpersonal associations. Perception has a significant role in establishing relations, for example, if a person perceives that his co-worker is not a good person, the relationship becomes bitter. In contrast, if the co-worker is perceived to be a good person it leads to a sweet relationship. In brief, it can be said that perception is the basis of relationship. If the perception happens to be wrong the interpersonal relations suffer so much so that the organisation becomes a centre of disagreements.

2.4.4 Basic Elements of Perception

Perception is known to be a process of sensory organs. The mind receives the information through the five sense organs that is nose, eyes, ears, tongue and skin. The stimulation is received by the organs through written messages, actions, oral communication, taste, touch, etc. Thus, perception starts with the knowledge of these stimuli. You can recognise the stimuli taking place only by paying attention to it. These messages are then further translated into actions.

Perception involves several elements (sub-processes) which are listed below:

1. **Stimuli:**

    Stimulus is the receipt of information that results into sensation. Knowledge and behaviour depend on senses and their stimulation. These senses are influenced majorly by this large number of stimuli. The social, family and the economic environment are the most important stimuli for the people. The psychological and physiological functions are impact of these stimuli. The intensive and extensive forms of stimuli have a much higher impact on the sensory organs. The socio-cultural environment, physical work environment and other factors have certain stimuli to influence the employee's perception. In organisational settings, the supervisor is supposed to form the stimulus situation for the employee's perceptual process.

2. **Attention:** The stimuli that is paid attention to purely depends upon the people's selection capacity and the intensity of the stimuli. Educated workers are observed to pay more attention to any stimuli, like, appeal for efficiency, announcement of bonus, motivation and training. It is the task of the management to find out suitable stimuli, which can be appealing to the employees at the highest level. Thus, an organisation must be aware of all the factors that affect the employee's attention. During the attention process, neural mechanisms and sensory gets affected and the receiver of the message becomes involved in understanding the stimuli. In an organisation, taking the employees to the attention stage is important for making them behave in a required and systematic manner.

3. **Recognition:** The incoming stimuli or messages are well recognised before they are transmitted into behaviour. Perception is a two-phase activity that is, receiving the stimuli and then translating the stimuli into action. The recognition process is highly solely dependent on the mental acceptability of the person. For example, if the car driver suddenly sees a child in front of his running car, he immediately stops the car. Thus, he recognises the stimuli, that is, the child's life is in danger. His mental process will recognise the danger if he pays attention to the stimuli. If he does not pay attention to the stimuli, then he won't be able to recognise the danger. Thus, after recognising the stimuli, he then translates the message into behaviour.

4. **Translation:** The organisation's management has to consider the various processes of translating the message into action. The employees need to be assisted in order to translate the stimuli into action. For example, in order to increase the overall production of the organisation, the announcement of bonus should be recognised as a stimulus, and thus the employee will be able to translate it into an appropriate behaviour. In simpler terms, employees should get motivated by the management which helps in the overall productivity of the organisation.

5. **Behaviour:** Behaviour is the outcome of the cognitive process which is a response to change in sensory inputs, like stimuli. Perceptual behaviour does not get influenced by reality however, it is an outcome of the perception process of the individual, his personality and learning, environmental factors and other external and internal factors at the workplace. The psychological feedback which may form an employee's perception may be his superior behaviour, raising of an eyebrow, movement of his eyes, his voice tone, etc. The employee's behaviour depends on perception, which is visible in the form of action, reaction or behaviour. The behavioural termination of perception may be covert or overt. The perception behaviour is thus a result of the cognitive process of the stimulus which can be a message or an action situation of management function. Perception is easily reflected in behaviour, which is visible in various forms of employee's action and motivation.

6. **Performance:** Proper behaviour leads to higher performance amongst employees. High performers become a source of stimuli and thus motivate other employees. A performance-reward relationship is formed to motivate people.

7. **Satisfaction:** High performance gives better satisfaction. The level of satisfaction is calculated based on the difference in performance and expectation. If the performance is more than expectation, people are delighted, but when performance and expectation are at par with each other, it results in satisfaction. On the other hand, if the performance is less than expectation, people get frustrated and thus it requires a more appealing form of stimulus for developing proper employee work behaviour and higher performance. It is important to understand the factors which influences the perception process and helps in moulding the employee's behaviour towards self-satisfaction and corporate objectives.

2.4.5 Factors Influencing Perception

The factors that control perceptual mechanism are of different kinds—external and internal factors.

I. External (exogenous) Factors

External perception factors are the features that influence whether the stimuli will be seen. The following external factors are defined as the principles of perception.

(i) **Size:** The larger the size of an external factor, the more it is expected to be perceived. A hiker will probably notice a fully grown fir tree than a seedling. For example, the maintenance engineer will concentrate more on a big machine than on a smaller one, even though the small machine has the same price as the big machine.

(ii) **Intensity:** The more intense the external factor, the more inclined it is to be noticed. Even the words in a memo from a boss to an employee can reflect the intensity principle. A memo that says "Please stop by my office at your convenience" would not make you as nervous as a memo that says "Report to my office immediately"!

(iii) **Status:** Perception is also influenced by the status of the person who is aware of things that are going around him. High status people can wield influence on the perception of an employee than the low status people. For example, when we are introduced to the divisional manager and foreman, we will probably remember the name of the divisional manager than the name of the foreman.

(iv) **Contrast:** External factors that are prominent against the background or those that are not what people anticipate are the most inclined to be perceived. Additionally to that, the contrast of objects with others or with their background may control how they are perceived.

(v) **Movement:** A moving factor is more likely to be perceived than a stationary factor. Soldiers in combat learn this principle very fast. Video games also show the principle that motion is quickly detected.

(vi) **Novelty and Familiarity:** Either a familiar or a novel factor in the environment can draw attention, depending on the situation. People quickly notice an elephant walking along a city street because it is a sight that is new and is hardly ever seen. You will probably be the first person to perceive the face of a close friend among a group of people walking toward you. A combination of these or factors that are same may function at any time to have an effect on perception. In combination with certain internal factors of the person doing the perceiving, they decide whether any particular stimulus will probably be noticed.

(vii) **Frequency:** The frequency principle defines that a repeated external stimulus gathers more attention than a single one. "A stimulus that is repeated has a better chance of catching us during one of the periods when our attention to a task is waning. In addition, repetition increases our sensitivity or alertness to the stimulus". Therefore the greater the frequency with which a sensory stimulus is presented, the greater the chances are that we draw its attention. Repetition is often used as a method in advertising and is the most common way of drawing attention. Repetition helps to increase the awareness of the stimulus. But it has certain drawbacks. Firstly, repeating the confusing information increases confusion. Secondly, its stimulus is presented as many times as you choose to filter it out completely to avoid becoming annoyed. At last, frequency undoubtedly increases the chances of selecting a stimulus by the receivers but it is no way linked to the accuracy of the interpretation of the information. Frequency only results in making people conscious of the stimulus.

(viii) Order: According to **Secord and Backman,** the order in which the objects or stimuli are presented is a significant factor in influencing selective attention. At times, the first part of information among many parts received, is given the most attention, thus making the other pieces of information less significant. Sometimes, the most important piece is left to the end, in order to intensify the curiosity and perceptive attention. For example, a writer of a communication may purposely develop to a major point by continuing through many smaller and less significant points.

II. Internal or Personal Factors

Internal perception factors are facets of the perceiver that influence perceptual selection. Some of the more significant internal factors consist of personality, learning and perception, and motivation.

(i) Personality

Personality has an interesting association with perception. In part, perception forms the personality; in turn, personality has an effect on what and how people perceive.

A part of the personality known as field dependence/independence gives a specific example of the relationship between personality and perception. A field-dependent person has a tendency to pay more attention to external environmental signs, whereas a field-independent person depends mostly on bodily sensations. For example, in a test where a subject has to decide whether an object is vertically straight, a field-dependent person will depend on cues from the environment, such as the corners of rooms, windows, and doors. A field-independent person will depend mostly on bodily cues, such as the pull of gravity, to make the same decision. A field-dependent individual requires more time to look for hidden figures that are set in complex geometrical designs than a field-independent individual. A field-dependent individual is influenced more by the background or the neighbouring design than is a field-independent individual. Field dependence/independence has some repercussions for organisational behaviour. For example, in comparison to a field-dependent employee, a field independent employee communicates more independently with others in the organisation, that is, a field-independent employee does not depend much on the cues that are sent from others to identify suitable interpersonal behaviour. Additionally to that, a field-independent employee seems to be more conscious of the important differences that he notices in others' roles, status and needs.

(ii) Learning and Perception

Another internal factor that has an effect on perceptual selection is learning, which can lead to the development of perceptual sets. A perceptual set is just what a person expects from the stimuli on the basis of his learning and experience that is related to the same stimuli. This is also called as cognitive awareness by which the mind organises information and forms pictures and compares them with prior exposures to similar stimuli.

In organisations, managers' and employees' past experiences and learning, strongly influence their perceptions. For example, visualise an architect, a lawyer, and a real estate appraiser—all employed by an international design and engineering company. These three persons may notice different things about the building. The architect may first notice the architectural style and the construction materials used in the building. The lawyer may quickly observe that the dimension and the advertising placed on the building breaches a zoning regulation. The appraiser may concentrate on the general condition of the building and of the surrounding area, the different aspects that would influence the building's price and saleability. Each individual focuses on a different aspect of the same general stimulus due to the person's training and work experiences. The culture into which a person is born decides several life experiences, and learned cultural differences influence the perceptual process.

(iii) Motivation

Motivation also plays a significant role in deciding what a person perceives. Generally, people perceive things that promise in satisfying their requirements that they have found rewarding in the past. They have a tendency to ignore events that are disturbing but will perceive dangerous ones. Summarising a significant aspect of the relationship between motivation and perception is the Pollyanna Principle, which defines that people process pleasant stimuli more efficiently and precisely than unpleasant stimuli. For example, an employee who gets both positive and negative feedback during a performance appraisal session with her boss may more easily remember the positive statements rather than the negative statements.

When an individual looks at a target and attempts to interpret what he or she sees, that interpretation is heavily influenced by the personal characteristics of the individual perceiver. Personal characteristics that affect perception include a person's attitudes, personality, motives, interest, past experiences, and expectations. For instance if you expect police officers to be authoritative, young people to be lazy, or individuals holding office to be unscrupulous, you may perceive them as such regardless of their cultural traits.

Characteristics of the target being observed, affects what is perceived. Loud people are more likely to be noticed in a group than quiet ones; so, are extremely attractive or unattractive individuals. Because targets are not looked at in isolation, the relationship of a target to its background also influences perception, as does our tendency to group close things and similar things together. For instance, coloured women or members of any other group that have clearly distinguishable characteristics in terms of features or colour are often perceived as alike in other, unrelated characteristics as well. A shrill voice is never perceived to be one of authority.

2.4.6 Attribution

This theory basically looks at how people make sense of their world; what cause and effect inferences they make about the behaviors of others and of themselves. **Heider** states that there is a strong need in individuals to understand transient events by attributing them to the actor's disposition or to stable characteristics of the environment.

The purpose behind making attributions is to achieve *cognitive control* over one's environment by explaining and understanding the causes behind behaviors and environmental occurrences.

Making attributions gives order and predictability to our lives; helps us to cope. Imagine what it would be like if you felt that you had no control over the world.

When you make attributions you analyse the situation by making inferences (going beyond the information given) about the dispositions of others and yourself as well as inferences about the environment and how it may be causing a person to behave.

Two basic kinds of attributions made:
- **INTERNAL - dispositional**
- **EXTERNAL - situational**

The attribution theory is a theory developed by psychologist, **Fritz Heider** that describes the processes by which individuals explain the causes of their behavior and events. A form of attribution theory developed by psychologist, Bernard Weiner describes an individual's beliefs about how the causes of success or failure affect their emotions and motivations. Bernard Weiner's theory can be defined into two perspectives: intrapersonal or interpersonal. The intrapersonal perspective includes self-directed thoughts and emotions that are attributed to the self. The interpersonal perspective includes beliefs about the responsibility of others and other directed affects of emotions; the individual would place the blame on another individual.

Individuals formulate explanatory attributions to understand the events they experience and to seek reasons for their failures. When individuals seek positive feedback from their failures, they use the feedback as motivation to show improved performances.

For example, using the intrapersonal perspective, a student who failed a test may attribute their failure for not studying enough and would use their emotion of shame or embarrassment as motivation to study harder for the next test. A student who blames their test failure on the teacher would be using the interpersonal perspective, and would use their feeling of disappointment as motivation to rely on a different study source other than the teacher for the next test.

Attribution theory identifies attributions made by people as the basis of their motivation. It explains the relationship between personal perception and interpersonal behavior.

Assumptions

1. They try to provide a logical explanation to all that is happening.
2. They attribute actions of individuals to internal or external causes.

3. These theories propose that individuals follow a fairly logical approach in making attributions.

Attribution theory tries to answer the "why" aspect of motivation and behaviour.

Locus of Control Attributions

- Those employees who believe that there is an internal control for all outcomes feel that they have the power to change or influence the outcomes by means of their ability, skill and efforts.

- Those who believe that external factors control all outcomes, factors like luck, chance, etc. are responsible for influencing outcomes.

- Employees with an internal locus of control are usually happier in their jobs, occupy managerial positions, and prefer the participatory style of management as compared with employees with an external locus of control.

- Managers with an internal locus of control are, in general, better performers, considerate towards their subordinates, are not over-stressed, and follow a strategic approach.

- However, some studies show that managers with an external locus of control are perceived to take more initiative and be more considerate.

- Besides having important implications for managerial behaviour and performance, attribution theory helps in explaining goal-setting behaviour, leadership behaviour and employee performance.

- The process of attribution plays an important role in the formation of coalitions within organisations. Members have been found to have strong internal attributions, such as ability and desire, whereas non-members have a perceived external locus of control.

- Other attributions: Bad luck attributions: when people blame their failures to external causes like bad luck, fate etc. it helps reduce the pain and disappointment associated with failure.

- When people attribute their success to internal factors, their expectations of success in the future tend to be higher.

Co-variation Model of Attribution

Co-variation principle states that people attribute behaviour to the factors that are present when a behaviour occurs and absent when it does not. Thus, the theory assumes that people make causal attributions in a rational, logical fashion, and that they assign the cause of an action to the factor that co-varies most closely with that action. Harold Kelley's co-variation model of Attribution looks to three main types of information from which to make an attribution decision about an individual's behaviour. The first is *consensus information*, or information on how other people in the same situation and with the same stimulus behave. The second is *distinctive information*, or how the individual responds to different stimuli. The third is *consistency information*, or how frequent the individual's behaviour can be observed with similar stimulus but varied situations. From these three sources of information, observers make attribution decisions on the individual's behaviour as either internal or external.

Three-dimensional Model of Attribution

Bernard Weiner proposed that individuals have initial affective responses to the potential consequences of the intrinsic or extrinsic motives of the actor, which in turn influence future behaviour. That is, a person's own perceptions or attributions as to why they succeeded or failed at an activity determine the amount of effort the person will engage in activities in the future. Weiner suggests that individuals exert their attribution search and cognitively evaluate casual properties on the behaviours they experience. When attributions lead to positive affect and high expectancy of future success, such attributions should result in greater willingness to approach to similar achievement tasks in the future than those attributions that produce negative affect and low expectancy of future success. Eventually, such affective and cognitive assessment influences future behaviour when individuals encounter similar situations.

Weiner's achievement attribution has three categories:

1.　Stable theory (stable and unstable).
2.　Locus of control (internal and external).
3.　Controllability (controllable or uncontrollable).

Stability influences individuals' expectancy about their future; control is related with individuals' persistence on mission; causality influences emotional responses to the outcome of task.

2.5 Learning

2.5.1 Introduction

You must have seen people in the process of learning and you must have also seen people behave in a particular way as a result of the learning. We can infer that learning has taken place if an individual behaves, reacts, and responds as a result of experience in a manner different from the way he formerly behaved. To explain and predict behaviour, we need to understand how people learn, so that we can apply the theories of learning for shaping employee behaviours. This section defines learning and presents the popular theories of learning. All complex behaviour is learned. It should be noted that, for organisations wishing to remain relevant and thrive, learning better and faster is critically important. Learning is the key to success—some would even say survival—in today's organisations. At the organisational level, continuous learning is increasingly important for the success of the organisation because of changing economic conditions. Given the current business environment, organisations must be able to learn continuously in order to deal with these changes and, in the end, to survive. Knowledge should be continuously enriched through both internal and external learning. For this to happen, it is necessary to support and energise organisation, people, knowledge, and technology for learning.

2.5.2 Meaning and Definitions of Learning

Learning is acquiring new, or modifying existing knowledge, behaviours, skills, values, or preferences and may involve synthesising different types of information. Learning is any relatively permanent change in behaviour that occurs as a result of experience

Learning itself cannot be measured, but its results can be. Learning is any relatively permanent change in behaviour that occurs as a result of experience.

Learning, as a noun, is the body of knowledge and wisdom that one learns, as a verb, it is the process of gaining understanding that leads to modification of attitudes and behaviours through the acquisition of knowledge, skills and values, through study and experience. Learning induces a persistent, measurable and specified behavioural change in the learner to formulate a new mental construct or revise a prior mental construct.

"Learning is a relatively permanent change in behaviour that occurs as a result of prior experience. It explains that change in behaviour indicates that learning has taken place and that learning is a change in behaviour".   **– E.R. Hilgard**

"Learning has taken place when an individual behaves, reacts, responds as a result of experience in a manner different from the way he formally behaved".   **– W. McGehee**

"As the process of having one's behaviour modified, more or less permanently, by what he does and the consequences of his action, or by what he observes".   **– N. L. Munn**

"Learning is a relatively permanent change in behaviour occurring as a result of experience".   **– R. C. Atkinson and R. J. Lindzey**

Learning through practice, education, training and experience brings a major change in a person's behaviour. It is related to acquisition of knowledge, skills, ability and expertise which are relatively permanent in nature. All changes do not reflect learning and temporary changes may be only reflective but fail to represent any learning. The experience or practice must be reinforced for occurrence of learning. If reinforcement does not accompany the experiences or practices, the temporary changes in a person's behaviour will disappear. Thus, it is reinforcement which makes a change as learning in an individual's behaviour.

2.5.3 Types of Learners

1. **Concrete Experience (CE):** A receptive, experience-based approach to learning that relies for a large part on judgements based on feelings. CE individuals tend to be empathetic and people-oriented. They are not primarily interested in theory; instead they like to treat each case as unique and learn best from specific examples. In their learning, they are more oriented towards peers than to authority and they learn best from discussion and feedback with fellow CE learners.

2. **Reflective Observation (RO):** A tentative, impartial and reflective approach to learning. They rely on careful observation of others and/or likely to develop observations about their own experience. They like lecture format learning so they can be impartial objective observers.

3. **Abstract Conceptualisation (AC):** An analytical, conceptual approach to learning logical thinking, rational evaluation. These learners are oriented to things rather than to people. They learn best from authority-directed learning situations that emphasise theory. They don't benefit from unstructured discovery type learning approaches.

4. **Active Experimentation (AE):** An active, doing approach to learning that relies heavily on experimentation. These learners learn best when they can engage in projects, homework, small group discussion. They don't like lectures, and tend to be extroverts.

2.5.4 The Process of Learning

To learn something a number of things need to happen. Problems at any level can lead to a learning disability. Here are the steps in the usual order. If the brain is not functioning correctly at any of these steps, we call it a learning disability.

Step 1. Attention: If you can't pay attention to something, you are not going to be able to learn. This learning disability has special status. It is called Attention Deficit Disorder.

Step 2. Perception: We perceive things through our eyes, ears, nose, mouth and skin. If we do not perceive them correctly, we can't learn. If you cannot perceive the difference between a toothbrush and a comb, you cannot learn to brush your teeth.

Step 3. Integration: Once you perceive something correctly, you need to do three things to make sense of it. You must place it in the right order, understand what the context is (abstraction), and then join it with other perceptions and your old memories (organisation). You can have a learning problem with any of these things.

(a) **Sequencing (ordering):** What is the difference between "god" and "dog"? It is the order of the letters. Reading requires constant attention to what direction you are going. Likewise many tasks such as math problems and computers require strict attention to ordering. A child might know the days of the week, but not be able to say them in order.

(b) **Abstraction (placing in context):** How do you tell the meaning of the word "run"? You need to know the rest of the sentence to know which of the many meanings apply. People with this problem have difficulty with all the concepts which they cannot see or hear. Understanding geometry concepts is a good example.

(c) **Organisation:** To live and learn efficiently, different concepts need to be put in order or importance. They have to be related to things we already know or else we cannot "retrieve" them from our minds when we need them. Without organisation, the brain works like a messy room. That is, you can't find anything that you are looking for and you get sidetracked by what you do find.

Step 4. Memory: Long-term memory is not affected in learning disabilities. Short-term memory can be. Even if you finally understand how to measure the height of a tree using angles and a tape measure, it will do you no good if you can't recall it. We all recall better when we repeat something over and over. People with short-term memory problems have to repeat things over and over until they finally have it stuck in their brain. However, once it is "stuck" in their mind, it stays there. Some people have auditory (hearing) memory problem. They can't recall what they hear. Others have visual (seeing) memory problems. They can't recall what they see.

Step 5. Output: Just as it may be hard to get information into the brain accurately and efficiently, it can also be hard to get information out of the brain. A common one is language problems where people cannot speak as well as they should for their intelligence. Others have horrible problems with the coordination of the small muscles of their hands which can cause problems like a learning disability for writing. Others have trouble making their larger muscles co-ordinate. They would be clumsy and have trouble with sports.

2.5.5 Determinants of Learning

1. **Motives (Drives)**

Motives prompt people to take actions as they are the primary energisers of behaviour. They are known to be subjective and thus represent the mental feelings of people.

2. **Stimuli**

A stimulus is an object that exists in an environment and they increase the probability of eliciting a specific response from people. They may be of two types as discussed below -

(i) **Generalisation:** Generalisation takes place when the similar new stimuli keep repeating. It is possible for the managers to predict human behaviour when stimuli are exactly the same. However, there is a negative implication of generalisation that a manager may make false conclusions and inferences based on the principles of generalisation. For example, generalisation leads to halo effect in perception.

(ii) **Discrimination:** In cases of discrimination, responses may vary to different stimuli. Discrimination has wide applications in an organisational behaviour in view of individual differences amongst various aspects. For example, a supervisor will respond positively to a high producing employee and will respond negatively to the less producing employee.

3. **Responses**

The stimuli results in responses be it in the physical form or in terms of perception, attitudes or some other phenomena.

4. **Reinforcement**

Reinforcement can be defined as anything which increases the strength of the response and also tends to induce repetitions of the behaviour that precedes the reinforcement. It is known as a fundamental conditioning of learning. There is no possibility of measurable modification of behaviour to take place without reinforcement.

5. **Retention**

Retention means remembrance of learned behaviour over time and converse means forgetting. Learning which is forgotten over time is called "extinction". When the response strength returns after extinction without any intervening reinforcement, then it is called as "spontaneous recovery".

2.5.6 Theories of Learning

(A) Behaviourist Theory

Consider learning as the association of stimulus and response (S-R) connection and the response and stimulus (R-S) connection.

1. Classical Conditioning

It is a type of conditioning in which an individual responds to some stimulus that would not ordinarily produce such a response. Classical conditioning is based on the premise that a stimulus initially does not elicit a response but gradually acquires the capacity to response. This type of learning is quite common and plays an important role in reactions such as of fear, taste, etc. In an organisational setting we can see classical conditioning operating. For example, at one manufacturing plant, every time the top executives from the head office would make a visit, the plant management would clean up the administrative offices and wash the windows. This went on for years. Eventually, employees would turn on their best behaviour and look prim and proper whenever the windows were cleaned even in those occasions when the cleaning was not paired with visit from the top brass. People had learnt to associate the cleaning of the windows with the visit from the head office.

Examples of Classical Conditioning

Individual	Stimulus	Response
	Watches favourite tennis player winning a tournament	Jumps with joy
	Touches a hot vessel	Moves away
	Hears good music	Hums and rocks gently

2. Operant Conditioning

It is a type of conditioning in which desired voluntary behaviour leads to a reward or prevents punishment. Operant conditioning, also called instrumental conditioning, refers to the process that takes place when our behaviour produces certain consequences. If our actions have pleasant effects, then we will be more likely to repeat them in the future. If, however, our actions have unpleasant effects, we are less likely to repeat them in the future. Thus, according to this theory, behaviour is the function of its consequences.

Examples of Operant Conditioning

Individual	Response	Stimulus
	Browses the internet	Obtains desired information
	Carries a credit card	Finds it convenient to shop
	Pays loan instalments promptly	Attracts no penalty
	Achieves sales targets	Obtains incentives and gifts
	Uses electricity carefully	Saves money

(B) Cognitive Theories

Cognitive theory consists of a relationship between cognitive environment cues and expectation. Learning is considered as developing a pattern of behaviour from bits of knowledge about and cognition of the environment. This learning is termed as S-S (Stimulus-Stimulus) Learning. Cognitive process assumes that people are conscious, active participants in how they learn. Cognitive theory of learning assumes that the organism learns the meaning of various objects, events and learned responses depending on the meaning assigned to stimuli.

(C) Social-learning Theory

People can learn through observation and direct experience. Also called observational learning, social learning theory, emphasises the ability of an individual to learn by observing others. The important models may include parents, teachers, peers, motion pictures, TV artists, bosses and others. An individual acquires new knowledge by observing what happens to his or her model. This is popularly known as vicarious learning. A learner acquires tacit knowledge and skills through vicarious learning. Social learning has considerable relevance in organisational behaviour. A great deal of what is learned about how to behave in organisations can be explained as the result of the process of observational learning. A new hire, acquires job skills by observing what an experienced employee does. Observational learning also occurs in a very informal, unarticulated manner. For instance, people who experience the norms and traditions of their organisations and who.

Points to Remember

- The characteristic set of thoughts, feelings, and behaviours that make a person unique is together known as the personality of an individual.
- Heredity, culture, family background, our experiences through life and the people we interact with, are the various factors that influence the personality.
- Attention, perception, integration, memory and output are the different steps through which the process of learning takes place.
- The three components of attitude
  - (i) Cognitive component
  - (ii) Affective component
  - (iii) Behavioural component
- A job attitude is a set of evaluation of one's job that constitute one's feelings toward beliefs about, and attachment to one's job.

  Personality arises from within the individual and remains fairly consistent throughout life.
- Perception is the organisation, identification, and interpretation of sensory information in order to represent and understand the environment.

Questions for Discussion

1. Define personality and the factors influencing it.
2. Describe the Myers-Briggs type indicator personality framework.
3. Describe how the Big Five traits predict behaviour at work?
4. Explain the relationship between attitude and behaviour.
5. Summarise the formation of attitude.
6. Define perception and explain the factors that influence it.
7. Define learning and list the three major theories of learning.

Chapter **3**...

Interpersonal Relations

Contents ...

Learning Objectives ...

➤ To study the meaning and importance of interpersonal relations

➤ To learn the basic guidelines for developing interpersonal relations

➤ To understand the meaning, sources and types of conflict

➤ To explain the types of intrapersonal and interpersonal conflict

➤ To elaborate the functional and dysfunctional aspects of conflict

➤ To study the various styles of conflict management

3.1 Interpersonal Relations

3.1.1 Introduction

A connection between individuals working together in the same organisation is called interpersonal relationship. A person spends around seven to eight hours at his place of work and it is practically not possible for him to work all alone. People need each other to converse with and talk about different issues at the workplace. Research says productivity increases many times, when people work in groups as compared to a person working alone. To have a healthy workplace, employees should get along well.

Interpersonal relation is an important part of the managerial job the world over and many studies have established their importance in formal organisations, particularly for effective decision-making and implementation of decisions.

The domain keeps on receiving the attention of academicians, managers and management consultants. In spite of interesting insights offered by many studies of interpersonal relations over the past four decades, more remains to be known about the underlying bases of interpersonal behaviour. Interpersonal relationships are social unions, connections, or affiliations between two or more individuals who may interact overtly, covertly, face to face or may remain unfamiliar with each other such as those in a virtual community who like to remain unknown and do not socialise outside of a chat room.

3.1.2 Importance of Interpersonal Relations

Interpersonal relationship refers to a strong relationship among people working together in the same organisation. Employees working together should share a special bond for them to give their level best. It is important that people be truthful to each other for a healthy interpersonal relationship and finally to create a positive ambience at the workplace.

Why interpersonal relationship at workplace?

Why do employees need to be cordial to each other?

1. A person spends around eight to nine hours in his organisation and it is nearly impossible for him to work all alone. Human beings are not machines who can work at a stretch. We require people to talk to and share our feelings. Imagine yourself

working in an organisation with no friends around. We are social animals and we require friends around. A person working alone is more stressful and anxious. They barely enjoy their work and come to work in the office just for the sake of it. Individuals working alone find their job very boring. It is important to have employees whom he can trust and share all his secrets without the fear of them getting leaked. We must have friends at the workplace who can give us truthful feedback.

2. **A single brain can't take all decisions alone.** We require people to talk about different issues, evaluate the pros and cons and arrive at solutions that benefit not only the employees but also the organisation on the whole. Employees can think together and give out better ideas and strategies. Strategies must be discussed on an open platform where every person has the freedom to convey his/her thoughts. Employees should be called for meetings at least once in a week to endorse open communication. Communication on a regular basis is important for maintaining a healthy relationship.

3. **Interpersonal relationship** has a direct impact on the organisational culture. Misunderstandings and confusions create negativity in the organisation. Conflicts lead you nowhere and in turn ruin the work environment.

4. **We need people around who can appreciate** our hard work and encourage us from time to time. It is important to have some employees who you can trust, who not only appreciate us when we do some good work but also point out our mistakes. A positive comment goes a long way in getting the best out of individuals. In an organisation, one needs to have people who are more like mentors than colleagues.

5. **It always pays to have individuals around who really care for us**. We need co-workers to fall back on when the times become difficult. If you do not talk to anyone in the organisation, no one would help you when you actually need them.

6. **An individual needs to get along with fellow workers** to finish the assignments within the stipulated time frame. A person working all alone is overstrained and never completes his tasks within the given deadline. It is important to encourage your fellow workers. You just can't do everything alone. Roles and responsibilities must be delegated as per the specialisation, educational qualification and interests of employees. A person requires help of his fellow employees to complete the assignments on time and for better results.

3.1.3 Developing Interpersonal Relations at Work

Interpersonal relationship refers to a strong association among employees either working together in the same team or same organisation. Employees must get along well for a positive and healthy ambience at the workplace.

1. **Do not treat office as your home:** There is a particular way of behaving in the organisation. It is important to be professional at work. Never behave badly with any

of your co-workers. Leg pulling, criticism, backbiting is not allowed. It is better to avoid someone you don't like rather than fighting or arguing with him/her. Your office co-workers can be your friends as well but one should know where to draw the boundaries. Excessive friendship is bad among the employees, which at times can ruin the relationship.

2. **An individual should not interfere in his colleague's work:** Superiors must create particular KRAs for all the employees and ensure that the job responsibilities do not overlap. Overlapping of job responsibility leads to employees interfering in each other's tasks and ultimately fighting over small issues. One should focus only on his work rather than trying to find out what the other employee is up to.

3. **Give space to your fellow workers:** Giving space in reality is important in all relationships. Overhearing anyone else's personal conversation is very unprofessional. An employee should not open envelopes, couriers or letters that do not belong to him. Such practices create disappointment amongst employees and eventually ruin relationships.

4. **Do not spread baseless rumours at workplace:** Even if you know something about someone, learn to keep things to yourself. Talk about it with the person concerned in private instead of publicising the whole thing. The organisation is not concerned with anyone's private matters.

5. **Pass on correct information to others:** If your manager has asked you to share some information with any of your co-workers, make sure it is shared in its desired form. Meddling with the data and playing with information ruin relationships among colleagues and cause confusions at the workplace.

6. **A team leader should not scold any of his team members in front of others:** It might be insulting for him/her. Call the person concerned either to your cabin or conference room. Avoid comparisons amongst team members. The employees must be strictly judged in accordance with their work and nothing else. The employees that work well should be suitably rewarded.

7. **Stay away from nasty politics at workplace:** Do not try to hurt anyone. It is absolutely fine to welcome someone who has done something remarkably well. Do not be jealous. It will hurt you in the long run. There should be healthy competition amongst the employees for a healthy environment at the workplace.

3.2 Conflicts

3.2.1 Meaning and Definition

Conflicts are the result of incompatible interests. Conflict occurs quite commonly in organisations. Research has estimated that 20 percent of the manager's time in any organisation is spent dealing with conflicts and its effects.

In the context of organisations, conflict can be defined as *a process in which one party perceives that another party has taken or will take action that is incompatible with one's own interests.*

Other definitions are –

- *"Conflict is a process in which an effort is purposefully made by one person or a unit to block another that results in frustrating the attainment of the other's goals or the furthering of his or her interests."*

- *"Conflict is a process that begins when, one party perceives that another party has negatively affected or is about to negatively affect something, the first party cares about."*

This definition describes the point in any on-going activity, which makes an interaction cross over to become an inter-party conflict. It encompasses the wide range of conflicts that people experience in organisations – incompatibility of goals, differences over interpretations of facts, disagreements based on behavioural expectations and the like.

This definition is also flexible enough to cover the full range of conflict levels, from overt and violent acts to subtle forms of disagreement.

There are many definitions of conflict. All these definitions have several common themes. Conflict must be perceived by the parties in to it; whether or not conflict exists is a perception issue. If no one is aware of a conflict, then it is generally agreed that no conflict exists.

Sociologists and Researchers define conflict as an interaction in which individuals and groups attempt to achieve their goals at the cost of others.

Conflict has been and is studied by almost all the social sciences like sociology, anthropology, psychology, politics, law and behavioural sciences. All of them are in agreement about the essential qualities of conflict. 'A's success is always at the cost of 'B'. If 'A and B' both achieve their goals then it is not conflict.

Sociologists and researchers define conflict as an interaction in which individuals and groups attempt to achieve their goals at the cost of others.

Sociologists who give more importance to interpersonal conflicts leading to neurosis and other mental illness define it as a situation in which a person is driven to engage in two or more mutually exclusive activities.

Behavioural scientists include both personal and social aspects in their definition. *"'Conflict' is a condition of objective incompatibility between values or goals; it is the behaviour of deliberately interfering with another's goal achievement; emotionally it is the cause of hostility."*

This definition states that –

1. Conflicts arise if values are discordant and
2. If goals are inconsistent.
3. Conflict is a deliberate action.
4. Conflict is interference in other person's achievement of goals.
5. Conflict is emotional enmity.

Conflict, competition and cooperation are three different types of social interactions sharing three common components.

1. Values of goals towards which actions are oriented.
2. Human groups related to each other in some degree for the achievement.
3. Pattern of action relating human groups to each other and to the achievement of goal values.

During conflict, interaction between relationship structures is direct and negative. Interaction towards the goal is reduced since eliminating the opposing group assures the goal.

In an organisation, conflict, competition and cooperation are usually inter-related. Members may cooperate with each other for achievement of work but they may be competing with each other to get to the senior's position. Simultaneously conflict may exist between members whose values differ vastly from each other.

> *It depends on the leader to use and convert conflict into a healthy organisational environment which leads to the achievement of goals.*

Similarly, in an organisational conflict, competition and cooperation are also inter-changeable.

It is possible to change conflict into competition and cooperation and vice-versa. It depends on the leader to use and convert conflict into a healthy organisational environment which leads to achievement of goals.

3.2.2 Steps in Conflict

The conflict process can be seen as comprising of five stages –
(i)   Potential Opposition or Incompatibility
(ii) Cognition and Personalisation
(iii) Intentions
(iv) Behaviour
(v)   Outcomes

Stage I: Potential Opposition or Incompatibility

At this stage, there is the presence of conditions that create opportunities for conflict to arise. They need not lead directly to conflict, but one of these conditions is necessary if conflict is to arise.

These conditions can be grouped into three general categories –
(a) Communication
(b) Structure
(c) Personal Variables

(a) Communication: A review of the research suggests that semantic difficulties (difficulties in understanding the meaning of words), insufficient exchange of information and noise in the communication channel are all barriers to communication and they are potential antecedent conditions to conflict.

Semantic difficulties arise as a result of differences in training, selective perception and inadequate information about others.

Research demonstrates that the potential for conflict arises when either too little or too much communication takes place.

The channel chosen for communication can have an influence on stimulating conflict. The process of filtering information and making use of new channels rather than previously established channels also leads to conflict.

(b) Structure: The structure includes variables such as size, degree of specialisation in the tasks assigned to group members, jurisdictional, clarity, member goal compatibility, leadership styles, reward systems, and the degree of dependence between groups.

Research indicates that larger the group and the more specialised its activities, the greater the likelihood of conflict. Tenure and conflict have been found to be inversely related. The potential for conflict tends to be greatest where group members are younger and where turnover is high. A lack of a precise definition of responsibility leads to emergence of conflict. Jurisdictional ambiguities increase inter-group fighting for control of resources and territory.

Groups within an organisation have diverse goals this itself is a major source of conflict.

Research tends to confirm that participation and conflict are highly correlated, because participation encourages the promotion of differences. Reward systems, are found to create conflict when one member's gain is at other's expense.

(c) Personal Variables: They include a person's individual value systems and the personality characteristics that account for individual idiosyncrasies and differences.

Certain personality types lead to potential conflict. For example, individuals who are highly authoritarian and dogmatic and who demonstrate low esteem, lead to potential conflict. Prejudice, disagreements over one's contribution are diverse issues, which can best be explained with the help of value differences. Differences in value systems are important sources for creating the potential for conflict.

Stage II: Cognition and Personalisation

In this stage, the potential for conflict or incompatibility becomes actualised. The antecedent conditions can only lead to conflict when one or more of the parties are affected by, and aware of the conflict.

Awareness by one or more parties of the existence of conditions that create opportunities for conflict to arise is a perceived conflict. Conflict results due to parties' misunderstanding of each other's true position.

> *Emotional involvement in a conflict creates anxiety, tension, frustration or hostility.*

Sometimes people perceive that there is a basis for conflict; however conflict will not arise unless the differences become personalised or internalised.

For example, X may be aware that Y and X are in serious disagreement over the interpretation of the policy, "Customer is the King" and are arguing for hours together. But if this episode does not make X tense or anxious and has no effect on X's relationship with Y then it can be concluded that the parties do not feel conflict.

Stage II is important because it is where conflict issues tend to be defined. At this stage, parties decide what the conflict is about. This is a critical event because the way a conflict is defined goes a long way towards establishing the sort of outcomes that might settle it.

Emotions play a major role in shaping perceptions. Negative emotions have been found to produce oversimplification of issues, reduction in trust, and negative interpretations of the other parties' behaviour. In contrast positive feelings have been found to increase the tendency to see potential relationships among the elements of problems, to take a broader view of the situation, and to develop more innovative solutions.

Stage III: Intentions

Intentions are decisions to act in a given way in a conflict episode. Intentions intervene between people's perceptions and emotions and their overt behaviour. In order to respond to other's behaviour we have to infer the other's intent.

Using the two dimensions of cooperativeness and assertiveness, five conflict handling intentions were identified by **Thompson.**

    (a) Competing   –   Assertive and Uncooperative
    (b) Collaborating   –   Assertive and Cooperative
    (c) Avoiding   –   Unassertive and Uncooperative
    (d) Accommodating   –   Unassertive and Cooperative
    (e) Compromising   –   Midrange on both assertiveness and cooperativeness

Cooperativeness means the degree to which one party attempts to satisfy the other party's concerns.

Assertiveness means the degree to which one party attempts to satisfy his or her own concerns.

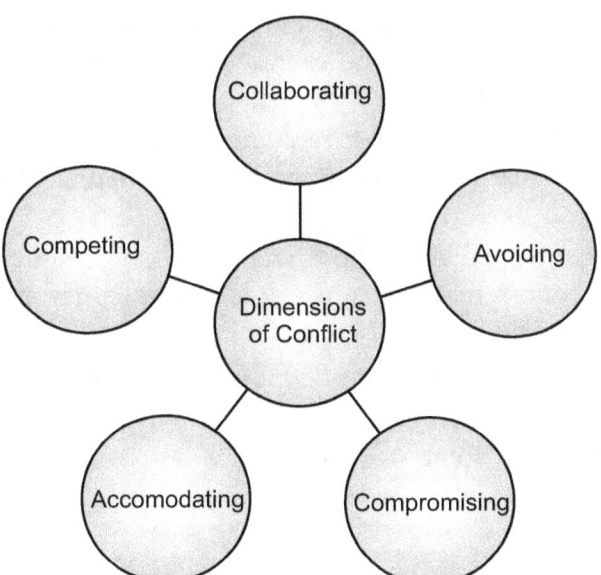

Fig. 3.1: Dimension of Conflict – Handling Intentions

Source: S. P. Robbins, "Organisational Behaviour, Concepts, Controversies, Applications" Prentice Hall of India, New Delhi 1997 Pg. 511.

Dimensions of Conflict – Handling Intentions

(a) **Competing:** When one person seeks to satisfy his or her own interest, regardless of the impact on the other parties to the conflict, he or she is competing. For example, a person who convinces another person that his conclusion is correct and another person's is wrong, that is, a person achieves his goal at the sacrifice of the other's goal. Many a times, in Indian organisations, the manager believes that he is always right and hence does not take the point of view of his subordinates, which then results in a common example of conflict.

(b) **Collaborating:** In collaborating, the intention of parties is to solve the problem by clarifying differences rather than by accommodating various points of view. Here the stance taken by all parties is to win and win rather than have an upper hand over another.

(c) **Avoiding:** It is the desire to withdraw from or suppress a conflict. Trying to ignore the conflict and avoiding others with whom you disagree are examples of avoiding. For example, many times during a performance appraisal the manager behaves as if there has been no difference between him and his subordinate.

(d) **Accommodating:** At times in order to maintain relationships, one party may be willing to place the opponent's interests above his or her own interest. Such an intention is called accommodating. For example, a person supports a colleague's opinion despite his reservations about it.

(e) **Compromising:** In compromising, there is no clear winner or loser. Each party intends to give up something. The solution, which is accepted, provides incomplete satisfaction to both the parties concerned.

These intentions can be called *conflict resolution styles*. The choice and use of the five conflict handling styles is likely to depend upon both the nature of the individual and the situational factors.

Intentions provide general guidelines for parties in a conflict situation. During the course of a conflict, people's intentions might change because of re-conceptualisation or because of an emotional reaction to the behaviour of the other party.

Research indicates that people have an underlying disposition to handle conflicts in certain ways. Individuals have preferences among the five conflict handling intentions. When confronting a conflict situation, some people want to win all at any cost, some want to find an optimum solution, some want to run away, others want to be obliging, and still others want to split the difference.

Stage IV: Behaviour

At this stage, conflict becomes visible. This stage includes the statements, actions and reactions made by the conflicting parties. Conflict behaviours are overt attempts to implement each party's intentions. At the same time, these behaviours have a stimulus quality that is separate from intentions. As a result of miscalculations or unskilled enactments, overt behaviours sometimes deviate from original intentions.

Stage V: Outcomes

Outcomes may be functional or constructive and dysfunctional or destructive.

Features of Conflict as stated by experts

1. Conflict occurs when two or more parties pursue mutually exclusive goals, values or events.
2. Conflict arises out of two different perceptions.
3. Conflict refers to deliberate behaviour. If interference is accidental there is no conflict.
4. Conflict can exist at the latent or overt level.
5. Conflict is different from competition. In competition both sides try to win, but neither side actively interferes with the other.

Indicators of Conflicts

1. Frequency and unwarranted arguments amongst employees.
2. Communication problems.
3. Destructive competition between departments.
4. An inflexible and insensitive attitude towards other members of staff.
5. Unfair criticism of certain individuals.

3.2.3 Types of Conflicts

In order to understand conflict, we need to understand the various types of conflicts.

These are as follows –

1. **Substantive Conflict:** This type of conflict is very common in organisations. It arises due to differences in perceptions and perspectives of people. Such a type of conflict is also beneficial as it forces people to think and discuss ideas openly and clearly.

   Such differences may allow innovation and also help the projects to be competitive. Substantive conflicts are a common phenomenon and they are welcome as the members are encouraged to openly discuss differences.

2. **Affective Conflict:** When people experience clashes of personalities, the resultant anger and frustration caused is called affective conflict. It is not unusual for people to experience affective conflict when team members of different projects come together or even similar projects come together and discuss common norms or behaviour.

   The clashes of personalities may be due to differences in ways of thinking, habits, work orientation and backgrounds. Affective conflict is likely to affect the work performance and productivity.

3. **Process Conflict:** Such type of conflict occurs as a result of differences in the ways of working or the processes or procedures adopted for working. For example, allocation of work, work responsibilities, job duties, and assignment of tasks are a result of process conflicts. These conflicts also affect the performance of work in a group.

3.2.4 Sources of Conflict

There are numerous situations happening in an organisation which leads to the creation of conflicts. Few of them are discussed as below –

1. **Competition of limited resources:** There is always a constraint for resource availability in most of the organisations and various departments in the firm keeps competing for these. Due to the limited availability of the resources, all the needs of the departments are not satisfied which leads to rising of conflicts amongst them.

2. **Diversity of goals:** Various groups and departments in an organisation have diversified goals, which lead to a conflict situation. For example, the marketing department of the firm would like to keep a higher stock of finished goods inventory so that they can supply for the increasing demand on time, whereas the finance department would like to minimise the inventory in order to reduce the carrying cost to the company.

3. **Task independence:** Various groups and departments in an organisation depend on each other for the successful completion of various tasks and this is known as interdependence. Because of this, the work of one group or department will get adversely impacted due to the poor performance of the other group, thus leading to conflicts.

4. **Differences in values and perception:** Differences in values and perception also lead to the generation of conflicts in an organisation. Labourers believe that the managers wants to exploit them and hence is paying lower bonuses whereas the management believes that by reinvesting the funds in the organisation itself will reap future benefits, which the labour force does not understand and this is what is known as differing perceptions. The R&D department takes it own time period for developing the products because of their orientation towards perfection whereas marketing department expects quick results so that it can beat the market competition. Thus, these situations lead to conflicts.

5. **Organisational ambiguities:** Often, there is some ambiguity about the precise job responsibility of the employees and thus there may also be conflict in performing the roles.

6. **Introduction of change:** When two organisations merge, it is a phase for organisational restructuring which may cause conflicts because of the two differing organisational cultures. Moreover, during these times, there is a power struggle which also leads to conflicts.

7. **Nature of conflict:** In an organisation, a faulty communication process where there is a noise in the system which causes distortion of the message resulting in deviations from the desired result of the communication, causes friction between the communicators and thus leads to conflicts.

8. **Aggressive nature of people:** Personality characteristics and idiosyncrasies in an individual also lead to conflicts especially in cases where an individual is highly authoritative, autocratic, arrogant and dogmatic.

3.2.5 Causes of Conflicts within Organisations

Conflicts taking different forms have different effects.

All organisational conflicts usually come under one of these categories –

* Conflicts of interest between functions, and
* Conflicts of authority involving manager and staff.

Let us now look at the underlying causes of conflicts.

1. **Grudges:** Much of the conflict occurs when people who have lost their face in dealing with someone because of their fault but attempt to get even with that person by planning to take some sort of revenge. By building a grudge with someone, employees are trying to get even with others and so much of the valuable organisational time and energy is lost. Many times, in the name of difference of opinion, the employee takes the advantage and uses the opportunity to take revenge and get even with other members.

2. **Malevolent Attributions:** Why did the other person want to cause harm? What are the intentions of the other party for provoking such behaviour and causing harm? Many times it may be due to the malevolent activities of others or malevolent motives of others. Whenever we feel we have suffered some harm or malice because of the intentions of others, we call it the malevolent attribution. This causes much harm as the members have malice and it is likely to impact behaviour and lose energy of the members involved.

3. **Destructive Criticism:** Negative feedback and destructive criticism can cause unnecessary harm and untold destruction. Most of the times, during the performance appraisals, when the bosses give negative feedback, it is likely to cause a negative impact on the subordinates and so, the work performance is likely to suffer. Today, more and more supervisors are taught to remain positive and speak positively to the subordinates and help them to develop from their mistakes and faults.

4. **Distrust:** Lack of trust is a very common cause of conflict. Many a times, when there is lack of trust and disbelief, superiors are likely to cause harm. Many bosses today are micromanaging, and do not give empowerment to the subordinates, due to the lack of trust between them. This is also likely to cause a lot of damage and harm to them.

5. **Competition over scarce resources:** Because organisations do not have unlimited resources in terms of money, inputs, equipment, infrastructure, there is always a conflict in relation to the scarce resources. For example, the marketing department of organisations has rivalry with the production departments, for the limited resources. Each feels that its department deserves more than the other departments and this causes rivalry and differences between them.

Specific causes are –

- Lack of coordination between employees from various departments; resulting in differing perceptions of objectives and roles
- Breakdown in communication lines and therefore barriers
- Poor team engagement
- Imprecise definition of goals
- Complex relationship between functions and sections
- Autocratic or dictatorial management style
- Personality difference among people
- Severe reductions in organisational resources
- Different perspectives and views
- Different perceptions
- Competition among members to do better than the others

3.2.6 Consequences of Conflict

The negative consequences of conflicts are that it causes negative feedback. However, these emotional reactions are only a part of the chain reaction that can cause harmful effects in organisations.

Due to conflicts, there is a lack of coordination among the personnel or the team members and it is likely to cause harmful effects in organisations and also cause stress.

Recently, in an FMCG company, when it was taken over by another company, the new organisation increased one layer in the organisational structure and so, as a result, the managers had to report to one more level rather than the Vice President directly which caused ego problems between them. They considered themselves inferior in status and as a result, five managers from such managerial posts left the organisation.

> ***Organisational Conflict has costly effects on organisational performance.***

In short, organisational conflict has costly effects on organisational performance.

Conflict, especially when it goes out of hand, is stressful, unpleasant, distracting, interferes with communication and can damage long-term relationships. That's quite a list, and it suggests that conflict is a serious issue, one that every manager and every organisation must take seriously.

3.3 Intrapersonal Conflict

Intrapersonal conflict is caused due to the tensions and frustrations within individuals. This happens because an individual is not clearly aware of his roles and thus he sets two mutually exclusively roles for himself. A person is expected to play a variety of roles during his entire lifetime. A role is an expectation which is placed on an individual by others (Katz and Kahn 1978). An individual occupying the roles becomes the role incumbent and then there are other people surrounding this individual and thus having certain expectations from him. As it is not practically possible to live up to everybody's expectations, it leads to anxiety and frustration in the role incumbent from within and these ultimately leads to intrapersonal conflict. Various types of role-related intrapersonal conflicts are discussed as below –

3.3.1 Role Related Intrapersonal Conflicts

1. **Intra-role conflict:** Intra-role conflict is experienced, when an incumbent is receiving conflicting messages from various role senders. This situation is very common in organisations which employs a dual authority system wherein the project head has different expectations as compared to a functional head and thus a role incumbent in unable to find solutions which can meet the various expectations. At times, intra-role conflicts occurs when the same person sends a role header conflicting or inconsistent expectations. For example, a customer service representative is instructed to handle maximum customers and also to provide detailed, complete timely and accurate information about the activities of the departments.

2. **Inter-role conflict:** An inter-role conflict is experienced when an individual is experiencing conflicts caused due to the multiple roles that he has to play in life. A common example of inter-role conflict is the conflict which is experienced by many employees when their working roles clash with their roles as a parent or a spouse (Nelson and Quick 1985). An individual who has to attend an important meeting at work and also a parent-teacher meeting at his child's school which is scheduled at the same time experiences inter-role conflict. This is caused due to different people with whom the role holder interacts, having different expectations from him.

3. **Person-role conflict:** Person-conflict is experienced when an individual has to perform various activities which are not a part of his value system. For example, this conflict is experienced by a highly ethical individual when he has to offer bribes to the clients to get an order. Also, a person trying to sell products of very low quality to a customer without actually disclosing the quality aspects of it may experience a person-role conflict. Similarly, a religious employee who is expected to work on a religious holiday experiences a person-role conflict.

Intrapersonal conflict has another form which arises due to the mutually exclusive goals that an individual sets for himself. There are three such types of goal conflicts.

3.3.2 Goal Related Intrapersonal Conflicts

1. **Approach-approach conflict:** When the incumbent is faced with two attractive goals and one has to be chosen over another, then this type of conflict arises. For example, when a person has to select between two equally attractive jobs or when a student receives admission calls from two very reputed institutions, it leads to approach-approach conflict.

2. **Approach-avoidance conflict:** When a person has to select between two goals and both are important, but one is attractive and the other is unattractive and thus avoidable, then it leads to approach-avoidance conflict. For example, a student who is scheduled to appear for his final exams in school the other day might experience this type of conflict if an important cricket match is scheduled to be relayed on the television before his scheduled examination.

3.   Avoidance-avoidance conflict: When an incumbent has to select between two equally unattractive but important goals, then it leads to avoidance-avoidance conflict. For example, an individual who has to make a choice between two jobs, one which is low paying and the other requiring relocation will experience this type of conflict.

Intrapersonal conflicts are known to be advantageous as they help us to select the right path and thus add on to our personal growth as well. They may also be equated with defining moments that puts across to us the challenges of choosing between the right and the wrong (Badaracco 1998). By creating appropriate and suitable job-person in an organisation, intrapersonal conflicts can be managed effectively because when there is a good fit between the individual's values and the organisation, the person is highly satisfied and attached to the organisation (O'Reilly et al. 1991).

3.3.3 Role Concepts: Role Identity, Role Perception, Role Expectations, Role Enacted, Role Ambiguity and Role Conflict

Roles: All the group members and employees plan out their respective roles as per their positions in the organisation. They not only behave in a specified manner but they also expect others to behave in a certain manner. Individuals in the group are assigned certain titles, jobs, and positions. The individuals are expected to perform certain roles and the perceived role is the role expected in practice by the individual himself which can be inaccurate. An enacted role is the way he actually behaves and the expected role is not the usual perceived role due to lack of clarity, role ambiguity and uncertainty. Role conflicts differentiate created roles from perceived roles. Job authority, duties and responsibilities are role factors which actually influence behaviour. When the perceived role, expected role and the enacted role are differently understood in reality it leads to distorted role behaviour, although theoretically they all are the same. The expected role may not properly be perceived due to the lack of clarity regarding job authority, duties and responsibilities. Role ambiguity is also caused due to various factors like the lack of clear job description. An employer or an individual may sink or swim when their enacted role is different from the expected role. Thus, at every level of management, role behaviour should be well defined and described in terms of individual characteristics, occupational levels and functional features so as to avoid creating role ambiguity.

At times, employees are required to perform more diverse roles than as expected. Most of the organisations have multiple role performing jobs. In order to understand role behaviour, it is important to note role perception, role identity, role enactment, role expectation, role conflict and role ambiguity.

Role identity: Role identity is formed when the behaviour and attitude is attached to the role together. Individual's behaviour is predicted as per their roles. When a situation demands a particular type of behaviour, it is related to role identity. Every position has its own type of role behaviour. For example, when an employee is promoted to managerial cadre, he will have a pro-organisation attitude, whereas when he was an employee, he may have been pro-union. Role identity is highly dependent on the socio-economic conditions prevailing inside and outside the organisation.

Role perception: When an individual is supposed to perform a set of activities or behaviour, it is known as role perception. It is a supposed role to be performed in a given situation. The employee's perception towards his job is influenced by various factors like environment, atmosphere, socio-cultural situations and other stimuli. Perceptions differ from person to person as people have different stimuli. Thus, role perception is an individual's view of how he expects to perform the task in the given situation. It is more of a psychological phenomenon than a real phenomenon.

Rule expectations: Role expectation is the behaviour which is expected by others from an employee. How other people believe an employee should perform the task in a given situation is known as role expectation. On the contrary, role perception is the behaviour presumed by an employee himself. Thus, perception is attached to an employee's understanding and own suppositions. It is his own belief regarding the role behaviour. Expectation is what others believe that how an employee would perform. Role expectation and role perception may be the same when others beliefs are similar to the employee's beliefs and this is known as role phenomena. In real, there are differences between role expectation and role perception because of the differences of attitudes amongst employees and also the differences of attitudes of other people towards employee behaviour. What the management expects from employees and what the employees expect from the management are role expectations. Similarly, what the management expects from itself and what employees expect from themselves are role perceptions.

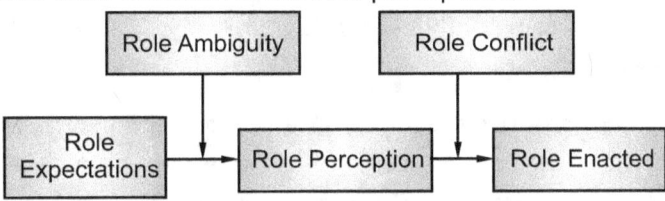

Fig. 3.2: Role Behaviour

Role enacted: The role enacted is known as the actual behaviour of individuals and the group members. The enacted role is dependent on the perceived role and the expected role and these roles tend to be in an equated form. If there is no difference between the expected role, enacted role and perceived role, the organisation will become free from role conflict and role ambiguity. Thus, there won't be any problems regarding responsibilities, duties, dissatisfaction, uncertainty, stress, deviation, tension and anxiety. There are very rare possibilities of equating these roles. An organisation desires to have equality of these roles for better performance.

Role ambiguity: Role ambiguity is created due to the differences between the expected role and the perceived role. Employees do not perceive what others are expecting from them. Role ambiguity occurs because of the lack of clarity regarding job descriptions, job duties and job lesions. An employee has to perform his duties as expected, discharge his expected responsibilities and also use his authority by the organisation.

Role conflict: Role conflict is created due to the differences between the perceived role and the enacted role. When an employee's perception is influenced by multiple directions and demands from multiple supervisors, then the employees tend to face uncertainty, unity of command and direction avoids role conflicts; however this is a rare phenomenon as in real, employees receive multiple directions and demands. Role conflicts may be intra-role conflicts and inter-role conflicts.

Intra-role conflict causes due to different directions being pointed to at the same time and inter-role conflict causes due to conflicting expectations. Intra-role is known as the first level conflict whereas inter-role is known as the second level conflict. An intra-role conflict is caused by production level multiple supervision, demand for various quantities by the sales manager, working conditions, repair problems and payment systems.

Inter-role conflict causes because of the position being occupied by the individuals. Multiple supervisors lead to multiple role expectations. One supervisor will expect quality, another supervisor will prefer quantity and yet another supervisor will desire smooth performance. Diverse expected roles cause multiple conflicting positions and thus it becomes difficult to reduce these conflicts.

Role behaviour depends upon the role conflict and role ambiguity. Less role conflict and role ambiguity leads to higher degrees of performance. Similarly, a higher amount of role conflict and role ambiguity lessens the performance. At times, employees may succumb to the strains and stresses of role conflict and role ambiguity.

3.4 Interpersonal Conflict

In organisations and group behaviours, interpersonal conflict is visible as employees have to act and react with other employees and this interdependence leads to interpersonal conflict. Interpersonal conflict is analysed under three heads, that is, transactional analysis, Johari Window and strategies for interpersonal conflict resolution.

3.4.1 Transactional Analysis

Transactional analysis is referred to people's interactions with regards to social transactions. Transactional analysis was developed by Eric Berne for psychotherapy in 1950, which was published in book form as 'Games People Play' in 1964. This analysis helps in providing a better understanding about how people react with each other while communicating and behaving with the society. Thomas Harris's book 'I am OK-You are OK' has gained popularity in transactional analysis. Behaviourists have discussed transactional analysis under two main heads, that is, Ego States and Life Positions.

Ego States: An ego state refers to the psychological analysis of interaction. It has been discussed by Freud for personality development. Ego is the reality between the morality of one self and the mere practical super ego. It keeps the impulsive ID and the conscience of the Superego within control. Transactional analysis makes use of this theory for identifying three important ego states, that is, ID (child), Ego (adult) and Superego (parent).

1.   Child State: In this state, a child acts like an impulsive child. The child's state is confronting, submissive, emotional, insubordinate, joyful or rebellious. People develop this state from experience and they possess all these qualities that are resealed spontaneously. People tend to behave like children when they realise the child state in them. They behave in an emotional manner and rebel against them when they are constantly hit by the latter. It is thus characterised by very immature and emotional behaviour. Employees under this state, generally says statements like, "You blame me only again and again", "Whatever you say, I will follow" and "I am getting mad because of the ill treatment of my boss". These are the numerous examples of a child state ID which should be properly used for motivating employees.

2.   Adult State: An adult state exists when people are calculative, rational, mature and factual. In this state, people gather relevant information, will analyse it carefully, interpret it, then will develop the alternatives and then select the best choices. It is characterised as fairness and objectivity. Under this state, emotional and dominant features are not exercised. For example, "We do the kind of job that we need", "This is high thinking, we should go into reality" is how these employees think and feel.

3.   Parent State: Parent state involves critical, protective, instinctive and controlled nurturing. This state involves superimposing rather than following real problems. People are domineering as they overact and desire protective and loving behaviour from their subordinates. They tend to treat others as children and behave in a mature way. Rules and regulations are to be followed strictly as many a times they are sceptical of other's capacities and thus the superego is observed in this state. For example, "Be careful with the rules", "Why do you not follow the rules" and other similar warnings and instructions are issued by them.

While interacting with other members of the society, people use any or all of the above described states and these states are effective for developing interpersonal relations. Transactional analysis based on state is useful and effective and these are known as positive and negative features of transactional analysis. The ego state is observed not only by the words used but also by the posture indicated, toned used, gestures and facial expressions.

Transactions based on ego state: People who are suing all the ego states are inclined to use one state predominantly. They commonly tend to use one of the three states, although all the skill states are important for effective interpersonal performance. Meantime, it should be noted that one state position contradicts the other state position. A person usually expects a response from another person in the state he needs the answer in transactions involving state positions that may conflict or confirm with the required behaviour. Transactions can be complementary, ulterior and crossed. Following are the basic factors of transactional analysis –

1.   Complementary Transactions: When the receiver and sender of the ego states are in reverse order, then it leads to complementary transactions. Following are the stages for complementary transactions: 1. Describe the behaviour, 2. Express the feelings, 3. Negotiate a change, 4. Empathise and 5. Indicate consequences. The manager asks and expects the employee to obey his orders but the employee denies them for that particular time although they perform it ultimately. If a manager is transacting in a parent-to-child pattern, employees tend to behave from a child state. If the manager is behaving in an adult-to-child pattern, then employees are not willing to oblige the manager. Adult-to-adult state is helpful for the managers to sit together with employees for sorting out the problems as these transactions are more effective in an organisation. Similarly, parent-child complementary transactions are also helpful for organisational performance.

2.   Crossed Transactions: Unlike complementary transactions, crossed transactions are non-parallel. A crossed transaction will occur when the message sent by one person's ego state is reacted to by an incompatible, unexpected ego state on the part of the other person. For example, the manager will behave in the parent-to-child ego state, whereas the employees will react only in the adult-to-adult ego state. The employees will be in another state, although the manager attempts to communicate from a basic ego state.

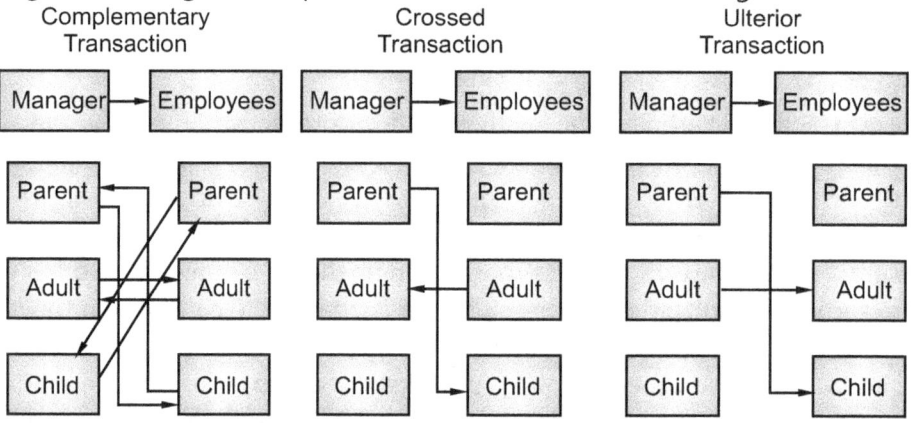

Fig. 3.3: Transactional Analysis

The manager attempts to explain the message and transactions in a parent-ego state or adult-ego state, but employees will receive it in a different-ego state and thus behave differently. If the manager expects them to perform a task, the employees may not follow his orders by flatly refusing and saying that they are not concerned about it. Communication blocks the accomplishment and leads to conflicts soon after the crossed transactions. If both the manager and the employee transacts at the same ego state then the problem may not arise. However, during crossed transactions, conflicts are bound to occur and they are also known as non-complementary transactions. A complementary transaction helps in increasing a cordial relationship.

3. Ulterior Transactions: The transactions happening between the employees and managers are influenced by various factors other than the ego state, although the ego state is realised in the transaction and a misunderstanding is observed. For example, the manager tells the employees that they are free to approach him any time as needed, but the employees feels that the manager is not willing to solve their problems. Apparently, the manager is behaving in a parental way although the employees realise it in an adult-ego state as shown in Figure 3.3.

Life positions: The ego state helps in understanding the life position. One's life position dominates a person's transactions while other positions are exhibited from time to time in various specific transactions. For example, "I am not OK - You are not OK, "I am not OK – You are OK", "I am OK – You are not OK", I am OK – Your are OK". The adult-to-adult transaction is "I am OK – You are OK". Any parallel ego state helps in maintaining cordial relations. Positive and negative attitudes towards one self and others help in deciding the levels of conflict. A crossed attitude increases the conduct.

Application of Transactional Analysis: Transactional analysis considers three ego states and three types of transactions, that is, complementary, cross and ulterior. Transactional analysis is applied in various forms which are known as stroking, conflict resolution, leadership, benefits and game play.

1. Stroking: Transactional analysis includes stroke, which simply means that right from the birth stage and throughout their lives, people need affection, cuddling, recognition and praise. In fact, everyone needs the stroke. If people do not receive positive strokes like praise and self-recognition, then they seek for negative strokes. Stroke is known to be the outgrowth of childhood experience. Stroke or recognition is required and desired for a healthy behaviour. The recognition or stroke may be verbal, physical or through eye contact. Managers give a pat on the employee's back in recognition of their performance. The parent-to-child stroke works better for motivating employees. Adult-to-adult communication is also effective for a healthy atmosphere. Stroke or recognition may occur due to certain conditions. For example, a manager shows his appreciation and gratitude to employees on achieving success. Unconditional strokes are presented without any conditions.

2. Leadership: A manager with a dominant attitude is known to become parental as he behaves more as an autocrat than a real parent. For effective performance, leaders should learn to adopt the parent-to-child ego state. An adult-to-adult approach gives more scope in employees for better performances.

3. Conflict Resolution: The parent ego state leads to follow up of rules and regulations and the child state avoids conflicts. Employees practicing the win-win outcome use the "I am OK – You are OK" state. Conflicts are better avoided through the parent-to-child state and also with the adult-to-adult ego state. The cross ego state creates conflicts which should be smoothed out through the parent-to-child approach.

4. Benefits: Transactional analysis that is based on the parent and child concept helps in creating a congenial atmosphere and benefits are observed in such a situation. Improved interpersonal communication creates benefits.

5.   Game Play: Transactional analysis discusses how people use their time. People learn to withdraw and intimate time development. The games that people play in their lives help in shaping up the atmosphere. People working with the spirit of a game actually achieve success in life as they are ready to win or lose the position. They use withdrawal, aggression, fixation and compromise in interpersonal behaviour.

3.4.2 Johari Window

Besides transactional analysis, Joseph Luft and Harry Ingham have also studied interpersonal behaviour. Johari, which is in the name of Joseph and Harry, has been developed for analysing interpersonal conflict. They have analysed interpersonal conflict and have suggested ways of solving conflicts. They have put emphasis on self as well as others, that is, self is related to "I or me" and others are concerned with "You or they". The interaction of 'I and you' is studied under this, wherein one should know about oneself and others. Knowing oneself includes knowledge of the people that they are coming across, the impact that they are having and the people that they are trying to influence. Many a times, people are not able to understand themselves and thus it is important to know themselves. The people who are related to an individual should provide feedback about their related attitudes and behaviour. There are four main components of the Johari Window – open self, hidden self, blind self and undiscovered self and these four windows are respectively known as public, private, blind and unknown arena.

	Known to Others	Unknown to Others
Known to Self	Public	Private
Unknown to Self	Blind	Unknown

Fig. 3.4: Johari Window

A person openly knows himself in open self. He knows everything about himself and about others too. There is known to be openness in their behaviour and attitude. Transparency is observed in their behaviour and is called as public arena wherein it has less scope for interpersonal conflict. Under hidden self, a person knows clearly about himself but fails to understand others. The person will remain hidden because of the fear of being known and criticised by others. In such a case, a person keeps his feelings secret and thus does not like to reveal his desires and feelings to others and this is called as private arena. This creates doubts and the chances of interpersonal conflicts are increased. In this system, the others do not pick up verbal and non-verbal responses. The blind arena is when one is not fully known to oneself, but is known to others. For example, the reader is unknown to self but is known to others. Since the followers are not willing to share feedback or communicate with the leader, it is unknown to the leader as well. The leader tends to shut his eyes to the available information or data, knowingly or unknowingly. A leader or person is unintentionally hurting the feelings of others whereas others are hesitant to express him the truth. There is no threat of conflict at present, but it would aggravate problems and thus holds a potential threat of interpersonal threat of interpersonal conflicts. In case of unknown arena, the person is not aware of himself and others too and he is in the dark about the real problem. The unknown facts may be seriously influencing the situation because doubts increase and conflicts are bound to incur because of the misunderstanding.

The Johari Window points out the interpersonal styles and the possible interpersonal conflict situations. It helps in solving conflicts through feedback, self-perception, disclosure and late strategies.

Feedback: Feedback helps in the configuration of the four arenas. In an organisation, the leader needs verbal and non-verbal feedback from his followers.

Subordinates in the organisation must be encouraged to give feedback to their leaders; this helps in increasing the mutual trust and confidence. It is actually the willingness of others to be frank and open to provide correct and fair feedback, Public arena, that is, known to others and known to self, provides feedback to the blind arena, that is, known to others and unknown to self. Thus, the superior receives the feedback from others and also from public arena. When subordinates express their perceptions and feelings, they should be heard and accepted which helps in removing the misunderstandings and doubts. Due to no feedback, managers are always in the dark and fail to realise that subordinates should be treated as family members. Feedback is more effective for solving the problem as it reduces the blind arena of the manager.

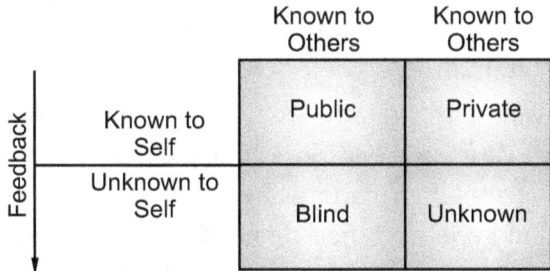

Fig. 3.5: Feedback Process

Disclosure: Disclosure is known as another process of Johari Window, that is, an extent to which a leader will willingly share his feelings with others and the subordinates should be looked at from their viewpoint. Only then, a manager can really understand them and make them understand his feelings. Potential conflict gets reduced if a person becomes more trustful of others and when he discloses relevant information about oneself. It should be realised that all the disclosures are not so useful and thus precautions must be exercised when disclosing the data. Disclosure is effective only when all the people, that is, the employees and the managers are at par and thus with this their attitudes and feelings are then comparable. They both have mutual confidence and trust in each other. Feedback and disclosure decreases the unknown arena which is known as the black spot as exhibited in Fig. 3.6. The public arena is increased by decreasing the blind arena through feedback and the private arena through disclosure. This helps in increasing the interpersonal behaviour and thus creates a healthy atmosphere in an organisation. In other words, the areas known to self and others should be increased in order to create a congenial atmosphere in an organisation.

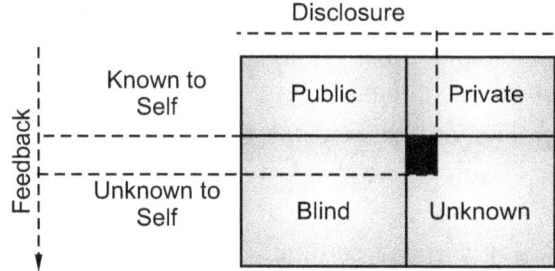

Fig. 3.6: Effect of Feedback and Disclosure

Strategies for Interpersonal Conflict Resolution

Apart from the transactional analysis and Johari Window, there are other strategies as well which are used for resolving the interpersonal conflict. They are known as lose-lose, win-lose, win-win, role set, linking pin and resolving conflicting groups.

1.   Lose-lose: Under this lose-lose strategy, both the parties involved will lose and this may take various forms. In order to resolve conflicts, a middle path is taken, wherein both the parties will lose the case to a certain extent. At times, one party may partially pay off the losses suffered by the opposite party. Judges and arbitrators are appointed to solve the problem; hence both the parties suffer in this. Lose-lose strategy shows the inaction of both the parties because they are fighting to lose! Although it is not a wise step to resolve, however there is no other alternative left before resorting to lose-lose strategy.

2.   Win-lose: In win-lose strategy, two parties are fighting to achieve success, however only one of them can win while the other party loses the conflict. For example, a manager may be very successful in suppressing the demand of the employees, or the employees will be successful in getting their demands redressed thus resulting in the loss of money by the organisation. Companies are supposed to pay more salaries and bonus to the employees. Conflicts are judgemental. This strategy has functional and dysfunctional consequences. It helps in creating a losing atmosphere because the losing parties remember the loss of the battle and thus take revenge whenever a situation arises.

3.   Win-win: In this strategy, both the parties involved in the conflict, win the battle and thus no one is a loser. Productivity, creativity and profitability are increased by mutual agreement. The manager asks striking employees to raise their productivity for claiming more bonuses, for which they go on strike. Profitability and production linked to bonus are the outcomes of the win strategy and it helps in eliminating any of the dysfunctional factors. It is associated with better experience, judgement and wise parties. Managements must try to exercise win-win strategies to resolve the conflicts because they create a healthy atmosphere in the organisation.

4. **Role set:** Overlapping and ambiguous role sets leads to various interpersonal conflicts. Robert L. Kahn is closely associated with the role set theory of the organisation. He suggested rearranging the overlapping and interlocking role sets in order to resolve conflicting problems. Kahn and his fellow associates have suggested that ambiguity and conflict tend to work more with a higher rank person.

5. **Linking pin:** Every group has a linking pin which is used in resolving the conflicts and it has an upward origination. Trade unions are linked with political parties which are headed by a person. There may be various linkages for resolving the conflicts like horizontal, influential, communicational, coordination and motivational. In Indian business houses, linkage is observed be it in group or out-groups.

6. **Resolving conflicting group:** Group conflicts can be resolved through delusions, avoidance, containment and confrontation. The avoidance strategy helps in keeping the conflict from surfacing by ignoring the conflict or by imposing a solution. The delusion strategy helps in cooling off the emotions and hostilities of both the parties through mutual co-operation. Under the containment strategy, some conflict is allowed to surface whereas other problems are contained by spelling out their solutions. The confrontation strategy plays a major role in bringing out all the issues into the open. The fighting group helps in directly confronting the issues. They ultimately resolve their problems through mediators.

3.5 Aspects of Conflict: Functional and Dysfunctional

The view of the integrator does not propose that all the conflicts are good; there is both positive and negative aspects to them. Boulding helps in recognising that some optimum level of conflict and associated personal stress, anti-tension are required for productivity and progress; however he portrays conflicts primarily as social and potential costs. Likewise, Kahn views that "one might as well make a case for interpreting some conflict as essential for the continued development of the mature and competent human beings, but they feel that conflict has a social cost".

Therefore, we can express that the conflicts that support the group's goals and improves its performance are known as functional conflicts. On the other hand, a conflict that hinders the group performance is a destructive and dysfunctional form of conflict, although the demarcation between functional and dysfunctional is neither precise nor clear.

3.5.1 Functional Conflicts

Looking at the conflict from a functional point of view, conflicts are supposed to serve the functions as mentioned below –

1. **Release of tension:** When conflicts are well expressed, it helps in clearing the air and reducing the tension which might otherwise stay suppressed. Suppression of

tension leads to distortion of truth, high mental exaggerations, sense of frustration and tension and biased opinions thus resulting in distrust. When members express themselves openly, they get some psychological satisfaction which also leads to reduction of stress amongst members.

2. **Analytical thinking:** When a group is facing some conflict, then the members display analytical thinking in identifying various alternatives. In the absence of conflict, they might not be creative or even might have been lethargic. The conflict may induce challenge to such opinions, views, policies, rules, goals and plans which need a critical analysis for justifying these as they are or making such changes as required.

3. **Group cohesiveness:** Inter-group conflict helps in bringing about solidarity and closeness amongst the group members. It helps in developing group loyalty and a greater sense of group identity for competing with the outsiders which increases the degree of group cohesiveness that can be utilised by the management for the attainment of organisational goals, in an effective manner. As cohesiveness increases, the differences are forgotten.

4. **Competition:** Conflicts promote competition and hence they increase the efforts too. Some people are highly motivated by conflict and severe competition and this leads to high level of effort and output.

5. **Challenge:** A conflict helps in testing the abilities and capacities of the individuals and groups. It helps in creating challenges for them for which they have to be creative and dynamic. If they can overcome the challenge, then it will lead them to look out for alternatives for existing patterns which further leads to organisational change and development.

6. **Stimulation for change:** At times, conflicts lead to changes amongst people, as when faced with a conflict, they might change their attitudes and be ready to change themselves too in order to meet the requirements of the situation.

7. **Identification of weaknesses:** During the arising of the conflict, it helps in identifying the weaknesses in the system and once the management learns about the weaknesses, it can always take the necessary steps to remove them.

8. **Awareness:** Conflicts throw light on different areas like what is the problem, who is involved in it and how to solve the same; and taking a cue from this, the management can accordingly take the necessary steps.

9. **High Quality Decisions:** During conflicting times, people tend to express their opposing perspective and views and this leads to high quality decision results. The people share their information and then check each other's reasoning for developing new decisions.

10. **Enjoyment:** Conflict adds the fun element to the team work, when it is not taken seriously. Most of the people find conflicts enjoyable as compared to competitive movies, games, sports, books and play.

3.5.2 Dysfunctional Conflicts

Following are the ways in which the dysfunctional aspects of the conflicts can be visualised –

1. **High Employee Turnover:** In case of individual and inter-individual conflicts particularly, some dynamic personnel may leave the company, if they happen to fail to resolve the conflict in their favour. In such a case, an organisation will suffer in the long run because of the loss of its key people.

2. **Tension:** At times, conflicts may lead to high level of tension amongst individuals and groups and there might come a stage when it becomes impossible for the management to solve the problem and this results in frustration, anxiety, hostility and uncertainty amongst the members.

3. **Dissatisfaction:** Conflicts result in discontentment to the losing party, who will be waiting for an opportunity for settling the score with the winning party. All this conflict results in lack of concentration on the job and thus even the productivity slows down.

4. **Climate of Distrust:** Conflicts lead to a climate of suspicion and distrust amongst the group members and the organisation as well. The degree of cohesiveness will be less as the discords will be more. Thus, the concerned people will have negativity towards each other and will try avoiding interaction with each other.

5. **Personal versus Organisational Goals:** Conflicts lead to distracting the attention of the organisational members from the organisational goals. They may waste their energy and time in finding ways and tactics to come out as winners in the conflict. Thus, here personal victory becomes more important than the organisational goals.

6. **Conflict as a Cost:** Conflict is not necessarily a cost for the individuals but it may weaken the organisation as a whole, if the management does not handle them in a proper manner. If the management suppresses the conflicts, they may acquire gigantic proportions in the later stages and if they fail to interfere in the early stages, then there might be unnecessary troubles in the later stages. Thus, it is a cost to the organisation because resignation of its people will weaken it completely and the feeling of distrust amongst members will have negative impact on its productivity.

3.6 Conflict Management

3.6.1 Meaning

Conflict management is a practice of being able to identify and handle the issues fairly, sensibly and efficiently. In businesses, since conflict is considered as an obvious part of the workplace, it is essential that there are people who understand the conflicts and even know how to solve them. This is highly a necessity in today's market than ever. Everyone is working hard to show how valuable they are to the organisation they work hard for, and sometimes this can lead to disputes within other members of the team.

3.6.2 Conflict Management Styles

Conflicts are obvious but how an employee resolves and respond to these conflicts will enable or limit his success. According to the Kenneth W. Thomas and Ralph H. Kilmann, following are the five conflict styles that a manager will follow –

1. **Accommodating:** An accommodating manager is the one who cooperates to the highest extent and this may be at his own expense and may actually work against his own objectives, goals and desired outcomes. This approach has proved to be effective when the other person has a better solution or if he is an expert.

2. **Avoiding:** Avoiding an issue is another way wherein a manager will attempt to resolve the conflict. This style fails to help the other team members to accomplish their goals and does not helps the manager who is avoiding the conflict and may not assertively pursue his or her own goals. However, this may work well when the conflict is trivial or when the manager has no chance of winning.

3. **Collaborating:** Collaborating managers teams up as partners or pair up in order to achieve their goals in styles. This is the way the managers break free the win-lose paradigm and thus seek the win-win. This turns to be effective for complex scenarios where managers needs to find a novel solution.

4. **Competing:** This is the win-lose approach wherein manager acts in a very assertive way to achieve his or her own goals without seeking cooperation with other employees, and it may be at the expense of those other employees. This approach may be appropriate for emergencies when time is the essence.

5. **Compromising:** Compromising is the lose-lose scenario where neither a manager nor a person really achieves what they want. This needs a moderate level of cooperation and assertiveness. It may be effective in scenarios wherein you need a temporary solution or where both sides have equally important goals.

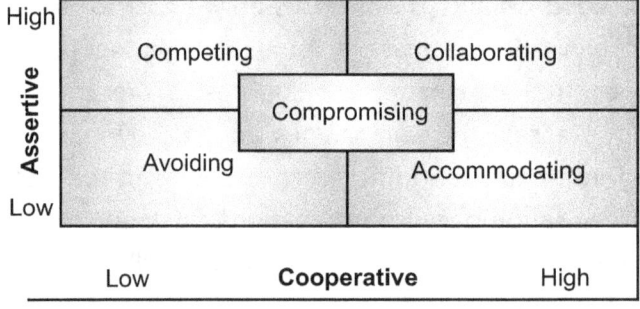

Fig. 3.7: Thomas-Kilmann Conflict Mode Instrument

3.6.3 Overcoming Conflict

Conflict seems inevitable. It appears far easier to become irrational, not seeking common ground and not taking the others' perspective needed to find a win-win situation. In other circumstances, third parties can be useful to break the deadlock.

One widely used way of helping out of such situations is by turning to alternative dispute techniques or common grounds for discussion.

Tips on Negotiating Win-Win Situations and managing conflict effectively

1. **Avoid making unreasonable offers:** In order to minimise the occurrence of conflict, each party should bargain and negotiate reasonably with the others. For probability of Conflict to be minimised, the negotiation should be just. For example, in the case of the Maruti Suzuki strike at Manesar, in Gurgaon, the supervisors were not willing to budge and stuck to their stand on the workers' lunch timings. This only aggravated the conflict and so, resulted in acute loss to life and property.

2. **Seek the common ground:** Many times conflicts occur when one party believes that the other party is in opposition to its own interests. This is not always so. There could be many common grounds of interest between them and those should be explored in detail, so that the effects of the conflicts are minimised. As far as possible, it is necessary to find common areas of interest between parties.

3. **Broaden the scope of issues considered:** While discussing the reasons for conflict and seeking a redressal of the same, it is necessary that conflicting issues be broadened to include bargaining powers. Like for an exchange of freezing the wages for the labour, the management can provide better canteen facilities, or a representation in the management for making decisions related to their areas of interest.

4. **Uncover the real issues:** Sometimes the real reason for the conflict may be hidden. It may show in some other way or in a superficial way. For example, a team member may show difference of opinion and so, there may be a reason for conflict or aggression, but however the real reason may be different, like getting even with the colleague or the peer. The process should help to clarify the real reason for the basis of the conflict and not the superficial one or the one that is really demonstrated.

Points to Remember

- A connection between individuals working together in the same organisation is called interpersonal relationship. Interpersonal relation is an important part of the managerial job world over and many studies have established their importance in formal organisations, particularly for effective decision-making and implementation of decisions.

- Interpersonal relationship refers to a strong relationship among people working together in the same organisation. Employees working together should share a special bond for them to give their level best. It is important that people be truthful to each other for a healthy interpersonal relationship and finally to create a positive ambience at the workplace.

- Interpersonal relationship refers to a strong association among employees either working together in the same team or same organisation. Employees must get along well for a positive and healthy ambience at the workplace.

- Conflicts are the result of incompatible interests. Conflict occurs quite commonly in organisations. Research has estimated that 20 percent of the manager's time in any organisation is spent dealing with conflicts and its effects.

- Conflict, competition and cooperation are three different types of social interactions sharing three common components.

- The negative consequences of conflicts are that it causes negative feedback. However, these emotional reactions are only a part of the chain reaction that can cause harmful effects in organisations.

- In organisations and group behaviours, interpersonal conflict is visible as employees have to act and react with other employees and this interdependence leads to interpersonal conflict. Interpersonal conflict is analysed under three heads, that is, transactional analysis, Johari Window and strategies for interpersonal conflict resolution.

- Transactional analysis is referred to people's interactions with regards to social transactions.

- Johari, which is in the name of Joseph and Harry, has been developed for analysing interpersonal conflict. They have analysed interpersonal conflict and have suggested ways of solving conflicts. They have put emphasis on self as well as others, that is, self is related to "I or me" and others are concerned with "You or they".

- Feedback helps in the configuration of the four arenas. In an organisation, the leader needs verbal and non-verbal feedback from his followers.

- Disclosure is known as another process of Johari Window, that is, an extent to which a leader will willingly share his feelings with others and the subordinates should be looked at from their viewpoint.

- Apart from the transactional analysis and Johari Window, there are other strategies as well which are used for resolving the interpersonal conflict. They are known as lose-lose, win-lose, win-win, role set, linking pin and resolving conflicting groups.

- The view of the integrator does not propose that all the conflicts are good; they are both positive and negative aspects to them. Boulding helps in recognising that some optimum level of conflict and associated personal stress, anti-tension are required for productivity and progress; however he portrays conflicts primarily as social and potential costs.

- Looking at the conflict from a functional point of view, conflicts are supposed to serve various functions.

- Conflict management is a practice of being able to identify and handle the issues fairly, sensibly and efficiently. In businesses, since conflict is considered as an obvious part of the workplace, it is essential that there are people who understand the conflicts and even know how to solve them.

- Conflicts are obvious but how an employee resolves and responds to these conflicts will enable or limit his success.

- Conflict seems inevitable. It appears far easier to become irrational, not seeking common ground and not taking the others' perspective needed to find a win-win situation. In other circumstances, third parties can be useful to break the deadlock.

Questions for Discussion

1. Discuss the meaning and importance of interpersonal relations.
2. Describe the basic guidelines for developing interpersonal relations.
3. Elaborate the meaning, sources and types of conflict.
4. Explain the types of intrapersonal and interpersonal conflict.
5. Elaborate the functional and dysfunctional aspects of conflict.
6. What are the various styles of conflict management?

Chapter **4**...

Group Dynamics

Contents ...

Learning Objectives ...

- ➢   To understand the meaning and nature of groups
- ➢   To illustrate the five-stage model of group development
- ➢   To study the various types of groups
- ➢   To learn the meaning of group norms, group conformity, group cohesion, group size, group think and group shift
- ➢   To identify the effects of group dynamics

4.1 Groups

4.1.1 Meaning of Group

A group may be defined as a collection of two or more people who work with one another regularly to achieve common goals. In a group, members are dependent on each other to attain common goals, and they communicate with one another regularly to follow those goals. Effective groups help organisations in achieving significant tasks. They particularly offer the potential for synergy, that is, the formation of a whole that is bigger than the sum of its parts. When synergy occurs, groups achieve more than the total of their members' individual capabilities.

Individuals make up the group and many groups make up the organisation. A group is a significant unit for sociological and psychological analysis to know about the organisational behaviour. It has an effect on the behaviour of its members, other groups, and the complete organisation. It is significant for a manager to understand how groups are formed. Group dynamics is related to the study of significant aspects related to group formation and group behaviour.

Group dynamics involves both kinds of groups—formal groups and informal groups. Formal groups are formed purposely by the organisation while informal groups are formed spontaneously.

Definitions

Group has been defined as under –

George C. Homans: "A group is any number of people who share goals, often communicate with each other over a period of time, and are few enough so that each individual may communicate with all the others, person to person".

John M. Ivancevich and Michael T. Matteson: "A group exists in an organisation when, its members (1) are motivated to join, (2) perceive the group as a unified unit of interacting people, (3) contribute in various amounts to the group processes (that is, some people contribute more time or energy to the group than others), and (4) reach agreement and disagreements through various forms of interactions".

In simple words, the term 'group' can be defined as: A group is a set of two or more people who have common goals or interests and communicate with each other to achieve their goals, are aware of each other and perceive themselves to be a part of a group.

More clearly, it can be said: A group is a set of two or more interdependent and communicating individuals who have a common goal.

4.1.2 Nature of Group

In order to know about group behaviour, one must analyse and understand the important features of groups. These characteristics may be referred to as elements or components of group.

1. **Membership:** Membership in a group is selective. A person is granted membership on the basis of common interest, willingness to co-operate, and conform to the group customs. An individual may be a member of many groups.

2. **Leadership:** A group cannot work without a leader. While a formal leader is recommended by the authority, the informal leader emerges from the group. The leader is given the power to make a decision, to take action, and to seek conformity.

3. **Formal Hierarchy or Status:** A group and its members have a certain position in the organisation depending upon the reason for which the group is formed and the task they carry out. However, circumstances are different in case of an informal group. In the same way, a group and its members have a socially defined position or rank. They have a high or low status, esteemed or ordinary status.

4. **Composition:** A group comprises different kinds of members. Most group activities need various skills and knowledge. The research shows that heterogeneous groups will probably perform more effectively. A group shares a common demographic trait, such as age, sex, race, educational level or length of service in the organisation.

5. **Specific Task:** Every group has its tasks to carry out. The task depends on the group's reason to serve.

6. **Interaction:** Group members communicate with each other. They interact in the form of discussion, decision-making, actions, and dealings with others. Communication is the important part in interactions.

7. **Group Norms:** Every group has its customs (values, standards, and beliefs) and members are expected to obey them. Norms are acceptable standards of behaviour within a group that are followed by the group's members. Norms keep the group members together. Norms might be in the form of external appearance, too, for example, uniform.

8. **Communication:** Communication is a significant process that keeps the group active and alive. All group processes and functions require communication.

9. **Group Cohesiveness:** Cohesiveness implies 'stick together' or 'help each other.' It refers to the group's magnetism towards its members. Goal, size of group, social and cultural homogeneity, personality characteristics, type of communication, and leadership are the controlling factors that influence the degree of cohesiveness.

4.1.3 Process of Group Development

The goal of most research on group development is to learn why and how small groups change over time. To do this, researchers examine patterns of change and continuity in groups over time.

Aspects of a group that might be studied include the quality of the output produced by a group, the type and frequency of its activities, its cohesiveness and the existence of group conflict. A number of theoretical models have been developed to explain how certain groups change over time.

In some cases, the type of group being considered influenced the model of group development proposed as in the case of therapy groups.

In general, some of these models view group change as regular movement through a series of "stages," while others view them as "phases" that groups may or may not go through and which might occur at different points of a group's history.

Attention to group development over time has been one of the differentiating factors between the study of ad hoc groups and the study of teams such as those commonly used in the workplace, the military, sports and many other contexts.

Stages in Group Formation

Bruce Tuckman reviewed about fifty studies of group development (including Bales' model) in the mid-sixties and synthesised their commonalities in one of the most frequently cited models of group development (Tuckman, 1965).

The model describes four linear stages (forming, storming, norming, and performing) that a group will go through in its unitary sequence of decision-making.

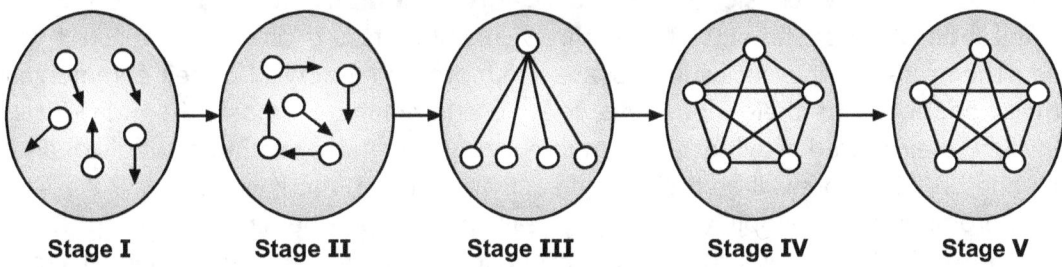

| Stage I | Stage II | Stage III | Stage IV | Stage V |

Fig. 4.1: Stages in Group Formation

Stage I - Forming: It is distinguished by a great deal of uncertainty about the group's reason, structure, and leadership. This stage is complete when the members think of themselves as a part of a group.

Stage II - Storming: This stage is one of the intra group conflicts. Members accept the existence of the group, but they resist the control put on one's individuality. Further, there is a disagreement over who will control the group. When this stage is complete there is a very clear hierarchy of leadership within the group.

Stage III - Norming: In this stage, close connections develop and the group shows cohesiveness. This stage is complete when the group structure solidifies and the group has gathered a common set of expectations of how can one define a correct group behaviour.

Stage IV - Performing: The structure at this point is completely functional and accepted. Group energy has moved from getting to understand each other to carrying out the task at hand. For permanent work groups (formal), performance is the last stage in their development.

Stage V - Adjourning: Adjourning is for temporary committees, task forces, teams, and related groups that have limited tasks to perform. In this stage, the group prepares for its dismissal. High task performance is no longer the group's main concern. Instead, attention is directed toward winding up the activities. The replies of group members differ in this stage.

It is difficult to determine the issue of group effectiveness. Under some conditions high levels of conflict are favourable for a high group performance. So we might expect to find circumstances where groups in stage II do better than those in stages III or IV. In the same way, groups do not always continue from one stage to the next. Sometimes, many stages continue at the same time, as when groups are storming and performing simultaneously. Sometimes, groups regress to the earlier stages. Thus, one should not always presume that all groups accurately follow this developmental procedure or that stage IV is always the most preferable. It is better to think of this model as a general structure. It reminds us that groups are active units and can help in understanding the problems in a better way, which will probably surface during a group's life.

4.1.4 Theories of Group Formation

1. Propinquity Theory

It comes from the classic theories of **George Homans**. It is based on activities, communications, and sentiments. These three constituents are directly connected to one another. The more activities individuals share, the more frequent will be their communication and the stronger will be their sentiments, the more interactions among the individuals, the more will be their shared activities and sentiments and the more sentiments individuals have for one another, the more will be their shared activities and communications.

Most probably those people who are physically placed together create a group. There are a lot of research theories which are supporting propinquity theory and several facets of group dynamics can be known by this theory. But the disadvantage of this theory is that it is not analytical and not capable of describing the difficult aspect of group formation.

2. Interaction Theory

This theory helps a lot in knowing about the individuals of group formation. In accordance with the interaction theory, it is not just propinquity, which brings people together, but it is a goal and mutual requirements, which bring them together. In order to attain group objectives, people require the co-operation from others; they have to co-ordinate with each other to solve work-related issues.

3. Balance Theory

Theodore Newcomb gives the balance theory of group formation. According to this theory, people catch the attention of each other because they have the same attitude towards common objects and goals. In the balance theory, both propinquity and interaction work together.

Here the person X interacts with the person Y because of common attitudes and values that is, once they form a connection they try to maintain it. For that they need to establish a balance between attraction and common attitude. In case this balance gets disturbed, the connection dissolves.

4. Exchange Theory

The exchange theory of groups is based on reward cost outcomes of interaction. A minimum positive level of an outcome must be there for attraction or affiliation to happen.

Rewards help to satisfy the needs, whereas cost involves anxiety and frustration, propinquity, interaction and common attitudes.

4.1.5 Types of Groups

There are many ways of classifying groups. The behaviour of group members will be affected by the types of groups in which they function. There are primary and secondary groups, formal and informal groups, membership and reference groups and in-groups and out-groups. Further, we can sub-classify the groups as command, task, interest and friendship groups. Each type of group has different characteristics and different effects on its member.

(a) Primary and Secondary Groups

C. H. Cooley defined and analysed a primary group. By primary groups, he means those characterised by intimate, face-to-face association and cooperation. Primary groups are those in which interpersonal relationship take place on a face-to-face basis and with great frequency. Primary groups are fundamental in forming the social nature and ideals of the individual.

Sometimes the terms small group and primary group are used interchangeably. But technically speaking, all primary groups are small groups, but not all small groups are primary groups, because small group has to meet only the criterion of small size. But besides being small in size primary group must have a feeling of loyalty and togetherness. Families are the most obvious example of primary groups, but this category also includes peer groups, recreational groups and work groups, and indeed any type of group in which individuals have some depth of involvement.

Organisational Behaviour scientists are keen about primary groups because the Hawthrone studies revealed their special significance. Because of frequent face-to-face interactions and close associations a work-group has qualities of a primary group. The workers behaviour is influenced and determined by the group.

The Japanese style of management has developed this quality of work-group as a primary group in a significant and most effective manner. The concepts of Industrial Families and Quality Circles (also a primary group) have led them to tremendous organisational success. To the Japanese, employment in an organisation is always a life-long affair. Earlier the industries were owned by families but now Japan has industrial families.

Secondary groups are likely to be more impersonal and more characterised by formalised or contractual relationships among members. Money, goods, services, and information can be achieved through our involvement in secondary groups.

Love, disappointment, depression, rage and elation are more likely to be expressed in primary groups, whereas expressions of emotion to members of secondary groups are more likely to be restrained or suppressed.

Hawthrone and many other studies pointed out the tremendous impact that the primary group has on individual behaviour.

(b) Membership and Reference Groups

Membership groups are formed informally and formally through membership cards or certificates. The Institute of Engineers is a membership group and is a secondary group.

Reference group is one in which individuals would like to belong or to identify themselves. The reference groups' values and opinions are important to the individual. The reference group serves a normative function to the individual; it also serves as a source of individual norms and attitudes.

(c) In- and Out-Groups

An 'in-group' represents a cluster of individuals who hold the prevailing or powerful values in high esteem, thus in-group represents 'power circle.'

The 'out-group' is one which does not have much influence on social thinking or powerful values.

(d) Open and Closed Groups

An open group is constantly adding and losing members whereas the membership is stable in closed groups.

In an open group, the frame of reference expands with the addition of the new members with new ideas and thereby the activity also expands but it is stable in a closed group.

Due to constant changes in an open group the perspective is limited to only the near future whereas in closed group, because of its stability, it has a longer time perspective.

(e) Formal and Informal Groups

A designed work group defined by the organisational structure is called formal group. A group that is neither formally structured nor organisationally determined and appears in response to the need for social contact is called an informal group.

Formal groups are established by the organisation and have a public identity and goal to achieve. Informal groups are formal on the basis of common interest, proximity and friendships.

Primary groups are likely to be informal, whereas formality is more often a characteristic of secondary groups. Structure of formal group makes a group more stable and enables it to resist drastic changes. The formal structures of religious organisations, work organisations and nations have enabled them to survive for centuries.

Different types of groups are relevant to the study of organisational behaviour, but the formal and informal types are most directly applicable. Formal and informal groups can be sub-classified as follows.

Forms of Formal Groups

1. Command Group: It is determined by the organisational chart. A command group consists of a superior and the immediate subordinates. The superior is granted formal authority over the other members of the group. The authority structure forms and determines the boundaries of division, departments and sections within the organisation and these departments or sections or divisions are known as command groups. The smallest command group consists of supervisor and his subordinates and the largest one consists of top management and the total personnel in the work force.

The chain of command as expressed by authority, responsibility, and accountability allocates the roles of each individual in the command group. It also spells out the member-authority relationship which exists between them. The superior of a particular group is the leader who performs important functions for his group. He sets goals for the group, suggests ways and means to get them and settles jurisdictional issues which arise between subordinates. The superior is an effective instrument for downward communication and an initiation for upward communication.

2. Functional Group

Functional groups are those groups whose primary task is to carry on the operations. In many cases, the functional groups may be congruent with the authority groups. Thus a single department in the organisation would probably be both command group and functional group. The department is a command group within the authority structure but the staff working in that department engaged in a particular activity and directed and coordinated by the same superior may form a functional group such as typist, clerk, salesman, etc. Thus a command group may have several functional groups.

The functional groups can be again classified into team, task and technological groups. The distinction between these groups involves the method, role allocation and role fulfilment.

(a) Team Group: Team group has no specified, fixed role to its individuals. The general role of the group is set and the members of the group are allocated the role according to the needs of the goal. Thus, roles of members in a team group are interchangeable without any clashes.

(b) Task Group: Those groups working together to complete a job task is called a task group. The task group is formally designed to work on a specific project or a job. Its interaction and structure are formally designed to accomplish the task. Task group's boundaries are not limited to its immediate hierarchical superior. It can cross command relationships. Role of the members are not interchangeable and if a superior does so there is personal resistance and friction between superior and the member.

(c) Technological Group: It is something different. Roles are assigned by the management. The position of the job is fixed and the methods are laid down and the speed of the work is fixed by some device. Thus members of the group have no choice over the method and the speed of the work.

(d) Status Group: Status group involves the members of the same status in an organisation. It includes a number of different ranking of positions. It makes distinction of a functional basis between manager and workers. In some cases, status distinction is made on the basis of facilities or amenities to be enjoyed by the members.

3.   Permanent and Temporary Formal Groups: Permanent formal groups are formed by the organisation on a permanent basis and exist so long as the organisation exists. Board of Directors, Departmental Units, Staff Groups and Standing Committees are examples of such groups.

Groups formed by the organisation to carry the particular work or to perform the specific task are temporary formal groups. These groups come to an end as soon as the task assigned to them is over.

4.   Committee Organisation: Committee is the most important type of formally organised group. Committee is a group of people who function collectively. Committees maybe referred to as teams, commissions, boards, groups or task forces. Committees are found in all types of organisations, for example, Governmental, Educational, Religious and Business Organisations.

Committees may act in service, advisory, coordinating, informational or final decision-making capacity. Committees may reduce conflict and promote co-ordination between departments and specialised subunits. If an individual is involved in the committee he will more readily accept and try to implement what has been decided. Thus, committee increases motivation and commitment. Committee also provides the opportunity for personal development.

Committees have certain disadvantages also –

1.   They are time-consuming as well as costly.

2.   Individuals may use the committee as a shield to avoid personal responsibility for bad decisions or mistakes.

Informal Groups: Formal groups have officially prescribed goals and relationships, but informal groups do not have such prescribed goals and relationships. We cannot separate formal and informal groups. Every formal organisation has informal groups and every informal organisation has a formal group. Thus, these two types of groups co-exist and they are inseparable.

Mayo and Lombard have classified informal groups on the basis of the functions of the group in determining standards of conduct and internal structures into three categories, that is natural, family and organised. Thus informal groups may be grouped as given below.

Forms of Informal Groups

1.   Cliques: The number of members of this group tends to be smaller. The object is to provide recognition to each other and exchange information of mutual interest.

Dalton has noted three types of cliques.

(a)   Vertical Cliques: Such cliques consist of people working in the same department irrespective of their rank difference. Such groups develop because of earlier acquaintance of people or the dependence of superior upon his subordinates for some formal purposes.

(b)   Horizontal Cliques: This group consists of people more or less of the same rank and working more or less in the same area. Such groups are formed cutting across organisational boundaries. Such members find some common points and keeping the objectives in mind, come together. This is the most common form of informal group.

(c) Random or Mixed Cliques: People from different ranks, departments and locations form such types of cliques. They have some common objectives in mind. The member may be residing in the same locality, travelling by the same bus or train or may be a member of the same club.

2. Sub-Cliques: The group consists of some member of a clique inside the organisation along with some other person outside the clique.

3. Isolates: Actually it is not a group. An individual who is not the member of any group is called isolate. Such isolates do not participate in any social activity organised by the group. They avoid people and people avoid them.

4. Interest Group: Those working together to attain a specific objective with which each is concerned are interest groups. Interest groups may also be formally designed. They are established on an informal basis according to the common interests or attitudes in the manner described by Newcomb's balance theory. Common interest may be sports, hatred of management, to support a peer or to seek increased benefits.

5. Friendship Group: Those brought together because they share one or more common characteristics. These groups are extended outside the work situation having attended the same college, holding of similar political views, similar age are the examples of common characteristics.

Person joins this group in the manner of exchange theory, which means rewards of such groups outweigh the cost. These groups are formed in order to satisfy needs for affiliation. Thus, informal groups provide a very important service by satisfying their member's social needs.

Classification by Sayes

Sayes gave another classification of informal groups from the stand-point of pressure tactics.

(a) Apathetic Group: They always show indifferent attitude towards formal organisation. They are not sincere to their demand and members do not actively engage in union activity.

(b) Erratic Group: This group is very sensitive to their demand. Easily inflamed and easily pacified. Thus, they are marked by inconsistent behaviour and centralised autocratic leadership. They engage in union activity without working. Deep-rooted grievances exist without any reaction from the group.

(c) Strategic Group: This group has a high degree of internal unity and good production record in the long run. They have a well-planned strategy for fighting with the management for their grievances. They build continuous pressure.

(d) Conservative Group: These groups consist of members having critical or scarce skills, though they have strong position by virtue of co-operation specific objectives and self assurance. They are least engaged in union activity.

4.1.6 Group Structure

When group members come together for the first time and start interacting, there are various differences that begin to appear between the members like differences in influence, status, ability, and role and so on. Thus, the pattern of relationship is established which is known as the group structure. It is obvious, that the pattern will change as per the stage of discussion or the nature of the task and the most influential person for one purpose may not be so for another. When there is no appointed leader in the group, the leadership thus, moves around amongst various group members. A structure that emerges in these ways is known as the invisible structure.

A visible structure exists when the group members agree upon division of roles, labour and responsibilities in order to get all the important tasks performed. For instance, you could distribute a set of roles to the group like, exchanging of information, asking for reactions, restating and giving examples, clarifying, confronting, and reality testing, synthesising and summarising, timekeeping, gate keeping and expediting, standard setting, evaluating and diagnosing, sponsoring and encouraging. These methods may be too demanding at a social level. Pyramiding is the structure which encourages participation, known as the sequence of stages involving individual work, later followed by discussion in pairs, then in fours and at last a final session with the entire group.

(a) Group Size

Group size varies from two people to a big number of people. Small groups of two to ten are considered as more efficient because each member has plenty of chances and engage themselves actively in the group. Big groups may waste time by determining the processes and trying to determine about who should participate next.

Evidence shows that as the size of the group rises, satisfaction increases up to a particular point. The increase in the size of a group beyond 10-12 members results in less satisfaction. It is becoming more difficult for members of big groups to recognise one another and experience cohesion.

(b) Group Roles

In formal groups, roles are always decided beforehand and then allotted to the members. Each role has particular responsibilities and duties. There are, though, emergent roles that develop naturally to meet the requirements of the groups.

These emergent roles frequently substitute the allotted roles, as individuals start expressing themselves and become more self-confident. Group roles can then be divided into work roles, maintenance roles, and blocking roles.

Work roles are task-oriented activities that engage in achieving the group's goals. They involve various roles such as initiator, informer, clarifier, summariser, and reality tester.

Maintenance roles are social-emotional activities that help members in maintaining their involvement in the group and increase their personal dedication to the group. The maintenance roles are harmoniser, gatekeeper, consensus tester, encourager, and compromiser.

Blocking roles are activities that create disorder in the group. Blockers oppose the group's concepts, disagree with group members for their own individual reasons, and have hidden plans. They rule over the discussions and verbally attack other group members, and divert the group by giving them unnecessary information.

Many a time, the blocking behaviour is not meant to be negative. At times, a member may share a joke so as to break the tension, or may question a decision that is taken in order to compel the group members to rethink about the issue. The blocking roles are aggressor, blocker, dominator, comedian, and avoidance behaviour.

Role conflicts come up when there is a confusion between the sent role and the received role which causes frustration and dissatisfaction, eventually leading to turnover; variation between the perceived role and role behaviour; and conflicting demands from different sources while carrying out the task.

(c) Group Norms

Norms define the limits of acceptable and unacceptable behaviour, which is shared by the group members. They are formed to facilitate a group's continued existence, make behaviour more predictable, avoid embarrassing circumstances, and communicate the values of the group.

Each group forms its own norms that decide from the work performance to the clothes to making comments in a gathering. Groups put pressure on members to force them to obey the group's standards and sometimes, to not perform at higher levels. The norms frequently reflect the level of commitment, motivation, and performance of the group.

The majority of the group agrees that norms should be suitable for the behaviour to be accepted. There must also be a mutual understanding that the group supports the norms. It should be seen that members do not defy the group norms from time to time.

If most of the members do not follow the norms, then they will ultimately change and will no longer serve as a model for assessing the behaviour. Group members who do not obey the norms are punished by being rejected, neglected, or asked to leave the group.

(d) Group Cohesiveness

Cohesiveness refers to the connection between the group members or unity, feelings of attraction for each other and the need to be a part of the group. Several factors influence the group cohesiveness – agreement on group goals, frequency of communication, personal attractiveness, inter-group competition, favourable assessment, etc.

The more difficult it is to get group membership the more cohesive the group will be. Groups also have a tendency to become cohesive when they are competing with other groups or face a serious external threat. Smaller groups and those who spend significant time together also have a tendency to be more cohesive.

Cohesiveness in work groups has several positive effects, including employee satisfaction, low turnover, absenteeism, and higher productivity. On the other hand, highly cohesive groups might be harmful for organisational performance if their goals are not aligned properly with the organisational goals.

Highly cohesive groups may also be dangerous for groupthink. Groupthink happens when members of a group put pressure on each other to take a final decision. Groupthink results in careless decisions, unrealistic assessments of alternative courses of action and a lack of reality testing.

Evidence puts forward that groups normally do better than individuals when the tasks involved require a number of skills, experience, and decision-making. Groups are often more flexible and can quickly collect, attain goals, and disband or move on to another set of goals.

Several organisations have found that groups also have several motivational aspects. Group members will probably take part in decision-making and problem-solving activities leading to empowerment and increased productivity. Groups finish most of the work in an organisation; thus, the effectiveness of the organisation is restricted by the efficiency of its groups.

4.1.7 Group Norms

As a group begins to develop, members begin to share the responses to specific issues or circumstances, and a strong 'group position' surfaces. Certain behaviours become acceptable, others do not; certain beliefs are appreciated and shared, others are not. As this value system develops, members get rewards for conforming to the rules and get punished for not conforming to them. From this the group norms appear: 'those attitudes, values and forms of behaviour that the group as a whole requires or expects of its members' (**Fester, 1976**).

Rules that a group makes purposely to regulate behaviours, or procedures could be considered as explicit norms, but in the true sense of the word, norms are implicit rather than explicit: that is, they only become famous when they are experienced. They are the ways of doing things that is considered as suitable or proper behaviour, and are particular to each group.

Because norms refer to the expected behaviour rewarded or punished by the group, there is a strong 'ought' or 'should' quality to them. The potential rewards and punishments may be open or a secret, but members are at least aware of their existence and may change their behaviour considerably because they either hope to get an approval or fear the group as a whole.

Some norms need more strict observance than others, with a corresponding difference in the extent of reward or punishment delivered. The more followers there are to a group norm, the greater will be the pressure to obey them. Conformity may be rewarded by acceptance, praise, approval, pay rises, promotion. Deviance or refusal to obey may be punished by rejection, criticism, hostility, ridicule, fines, ostracism or expulsion.

Norms, created as they are during the course of group communication as people learn to 'fit in', are also influenced by the culture of the society in which the group continues to live. **Luthans** (**1985**) said that group norms will be strongly implemented if they –

- Ensure a group's success or existence.
- Reflect the choices of the leader or other powerful members.

- Simplify or predict the behaviours that are expected of members.
- Reinforce particular individual roles.
- Help the group to stay away from interpersonal conflict.

Classification of Group Norms

1. **Positive norms**
   - Viewing self and group with pride;
   - Wanting to improve on past performance;
   - Sharing information and working co-operatively; leaders as helpers and developers of subordinates; saving money to decrease the costs;
   - Maximising customer satisfaction;
   - Supporting and encouraging innovation and change, training and development seen as important.

2. **Negative norms**
   - Negative view of organisational goals;
   - Near enough is good enough;
   - 'Every man for himself';
   - Secrecy;
   - Leaders as policemen;
   - Lack of concern for cost effectiveness;
   - Customers are obstacles to be avoided;
   - Support the status quo;
   - Discourage experimentation;
   - Training and development a non-essential luxury;
   - Closed and defensive interpersonal communication.

How norms are developed

The experts state that norms evolve in an informal manner as the group or organisation decides what it takes to be efficient. In general, norms develop in different combinations of the following four ways.

1. **Explicit statements by supervisors or co-workers:** For example, a group leader might clearly set norms about not drinking alcohol at lunch.

2. **Critical events in the group's history:** Sometimes there is an important event in the group's history that establishes a significant model. For example, a key recruit may have decided to work elsewhere because a group member said several bad things about the organisation.

   Thus, a norm against such "sour grapes" behaviour might develop.

3. **Primacy:** The first behaviour pattern that appears in a group usually sets group expectations.

If the first group meeting is marked by a very formal communication between the supervisors and employees, then the group usually expects future meetings to be carried out similarly.

4. **Carryover behaviours from past situations:** Such carryover of individual behaviours from past situations can raise the predictability of group members' behaviours in a new environment and facilitate in accomplishing the task.

4.1.8 Group Conformity

The group members must conform to the norms and beliefs of the group. Conformity means adjusting one's own behaviour as per the norms of the group. People belonging to various groups and norms vary from group to group wherein they conform to the important group norms and leave others.

Conformity to group norms indicates the dedication and commitments to the group's progress and process. Norms help in bringing about group bonding, cohesion, identity and to some extent, control. Members, who do not conform as per the group norms and expectations, act in direct conflict to group values. Members, who desire group affiliation, acceptance and connection to the group tend to conform, and are called conformists. In conforming, they tend to avoid the negative consequences of ostracism and rejection or any other group sanction that they impose. Few group members move continually between conforming to group norms and not confirming or violating group norms and these members are called sliders. Other group members violate and defy group norms continually and do not shy away or fear from retribution in the form of ostracism, rejection or imposition of sanctions by the group and these are called as non-conformists. Sliders and non-conformists may seek to satisfy an individual's needs inherent in any one of the individual roles.

4.1.9 Group Cohesion

Group cohesion is a sense of togetherness or community within a group. A cohesive group is one in which the members get incentives for staying with the group and share a feeling of relatedness and belongingness. During the early stages in the group, the members do not know each other well enough for a true sense of community that needs to be formed. Usually, there is some kind of awkwardness till members become acquainted. Though participants talk about themselves, it is more likely that they are presenting their public selves rather than deeper aspects of their private selves. Genuine cohesion typically arrives after groups have struggled with conflicts, have shared common pains and have committed themselves to take significant risks. However, the foundations of cohesion can begin to take shape during the initial stage.

Few indicators of this initial degree of cohesion are cooperation amongst members, an effort to make the group a safe place, a willingness to show up for the meetings and be punctual, talking about any feelings of lack of trust or fears trusting, caring and support, evidenced by willing to listen to others and thus accept them for who they are and a willingness to express perceptions of and reactions to others in the here-and-now context of group interactions. Genuine cohesion is not a fixed condition which is arrived at automatically. In fact, it is a continuous process of solidarity which members earn through risks which they take with one another. Group cohesion can be maintained, developed, and increased in various ways. Following are a few suggestions to enhance the group cohesion –

•   If all the group members shares meaningful aspects about themselves, then they learn to take risks and thus increase the group cohesiveness. For instance, by modelling, by sharing their own experiences as to what is occurring in the group, leaders can encourage risk-taking behaviour. When group members do not take risks, they can be reinforced with sincere support and recognition, which will help in increasing their sense of closeness to the others.

• Individual goals and group goals can be jointly determined by the group members and the leader. If the group is without any clearly stated goals, then it leads to animosity and fragmentation of the group.

• Cohesion can be increased by inviting all the group members to become active participants. Members who are withdrawn and silent can be encouraged to express their reactions towards the group. These members may be observers and may not be verbally contributing to the group for various reasons and these reasons can be productively examined in the group.

• Cohesion can be built with the group members by sharing the leadership role. In autocratic groups, all the decisions are made by the leader. A cooperative group is more likely to develop if the members are encouraged to initiate discussion of issues that they want to explore. Moreover, instead of fostering a leader-to-member style of interaction, group leaders can promote member-to-member actions. This is possible by requesting the members to respond to each other, by encouraging feedback and sharing and by searching for ways to involve as many members as possible for group interactions.

• Conflict is inevitable in groups. It is needed for group members for recognising sources of conflict and dealing openly with them whenever they arise. A group can be strengthened by accepting the conflicts and honestly working through interpersonal tensions. Members must be asked to predict as to how they are handling conflicts in the group when it arises and talk about their typical ways of dealing with the same. Then, it can be noted whether they are willing to commit for working on more effective ways of dealing with conflicts within the group.

• Group cohesion and attractiveness are related. It is usually accepted that the greater the degree of attractiveness of a group to its members, the greater the level of cohesion will be. If the group deals with matters that interest the members, and if they feel that they are respected and supported, then the chances are high that the group will be perceived as attractive.

• Members can be encouraged to disclose their feelings, ideas and reactions to what occurs within the group. The expression of both the positive and the negative reactions should be encouraged and if this is done, then an honest exchange can take place which is important if a sense of group belongingness is to develop.

4.1.10 Group Size

The size of the group definitely affects the group's overall behaviour; however the effect depends on what dependent variables you look at.

For example, the evidence indicates that smaller groups are faster at completing the tasks than the larger groups. But, if the group is engaged in problem solving, then large groups consistently get better marks than their smaller counterparts. It is relatively hazardous to translate these results into specific numbers, but we can offer some parameters. Larger groups (with a dozen or more members) are good in gaining diverse input. So, if the group's goal is fact finding, then larger groups should be more effective, whereas, smaller groups are better at doing something productive with the inputs. Thus, groups of around seven members, tend to be more effective for taking actions.

Social loafing is one of the most important findings which are related to the size of the group. Social loafing is the tendency for individuals to expend lesser efforts while working collectively then while working individually. It straightaway challenges the logic that the group's productivity as a whole should be at least at par with the sum of the productivity of every individual of that group.

The cause for the social loafing effect may be because of the belief that others in the group are not carrying their fare share. If others are seen lazy, then you can re-establish equity by reducing your efforts. Another explanation to this is the dispersion of responsibility because the group's results cannot be attributed to just one single person as the relationship between the individual's input and the group's output is clouded. At such times, there will be a reduction in efficiency wherein individuals thinks that their contribution cannot be measured.

The research on group size leads us to two additional conclusions, that is, groups with an odd number of members tend to be preferable to those with an even number and groups made up of five or seven members does a good job of exercising the best elements of both small and large groups.

4.1.11 Group Think

Group think is related to group conformity as it occurs when group members relinquish their critical beliefs and evaluate thinking and their standards of invention and think only in relation with the group's beliefs, values and standards. There are three major factors that inspires group think, that is, the unrealistic beliefs of the group's power, close-mindedness and pressure to agree.

1. **Unrealistic beliefs about the group's power:** Groups may start believing that because of the group power they are invincible. They internalise the mistaken notion that the group's collective power can shield and protect them from any retaliation, threat and retribution. Thus, group members may be convinced to take extreme risks. They are bound to do risky things when they are in group and might not do well when they are alone. This is called as risky drift. It is a shift in the degree and level of

risk that the group member is ready to take due to the unrealistic belief in the group's power. For instance, gang members are ready to commit extremely terrible acts without regard to the consequences which they may not do as individuals, due to their belief in and allegiance to the gang power. Sorority and fraternity members take risks when they are with their sorority sisters and fraternity brothers which they may not take as individuals. On the battlefield, soldiers perform acts of heroism and bravery which they may not perform as individuals. Usually, bullies are surrounded by other bullies or supporters and may not bully if alone.

2. **Close-Mindedness:** Group members may discount and disregard warnings and indications of adverse consequences or negative outcomes of acting, in some certain ways. There is a quality of single mindedness about following through an action sanctioned by the group regardless of information that must cause group members to reconsider, rethink and revise their actions. In certain situations, when somebody outside the group is victimised as a result of group think, then the tendency is to rationalise behaviour, and if needed, verify and stereotype the perceived enemy to justify actions against the victim. For example, when a group of students may bully another student, then they may disregard the possibility of expulsion or suspension from school and they may justify their actions by labelling the bullied students in ways that will showcase that the victim deserved or invited this kind of a negative treatment.

3. **Pressure to Agree:** The group does not tolerate dissent and demands loyalty from its members. Group members puts pressure on other group members in order to conform to the group's expectations and norms when such members appear to be drifting away from the group's expected ways of behaving and thinking. Members yield to the group's pressure in order to gain favour and acceptance with the group and to avoid ostracism and rejection by the group. Group members having high affiliation needs are most vulnerable to this group pressure to conform.

Although "group think" is often viewed as a negative phenomenon because it is frequently associated with group coercion to do desirable or undesirable things, "group think" can also be positive at times and can give desirable outcomes. The three major factors to conform apply to the positive view of "group think" just like the way they apply to the negative view. For instance, a child who is underachieving and unmotivated in school, but he wishes to join some sport team, may be granted a membership only if he conforms to the academic standards set by the team. In the child's mind, it may seem unrealistic to meet the requirement of the high academic standards while simultaneously practicing enough to win the game. The child may complain and protest about stress and fatigue but the team may continue to insist on very high academic performance. The team may strengthen its resolve to promote each player as a scholar athlete and may institute a policy of reviewing and receiving on-going teacher progress reports for each team member, thus penalising those who fall below a certain grade cut off.

This stands to be a positive example of group think because the members are expected to act in agreement with the group values.

4.1.12 Group Shift

It is sensed that while discussing a given set of alternatives and arriving at a solution, group members tend to exaggerate the initial positions that they are holding. In some situations, caution dominates and there is a conservative shift. However, mostly, the evidence indicates that groups tend towards a risky shift.

While comparing the group decisions with the individual decisions of the group members, evidence suggests that there are differences. In few cases, the group decisions turn out to be more conservative than the individual ones.

What actually happens is that the group discussion leads to a significant shift in the positions of members towards a more extreme position in the direction in which they were already leaning before the discussion. Thus, the conservative types tend to become more cautious and the aggressive types tend to take more risk. The group discussion tends to exaggerate the initial position of the group.

Actually, the group shift can be viewed as a special case of group think. The group's decision reflects the dominant decision-making norm which develops during the group's discussion. It all depends on the dominant pre-discussion norm, whether the shift in the group's decision is toward greater caution or more risk.

The greater occurrence of the shift towards risk has generated various explanations for the phenomenon. For instance, it is been argued that discussion creates familiarisation amongst the members. As they become more comfortable with one another, they also become more daring and bold. Another argument is that most societies around the developed nations value risk, that they admire individuals those are willing to take risks, and that the group discussion motivates the members for showing that they are at least as willing as their peers to take risks. However, the most plausible explanation of the shift toward risk seems to be that the group diffuses responsibility; group decisions free any single member from accountability for the group's final choice. Greater risk can be taken because even if the decision fails, the blame won't come on any one member.

So in order to use the findings on group shift, one must recognise that group decisions exaggerate the initial position of the individual members, that the shift has been shown more often to be toward greater risk and that whether a group will shift toward greater risk or caution remains a function of the member's pre-discussion inclinations.

We may now turn to the techniques by which groups make decisions and these techniques reduce the sonic of dysfunctional aspects of group decision-making.

4.2 Group Dynamics
4.2.1 Introduction

We are all members of some groups whether we stay at home, study in colleges or universities, or work in different companies. There are no reasons about why people join groups. The most accepted reasons for joining groups are associated with our needs for security, food, clothes, sex, affiliation, power, esteem, huddling and task functions. Hence, many individuals belong to a group whether the group size is big or small. In recent years, numerous scientific studies have been undertaken to understand how these small groups work in the organisations. A social process by which individuals communicate with each other in a small group is called as group dynamics.

In a group, communication is not always governed by formal rules and regulations. In these small groups social requirements between members may also play a significant role in communication. In order to satisfy the social requirements such as affiliation, expression, friendship, people form small groups on the job itself. Small groups develop specific norms of behaviour which bring discipline and order among the members. The group may implement stronger control over their members of a business organisation. The study of group dynamics is significant because of the fact that several individuals have a tendency to act differently as a person than as group members.

4.2.2 Meaning

Kurt Lewin popularised the concept of group dynamics in 1930. Group dynamics refers to the changes which occur within a group and is related with communication and the forces obtained between group members in a social setting. The word 'dynamic' is a Greek word which means 'study of forces' that functions within a group for social communication. It is the study of forces working within a group. When the word group dynamics is used in the study of organisational behaviour, the importance is on how the information is used for achieving some purposes.

However, over the period of time, there have been different confusing connotations. According to one point of view, group dynamics explains how a group should be organised. Here it refers to democratic leadership, members' participation and overall co-operation. There is another point of view of group dynamics revealing what different methods should be accepted to make groups more useful to its members and the organisation. It suggests different methods like role-playing, brainstorming, buzz groups, group therapy, sensitivity training, team-building, transactional analysis, and allied methods. It is concluded from these descriptions that group dynamics is the field of enquiry that deals with the nature and development of small groups, communication among members, group and intergroup behaviour. It is possible to describe and predict a big part of individual behaviour within a group. The significant assumptions underlying the study of group dynamics are –

1. **Groups are inevitable and spontaneous:** Whenever two or more employees communicate often and share common values and customs, they tend to form groups. Since job performance needs frequent communication among employees, it is unavoidable that they create their own groups. Numerous informal groups continue to exist. All organisations study the formal and informal group behaviour.

2. **Groups may produce both bad and good results:** Group members' values and norms encourage or resist the goals of the formal organisations. It depends on to

what extent the principles and norms of an informal group's members match with the formal organisation's that are needed by the management of the organisation for its own work. If group norms, values and sentiments do not match with those needed by the organisation, then the informal group members both personally as well as collectively are likely to work to defeat the organisational goals. The formal organisation will get the co-operation and support of a person as well as members of informal groups to the extent they perceive that they will be advancing towards attaining their personal as well as organisational goals.

3. **Groups mobilise powerful forces that produce effects of utmost importance to individuals:** Groups are bound together because of common norms, beliefs, values, pattern of interaction, communication and emotional bonds. It shows the classification of a member with the group and its other members. Since group members feel that their membership with the group is important, they observe the group norms and values which implement a strong influence on their work and behaviour.

4. **Proper understanding** of the group dynamics allows the possibility that there will be more positive results from the groups. It is a fact that informal groups implement a strong influence on the employees' work performance at the place of work; management can get their support for increasing organisational efficiency by having a proper understanding of properties of different groups and their inter- and intro-group associations. It is only by gaining an insight of the working group that the management can change the individuals' and members' group behaviour in the required direction.

4.2.3 Components of Group Dynamics

All groups have established norms, that is, standards of behaviour that are acceptable by a group and which are shared by the group's members. Norms are rules of behaviour or the correct ways of action which are accepted to be legal by the group members. Norms tell members what they ought and ought not to do under particular situations. These are also referred to as a set of beliefs, feelings and attitudes that are generally shared by the group members. Norms provide three functions in groups – predictive, control and relational. Predictive norms provide a basis for understanding the behaviour of others and for determining one's own behaviour. Control norms regulate the behaviour of members. When a member disobeys a norm, other members will probably implement sanctions and this may be informal remarks or physical. Finally, relational norms define relations among roles. According to **Robbins** high status members are expected to play leadership roles, low status members are not allowed from doing so.

According to **Hackman** group norms have five characteristics –

1. Norms sum up and make the group influence processes simpler. They sum up and highlight those things that group feels is significant to control.
2. Norms are usually formed only for behaviours which are considered significant by most group members.
3. Norms apply only to behaviour, and not to private principles and feelings. It is enough if there is behavioural compliance from the members.

4. Norms usually develop slowly, but the process of development can be made shorter if the members of the group so desire. If, for any reason, the group members decide that a specific norm is not wanted, they may simply agree to accept such norms by announcing that 'from now on' the norms exists.

5. Not everyone can apply all the norms in the group in the same way. High status members enjoy more freedom to stray from the law than do other members.

4.2.4 Inter-Group Dynamics

Inter-group dynamics refers to relationships between groups or departments, within a system or organisation.

The effectiveness of any group is dependent on the relations between different groups in the environment. Groups, like individuals, make social comparisons with one another and make control demands on one another. Members of one group often have active contacts with members of another body. Top executives meet with their board members, union representatives confer with management and the public relations unit needs information from program units. Such interactions across the boundaries of groups can develop in unexpected ways, and often they are marked by tension because it isn't always clear what rules should be followed. These ambiguities may lead to strong responses, and groups' connections may be burdened with conflict and hard feelings.

On the positive side, inter-group conflict and rivalries can result in increased motivation through competition and can also increase the cohesion within each group. However, when competition escalates into destructive conflict, 'winning' becomes more important than reaching organisational goals.

Points to Remember

- A **group** is defined as two or more individuals, interacting and interdependent, who have come together to achieve particular objectives.
- A five-stage model of group formation has been developed and identified. The first stage is known as 'forming', second is 'storming', third is 'norming' and the fourth is 'performing'. The fifth stage is the stage of 'adjourning' which mentions how the group may cease to exist because they may have been formed for a specific project or an assignment.
- The success of a group usually depends on several factors such as group member resources, structure, group processes and group tasks.

Questions for Discussion

1. Discuss the meaning and nature of groups in organisation.
2. Describe the various types of groups.
3. What are the distinct stages in group development?
4. Explain group dynamics and inter-group dynamics.
5. Write short notes on the following –
(i) Group Norms	(ii) Group Conformity
(iii) Group Cohesion	(iv) Group Size
(v) Group Think	
(vi) Group Shift	

***

Chapter 5...

Motivation and Leadership

Contents ...

Learning Objectives ...

➢ To understand the meaning, importance and types of motivation

➢ To identify four early theories of motivation and evaluate their applicability today

➢ To apply the effects of motivation on work behaviour

➢ To understand the meaning and importance of leadership

➢ To distinguish between leaders and managers

➢ To discuss the various leadership styles

➢ To illustrate the theories of leadership

5.1 Motivation

5.1.1 Introduction

A majority of employees working in organisations today have no enthusiasm for their work. Motivation is an important issue today. It is therefore the most frequently researched topic in organisational behaviour. What motivates people to excel? Is there anything organisations can do to encourage their employees? The theories of motivation attempt to answer these questions.

5.1.2 Definitions of Motivation

Motivation is a psychological feature that arouses an organism to act towards a desired goal and elicits, controls, and sustains certain goal-directed behaviours.

It can be considered a driving force; a psychological one that compels or reinforces an action toward a desired goal. For example, hunger is a motivation that elicits a desire to eat.

Motivation has been shown to have roots in physiological, behavioural, cognitive, and social areas.

Motivation may be rooted in a basic impulse to optimise well-being, minimise physical pain and maximise pleasure. It can also originate from specific physical needs such as eating, sleeping or resting.

5.1.3 Types of Motives

> **Motive:** *An emotion, desire, physiological need, or similar impulse that acts as an incitement to action.*

1. **Primary Motives**
   - When a motive is not learned and it is physiologically based.
   - The most common primary motives are hunger, thirst, sleep, sex, avoidance of pain and maternal concern.
   - Although primary motives take precedence over the other kinds of motives in some theories of motivation, secondary motives do dominate over the primary motives in certain situations.

2. **Secondary Motives**
   - Learned secondary motives play a very important role in understanding motivation in a complex and economically advanced society.
   - Some important secondary motives are power, achievement and affiliation. Security and status motives are also important secondary motives.

3. **General Motives**
   - General motives include those which are neither purely primary nor purely secondary, but rather in between.
   - These motives are not learned, but also not based on physiological needs.
   - General motives also called "stimulus motives," stimulate tension within an individual.
   - The motives of curiosity, manipulation, and motive to remain active and to display affection are examples of general motives.
   - Curiosity, manipulation, and motive to remain active: These result in innovations and better ways of doing things.
   - The affection motive: Love is part primary and part secondary motive. Therefore to avoid confusion it is included as a general motive.

> *Motivation is an inner drive to behave or act in a certain manner.*

Motivation is an inner drive to behave or act in a certain manner. It's the difference between waking up before dawn to pound the pavement and lazing around the house all day. These inner conditions such as wishes, desires, goals, activate to move in a particular direction in behaviour.

In summary, motivation can be defined as the purpose for, or psychological cause of, an action.

5.1.4 Importance of Motivation

"Motivation is the core of management" and by motivating the workforce the management creates "the will to work" which is required for attaining organisational objectives.

Managers realise that human beings have a lot of potential, and in a group setting, they use only a small part of that potential. By being capable of harnessing the full potential of the individual through the right managerial plans and practices, that is, through motivation, managers can set their subordinates to do things which are directed towards organisational goals. A motivated employee makes the organisation successful and gives great benefits to it. Some of these are –

1. Motivated employees put all their efforts in attaining the goals of the organisation and co-operate voluntarily with the management.

2. Motivated employees raise the possibility of the work being completed within the selected time and budget cost.

3. Motivated employees are quality-driven. Not only are the employees motivated to carry out the selected task, but they also look for better ways to do a job.

4. Motivation inspires employees to make the best possible use of different factors of production. They work sincerely to give their full abilities and potential so as to minimise the waste and cost.

5. Motivated employees have a tendency to be more well-organised by improving their skills and knowledge, which results in improved productivity.

6. Motivated personnel have a positive effect on productivity and lead to higher levels of job satisfaction. The opportunities available to satisfy the needs of the employees make the employees loyal and committed towards the organisation.

7. A motivated employee has a drive to perform well and is ready to do it. The motivated employee is easy to deal with resulting in a lesser number of complaints and grievances.

8. Motivated employees show a lower rate of absenteeism and turnover. This is because of the positive relationships that prevail in the organisation because of higher productivity and income. This results in lesser friction among the employees themselves and between the management and the employees.

5.1.5 Types of Motivation

Motivation is usually considered to be of two types – positive and negative motivation. When a manager wants to get more work done from the subordinates, he will have to motivate them to enhance their performance. They can either be given incentives for more work which may be in the form of a reward, better reports or recognition, etc., or he may inculcate fear in or he may compel his employees for getting the work done. It is known that under the same set of external factors, all employees are not motivated uniformly. Some experts of OB are of the view that employees are motivated by external factors such as rewards or fear and some experts are of the view that motivation is self-generated without applying any external factors. Two types of motivation are described below and they are as follows.

1. **Positive and Negative Motivation**

    Positive Motivation: Positive motivation or incentive motivation is based on rewards. Employees are provided with incentives for attaining the desired goals. The incentives may be in the form of more pay, promotion, recognition of work, etc. Employees are motivated when they are given incentives and they try to improve their performance, readily. Real and positive motivators are accountable for achieving a high standard of performance and the participation of the employee as a responsible citizen in the community. Positive motivation is attained by the co-operation of employees as then they have a feeling of belongingness and contentment. Some positive motivation methods which enhance the standards of performance and lead to good team spirit and pride are –

    1. Praise and credit for work done well.
    2. A genuine interest in the welfare of the subordinates.
    3. Delegation of authority and responsibility to subordinates.
    4. Participation of subordinates in the decision-making process.

    Negative Motivation: Negative or fear motivation is based on fear or the use of force, power or threats. Fear is the reason why employees act in particular ways. In case, they do not act according to what is required of them, then they may be punished with demotions or lay-offs. This fear acts as a push mechanism. The employees do not co-operate readily, but rather they work to not get punished. Through fear, employees work on to a level where punishment can be avoided, but this kind of motivation is the reason for the anger and frustration and may usually become a cause of industrial conflict. On the other hand, it has been found that the fear of punishment and the actual punishment result in controlling individual misconduct and has contributed towards positive performance in several circumstances, but it is not suggested as a feasible option in the existing business and industrial environment. This technique is highly controversial and it has been proposed that while punishment has some immediate and short-term effect in changing behaviour, the long-term effects are highly doubtful. In the context of work and organisations, no one likes to be judged or threatened to be removed from his employment. If a worker is punished for the behaviour that is not desired and it seldom happens, then it will have a negative effect on his morale, make him bitter and will have a negative effect on his social interaction, his loyalty may result in poor performance, poor productivity and poor quality.

    Some authors tend to describe motivation as either intrinsic or extrinsic.

2. **Intrinsic and Extrinsic Motivation**

    Intrinsic Motivation: Intrinsic motivation causes people to do something spontaneous because they are happy from the activity itself. Intrinsic motivated people engage in any particular behaviour because to them such behaviour is pleasant, challenging, interesting, fulfilling and meaningful. When an activity is an intrinsic motivator, a person sees it as a chance to learn something new, make significant contributions and be creative.

Intrinsic motivation comes from the feeling of achieving something and it is regarded as the state of self-actualisation in which the satisfaction of accomplishing something meaningful motivates the employee further so that this motivation is self-generated and is free of financial incentives. An example of an intrinsic motivation is the practice of retired doctors, who are free in the hospitals because it gives them a sense of achievement and happiness. Some intrinsic motivators are praise, recognition, responsibility, esteem, power, status, challenges and decision-making responsibility.

Extrinsic Motivation: This kind of motivation is brought about by external factors that are mainly financial in nature. It is based upon the supposition that behaviour which is an outcome of positive rewards tends to be repeated; though, the reward for the desired behaviour should be adequately powerful and changeable so that it enhances the possibility of occurrence of the desired behaviour.

Extrinsic motivation thus, requires the offer of the results of an act, so that satisfaction comes not from the activity itself but from the extrinsic results to which the activity shows the way. For an extrinsically motivated person, work is only a means that is required to be completed so as to obtain the rewards that are connected to the job, which may be money or something else. Extrinsic motivation is required because –

1. The right intrinsic motivation is difficult to create for all.
2. Not all intrinsic motivation is always ethical or desirable.
3. Organisations require a common denominator for all the efforts.

Some financial benefits like higher pay, fringe benefits, retirement plans, stock options, profit sharing schemes, paid vacations, health and medical insurance, sympathetic supervision, and people-oriented firm policies are all factors of extrinsic motivation.

Thus, it is important for managers to take into consideration the internal and external incentives when motivating their employee. It has been seen that managers who are more helpful and less controlling appear to bring out more intrinsic motivation from their employees.

5.1.6 Effects of Motivation on Work Behaviour

Motivation is a very significant for an organisation because of the following benefits it provides.

1.   Puts human resources into action

Every problem requires physical, financial and human resources to achieve the goals. It is through motivation that human resources can be used. This can be done by motivating employees to willingly work. This will help the enterprise in securing the best possible utilisation of resources.

2.   Improves level of efficiency of employees

The level of a subordinate or an employee does not only rely on his qualifications and capabilities. For achieving his best work performance, the gap between ability and willingness has to be closed which helps to improve the level of performance of subordinates. This will result in –

(a)   Increase in productivity,

(b)   Decreasing the cost of operations, and

(c)   Improving overall efficiency.

3.   Leads to achievement of organisational goals

The goals of an enterprise can be attained only when the following factors happen.

(a)   There is best possible utilisation of resources,

(b)   There is a co-operative work environment,

(c)   The employees are goal-oriented and they behave in a good way,

(d)   Goals can be attained if co-ordination and co-operation takes place at the same time which can be effectively completed through motivation.

4.   Builds friendly relationship

Motivation is a significant factor which makes the employees happy. This can be prepared by framing an incentive plan for the benefit of the employees. This could start the following things –

(a)   Monetary and non-monetary incentives,

(b)   Promotion opportunities for employees,

(c)   Disincentives for inefficient employees.

In order to build a pleasant, friendly atmosphere, the above steps should be taken by a manager. This would help in –

(i)   Effective co-operation which brings stability,

(ii)   Industrial dispute and unrest in employees will decrease,

(iii) The employees will be flexible to the changes and there will be no resistance to the change,

(iv) Providing a smooth and sound concern, in which personal interests will match with the organisational interests,

(v)   This will result in profit maximisation through increased productivity.

5.   Leads to stability of workforce

Stability of workforce is very significant from a reputation and goodwill viewpoint. The employees can remain loyal to the company only when they feel that the management is participating in the organisational activities. The skills and efficiency of employees will always be beneficial to the employees. This will lead to a good public image in the market which will catch the attention of competent and qualified people into a concern. As it is said, 'old is gold' which suffices the role of motivation here, the older the people, more the experience and their adjustment into a concern which can be advantageous to the company.

From the above discussion, it can be said that motivation is an internal feeling which can be understood only by the manager since he is in close contact with his employees. Requirements and desires are inter-related and they are the driving force to act. These requirements can be understood by the manager and in view of that he can outline motivation plans. We can say that motivation is thus a continuous process since the procedure of motivation is based on the requirements which are unlimited. The process has to be continued throughout.

5.2 Theories of Motivation

5.2.1 Hierarchy of Needs Theory

Content theory of human motivation includes both Abraham Maslow's hierarchy of needs and Herzberg's two-factor theory. Maslow's theory is one of the most widely discussed theories of motivation.

The American motivation psychologist Abraham H. Maslow developed the hierarchy of needs consisting of five hierarchic classes. According to Maslow, people are motivated by unsatisfied needs. The needs, listed from basic (lowest-earliest) to most complex (highest-latest) are as follows –

1. Physiology (hunger, thirst, sleep, etc.)
2. Safety/Security/Shelter/Health
3. Belongingness/Love/Friendship
4. Self-esteem/Recognition/Achievement
5. Self-actualisation

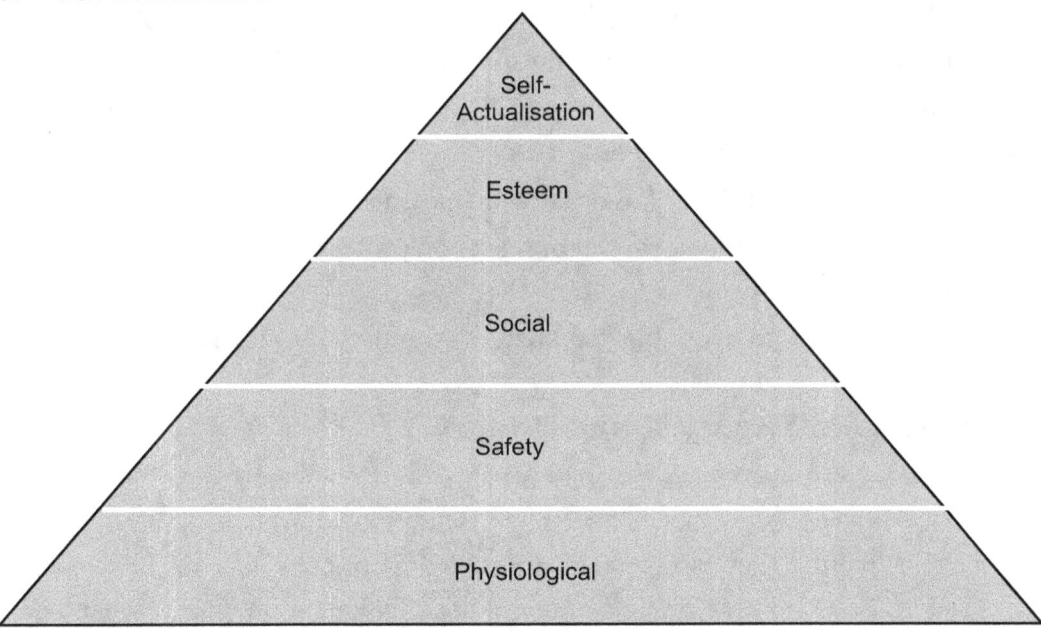

Fig. 5.1: Maslow's Hierarchy of Needs

Maslow's Hierarchy of Needs

The basic requirements build upon the first step in the pyramid: physiology. If there are deficits on this level, all behaviour will be oriented to satisfy this deficit. Essentially, if you have not slept or eaten adequately, you won't be interested in your self-esteem desires. Subsequently we have the second level, which awakens a need for security. After securing those two levels, the motives shift to the social sphere, the third level. Psychological requirements comprise the fourth level, while the top of the hierarchy consists of self-realisation and self-actualisation.

> *Motivation is the processes that account for an individual's intensity, direction, and persistence of effort toward attaining a goal.*

Hierarchy of Needs Theory: Within every individual there exists a hierarchy of five needs –

- **Physiological:** Hunger, thirst, shelter, sex, and other bodily needs.

- **Safety:** Security and protection from physical and emotional harm.

- **Social:** Affection, belongingness, acceptance, and friendship.

- **Esteem:** Internal esteem factors such as self-respect, autonomy, and achievement; and external factors such as status, recognition, and attention.

- **Self-actualisation:** The drive to become what one is capable of becoming; includes growth, achieving one's potential, and self-fulfilment.

> *As each need is substantially satisfied, the next need becomes dominant.*

Maslow's Hierarchy of Needs theory can be summarised as follows –

Human beings have wants and desires which influence their behaviour. Only unsatisfied needs influence behaviour, satisfied needs do not.

Needs are arranged in order of importance to human life, from the basic to the complex.

The person advances to the next level of needs only after the lower level need is at least minimally satisfied.

The further the progress up the hierarchy, the more individuality, humaneness and psychological health a person will show.

5.2.2 McGregor's Theory X and Theory Y

Douglas McGregor introduced Theory X and Theory Y which are diagonally opposite to each other. McGregor is aware that human beings are rational in their thought process and they are social by nature. They display a very high degree of behaviour relating to achieving self-actualisation. There is interaction of variety of need fulfilment phenomenon and complex nature displayed by an individual in different situations.

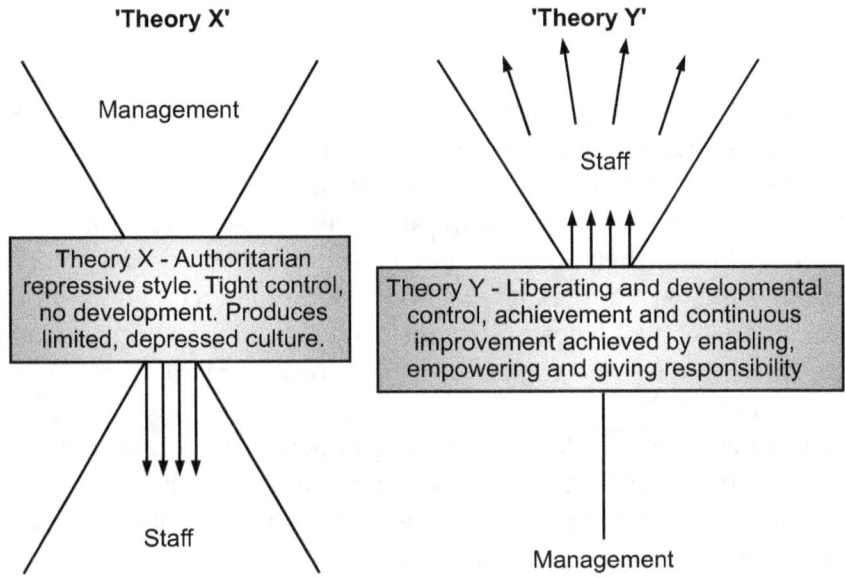

Fig. 5.2: McGregor's Theory X and Theory Y

Theory X

Theory X is a traditional theory McGregor assumed with respect to **managerial action.** Management is responsible for organising various elements of an enterprise like money, material, equipment and people. With respect to people, it is a process of directing people, their efforts, motivating them, controlling their actions, modifying their behaviours so that they fit in with the organisations. In Theory X, McGregor assumed that people would be passive therefore management must persuade, reward and punish the worker to achieve the desired behaviour of workers.

Human Nature: McGregor further stated that humans have an indolent nature; he has a tendency to work to the minimum. McGregor summarises that workers as they lack ambition, dislike responsibility, prefer to be led. An individual is self-centred and indifferent to organisational needs, by nature he resists change. Lastly he is gullible and not very bright. In Theory X, McGregor states that those who subscribe to the views expressed above, the manager will have to structure, control and closely supervise employees. External control has to be exercised towards immature and irresponsible behaviour of employees, so that their energies can be regulated towards productive work. Theory X is applicable to traditional organisational behaviour and characterised by centralised decision making hierarchical pyramid and external control.

After Theory X was proposed, McGregor observed that some changes in human nature have taken place. It was not due to the changes in human behaviour and reactions to various situations but due to change in industrial organisations, management policies and practices that have tremendous effect on human nature. At this point he proposed Theory Y as under –

Theory Y

(a) Expenditure of physical and mental efforts on the part of employees is as natural as play or rest. The average human being does not inherently dislike work.

(b) Worker seeks direction and exercises self control. He dislikes punishment.

(c) Commitment to organisational objectives is associated with rewards like pay promotion etc., ego satisfaction and satisfaction of self-actualisation needs.

(d) An average human being learns under proper conditions. He accepts and seeks responsibilities. At times, it will be seen that certain individuals display phenomenon like avoidance of responsibility, lack of ambition and lay undue stress on security. McGregor suggested that these are due to inherent human characteristics.

(e) Capacity to exercise high degree of imagination, ingenuity and creativity is widely distributed among workers that must be identified and fully utilised.

(f) Intellectual potential of workers is partially utilised. In the above situation McGregor recommends that the organisation should reorient based on human behavioural change. More cooperation, maximum output with minimum control and self-direction is predominant among workers. It is also seen that there is no conflict between individual and organisational goals. The emphasis is on very smooth running of organisation with greater participation of individuals.

Assumptions about Human Nature that underlines Theory X and Theory Y propagated by McGregor

Basis of Distinction	Theory X	Theory Y
Attitude towards work	Work is inherently distasteful to most people.	Work is as natural as play.
Acceptance of responsibility	Most people are not ambitious, have little desire for responsibility and prefer to be directed.	People willingly accept responsibility, display extreme degree of self control, which is necessary for achieving goals.
Creativity	Most people have little capacity for creativity in solving organisational problems.	The capacity of creativity in solving organisational problems is widely distributed in the population.
Motivation	Only satisfaction of physiological and safety needs will motivate workers.	Motivation occurs at social, self esteem and self- actualisation level.
Control	Control is the only means to achieve organisational objectives.	With proper motivation people may be self-directed and creative.
Leadership	Autocratic leadership.	Democratic and supportive leadership.

It is unusual to find exclusively Theory X people or Theory Y people in any organisation. There would always be a mix of both types of employees in varying proportions. Managers therefore will have to tailor their motivational techniques in an appropriate manner suiting behavioural patterns.

5.2.3 Motivation-Hygiene Two-Factor Theory

Frederick Herzberg's two-factor theory, also known as intrinsic/extrinsic motivation, concludes that certain factors in the workplace result in job satisfaction, but if absent, they don't lead to dissatisfaction but no satisfaction. The factors that motivate people can change over their lifetime, but "respect for me as a person" is one of the top motivating factors at any stage of life.

*   Proposed by psychologist Frederick Herzberg.
*   Also known as motivation-hygiene theory: Intrinsic factors are related to job satisfaction, while extrinsic factors are associated with dissatisfaction.
*   Intrinsic factors, such as advancement, recognition, responsibility, and achievement seem to be related to job satisfaction. Employees who felt good about their work tended to attribute these factors to their own selves. On the other hand, dissatisfied respondents tended to cite extrinsic factors, such as, pay, company policies, and working conditions.
*   Herzberg felt that the opposite of satisfaction is not dissatisfaction. Removing dissatisfying characteristics from the job does not necessarily make the job satisfying.

Herzberg felt that the opposite of satisfaction is not dissatisfaction.

He distinguished between –

Motivators (for example, challenging work, recognition, responsibility) which give positive satisfaction, and hygiene factors (for example, status, job security, salary and fringe benefits) that do not motivate if present, but, if absent, result in de-motivation.

The name 'hygiene factors' is used because like hygiene, the presence will not make you healthier, but absence can cause health deterioration.

The theory is sometimes called the "Motivator-Hygiene Theory" and/or "The Dual Structure Theory."

Herzberg's theory has found application in such occupational fields as information systems and in studies of user satisfaction.

Contrasting views of Satisfaction and Dissatisfaction

*   **Traditional view:** Satisfaction and dissatisfaction are opposite to each other.
*   **Herzberg's view:** Motivators lead to satisfaction or to no satisfaction.
*   **Hygiene factors:** Factors – such as company policy and administration, supervision, and salary – that, when adequate in a job, placate workers. When these factors are adequate, people will not be dissatisfied.

- If we want to motivate people on their jobs, Herzberg suggested emphasising factors associated with the work itself or to outcomes directly derived from it, such as promotional opportunities, opportunities for personal growth, recognition, responsibility, and achievement, that is, characteristics that people find intrinsically rewarding.

5.2.4 Goal-Setting Theory of Motivation

In the period of the '60s, Edwin Locke had put forward the goal-setting theory of motivation. This theory, states that goal-setting is majorly linked to task performance. It states that challenging and specific goals along with appropriate feedback contributes to better and higher task performance.

In other words, goals helps in indicating and giving directions to the employees about what needs to be done and how much efforts are required to put in.

Following are the important features of goal-setting theory –

1. The main source of job motivation is the willingness to work towards attainment of goals. Particular, clear and difficult goals are greater motivating factors than general, easy and vague goals.

2. Clear and specific goals leads to better performance and greater output. Measurable, unambiguous and clear goals accompanied by a deadline for completion avoids misunderstanding.

3. Goals must be challenging and realistic as it gives a feeling of triumph and pride to an individual when he attains them and sets him up for the accomplishment of the next goal. The more challenging the goal, the greater is the reward and the passion also increases for achieving it.

4. Appropriate and better feedback of results directs the employee's behaviour and contributes to higher performance than absence of feedback. Feedback is a means of making clarifications, gaining reputation and regulating goal difficulties. It helps the employees to work with more involvement and leads to greater job satisfaction.

5. Employee's participation is goal may not always be desirable.

6. However, participation of setting goal makes the goal more acceptable and leads to more involvement.

7. Goal setting theory as various eventualities as below –

   (a) Self-efficiency: Self-efficiency is an individual's faith and self-confidence which he has in him for performing the task. Higher the level of self-efficiency, the greater will be the efforts that an individual will put in when he faces challenging tasks. Whereas, lower the level of self-sufficiency, lesser will be the efforts put in by an individual or else he might even quit while facing challenges.

   (b) Goal commitment: Goal-setting theory assumes that an individual is committed to the goals and this is based on the following factors as mentioned as follows.

- Goals are made known, open and broadcasted.
- Goals set should be set by an individual rather than designated.
- Set goals of an individual should be consistent with the organisational vision and goals.

5.2.5 Process Theory

Process theory is a commonly used form of scientific research study in which events or occurrences are said to be the result of certain input states leading to a certain outcome (output) state, following a set process.

Process theory holds that if an outcome is to be duplicated, so too must the process which originally created it, and that there are certain constant necessary conditions for the outcome to be reached. When the phrase is used in connection with human motivation, process theory attempts to explain the mechanism by which human needs changes. Some of the theories that fall in this category are expectancy theory, equity theory, and goal-setting.

In management research, process theory provides an explanation for 'how' something happens and a variance theory explains 'why'.

5.2.6 Vroom Expectancy Theory

Like the needs-goal theory, motivation strength is determined by the perceived value of the result of performing behaviour and the perceived probability that the behaviour performed will cause the result to materialise.

> *People tend to perform the behaviours that maximise their rewards over the long term.*

As both of these factors increase, so does motivation strength, or the desire to perform the behaviour. People tend to perform the behaviours that maximise their rewards over the long term.

- An employee will be motivated to exert a high level of effort when he or she believes that effort will lead to a good performance appraisal; that a good appraisal will lead to organisational rewards such as a bonus, a salary increase, or a promotion; and that the rewards will satisfy the employee's personal goals.

    The theory, therefore, focuses on three relationships –

- **Effort-performance relationship:** The probability perceived by the individual that exerting a given amount of effort will lead to performance.

- **Performance-reward relationship:** The degree to which the individual believes that performing at a particular level will lead to attainment of a desired outcome.

- **Rewards-personal goals relationship:** The degree to which organisational rewards satisfy an individual's personal goals or needs and the attractiveness of those potential rewards for the individual.

5.2.7 Porter-Lawler Theory

The Porter-Lawler Theory accepts the premises that felt needs cause human behaviour and that the effort expended to accomplish a task is determined by the perceived value of rewards that will result from finishing the task and the probability that those rewards will materialise. The model holds that performance in an organisation is dependent on three factors –

1.   An employee should have the desire to perform, that is, he must feel motivated to accomplish the task.

2.   Motivation alone cannot ensure successful performance of a task. The employee should have the abilities and skills required to successfully perform the task.

3.   The employee should have a clear perception of his role in the organisation and an accurate knowledge of the job requirements. This will enable him to focus his efforts on accomplishing the assigned tasks.

Important Variables in the Model

*   **Effort:** This denotes the amount of energy expended by an individual to perform a specific task. Motivation is the force that drives an individual to make an effort to perform a certain task.

*   **Performance:** Making an effort does not deliver effective performance on its own. Performance also depends on his abilities and skills and the way he perceives his role in accomplishing the task.

*   **Rewards:** Maybe intrinsic or extrinsic in nature. Intrinsic rewards are less likely to be affected by disturbing or negative thoughts and influences of others; while for extrinsic rewards, it is difficult to establish a relationship between rewards and performance.

*   **Satisfaction:** Depends upon whether the actual reward offered falls short of, matches or exceeds what the individual perceives as an equitable level of reward.

5.2.8 Equity Theory

Equity theory looks at an individual's perceived fairness of an employment situation and finds that perceived inequalities can lead to changes in behaviour. When individuals believe that they have been treated unfairly in comparison with their co-workers, they will react in one of four ways.

> *Equity theory looks at an individual's perceived fairness of an employment situation and finds that perceived inequalities can lead to changes in behaviour.*

1.   Changing their work inputs to better match the rewards they are receiving.

2.   Ask for a raise or take legal action.

3.   Change their perception of the situation.

4.   Quit.

- Individuals compare their job inputs and outcomes with those of others and then respond to eliminate any inequities.
- If we perceive our outcome-input ratio to be equal to that of the relevant others with whom we compare ourselves, a state of equity is said to exist. We perceive our situation as fair—that justice prevails.
- When we see the ratio as unequal, we experience equity tension.
- When we see ourselves as under-rewarded, the tension creates anger; when over-rewarded, the tension creates guilt. This negative state provides the motivation to do something to correct it.

Important Variables in Equity Theory

The referent chosen is an important variable in equity theory.

1. **Self-inside:** An employee's experiences in a different position inside his or her current organisation.
2. **Self-outside:** An employee's experiences in a situation or position outside his or her current organisation.
3. **Other-inside:** Another individual or group of individuals inside the employee's organisation.
4. **Other-outside:** Another individual or group of individuals outside the employee's organisation.

Employee's Choices when Inequity is perceived

1. Change their inputs, that is, don't exert as much effort.
2. Change their outcomes, that is, if paid on piece-rate basis, they can increase their quantity of units produced.
3. Distort perceptions of self, that is, "I now realise that I work a lot harder than others."
4. Distort perceptions of others, that is, "his job isn't as desirable as I previously thought it was."
5. Choose a different referent, that is, make comparison with someone who isn't as well of.
6. Leave the field, that is, quit the job.

Propositions Relating to Inequitable Pay

1. Given payment by time, over-rewarded employees will produce more than will equitably paid employees.
2. Given payment by quantity of production, over-rewarded employees will produce fewer, but higher-quality, units than will equitably paid employees.
3. Given payment by time, under-rewarded employees will produce less or poorer quality of output.

4. Given payment by quantity, under-rewarded employees will produce a large number of low-quality units in comparison with equitably paid employees.

    - **Distributive justice:** Perceived fairness of the amount and allocation of rewards among individuals.

    - **Procedural justice:** The perceived fairness of the process used to determine the distribution of the rewards. These are particularly relevant to OCB (Organisational Citizenship Behaviour).

5.3 Motivation Applied

5.3.1 Financial Motivators

Incentives have the power to motivate employees towards a set target. These incentives can be classified as financial and non-financial. In the context of financial and non-financial motivators, it is said that, "financial and non-financial incentives are required to motivate the workers for harder work just as both the right and left feet are essential for walking." In simpler words, both are of the same importance and it is important to implement both simultaneously.

(A) Financial or Monetary Incentives

Financial incentives are the ones which are evaluated in terms of money. This does not mean that all the incentives should be in money form, but some such facilities can be provided as can be evaluated in money terms, like facility of a servant, rent-free house, car, etc. Generally, financial incentives are helpful to satisfy the safety and psychological needs. Following can be included amongst the chief financial incentives –

1. **Pay and Allowances:** Pay and allowances are known as the chief monetary incentives for every employee as salary includes basic pay and dearness allowance along with other allowances. The employees remain motivated with the annual increment in pay and allowances.

2. **Productivity Linked Wage Incentive:** The employees feel motivated by linking productivity with their salary. In simpler words, the salary increment will be in direct proportion of the productivity increase.

3. **Bonus:** Bonus is referred to as the extra pay in addition to their regular remuneration which is as a reward of their good services. This helps in establishing cordial relations between the owners and employees. It may be in the form of cash or in kind and it is getting prevalent in almost all industries.

4. **Profit Sharing:** The profits earned by an organisation are the outcome of the two parties, that is, the owners and the employees. The owners invest the money whereas the employees provide services to fulfil its objectives. Consequently, the owners get profit in lieu of their investment whereas the employees get their salaries for providing the services. Although, the employees naturally get their remuneration as a reward for their services, sometimes they are made a part of the

profit earned by the organisation with the hope that they will provide services with full labour, potential and honesty. The profit plan thus is known as profit-sharing.

5. **Co-partnership:** Co-partnership is known as a developed form of profit-sharing. It is based on the establishment of the industrial democracy and worker's participation in management. In this plan, the employees render their services to the company and they are also the partners in the equity capital. Consequently, the employees are entitled to get dividend and also equal participation in management besides their regular pay. The company's equity shares may be issues to the employees in the following two ways –

   (i)   On cash payment basis,

   (ii) In lieu of any incentive otherwise payable in cash like issue of shares under profit-sharing plan or payment of bonus in the form of shares.

6. **Retirement Benefits:** If the employees are offered financial security after their post-retirement period, their future will be secured, and this will definitely motivate them to give in their best. Gratuity and provident fund are the best examples for post-retirement benefits.

7. **Prerequisites:** Prerequisites are the facilities which an employee gets free from the employers and these facilities play a major role in motivating the employees.

5.3.2 Non-Financial Motivators

Non-financial incentives are indirectly related with money and help in satisfying the top hierarchy needs like esteem, social and self-actualisation needs. As per **Dublin**, *"Non-financial motivators are in the form of mental reward"*. As per **Chester Barnard**, *"Common feeling that material reward (like money) becomes ineffective after a certain extent"*. This means that non-financial rewards are more effective than the financial rewards for motivating materially prosperous persons. Following are the factors that are primarily helpful in motivating the employees with the non-financial rewards.

1. **Status:** Status refers to the rank or the position of a person in an organisation and this can high or low. An employee's rank is directly linked with his responsibility, authority and other facilities. As everybody has a wish for a higher status, the employees can be motivated by raising their position or rank. The attainment of the higher status fulfils the social, psychological and esteem-related needs.

2. **Organisational Climate:** Organisational climate refers to the working system of the organisation which includes the receipt of awards, individual freedom, the importance of employees, etc. Everybody likes to work in a better organisational climate and thus the manager can motivate the employees by providing a better organisational environment.

3. **Career Advancement Opportunity:** Career advancement opportunity refers to promotions. Training and development facilities need to be provided for promoting the employees. Thus, the managers can clear their way to promotion by providing such facilities. With this, the employees definitely get motivated.

4. **Job Enrichment:** Job enrichment refers to the increasing of work importance. Such a job must have (i) Responsibility, authority and a wide scope for challenges, (ii) there should be a need of higher knowledge and experience, (iii) opportunities should be available for personal development and iv) there must be absolute freedom to take decisions. Employees' feelings provide for getting such jobs and thus job enrichment enhance employee's interest in their work and they start getting motivated automatically.

5. **Employee Recognition Programmes:** Every employee wishes to have his own identity, be distinctive and thus be considered as an important part of the organisation. Following are the examples which help in the employee's recognition –

    i) Congratulating the employee for good work performance.

    (ii) Displaying employee's achievements on the information board and publishing them in the magazine of the organisation.

    (iii) Awarding certificates of merit and the ceremonial functions of the organisation for better work performance.

    (iv) Presenting mementos.

    (v) Honouring those offering valuable suggestions.

6. **Job Security:** Job security is known as an important non-monetary motivator. Job security means a feeling of stability and permanence. For example, if an employee has a sense of insecurity in his mind that he will be removed from his job any time, then he will not be able to work whole-heartedly as this will continue to trouble him always. Whereas, if he has a feeling of security and knows that he will not be removed from the job so easily then he will give his best at work without any worries. This helps in increasing his efficiency and is the prime reason why people prefer a permanent job with less salary to a temporary job with more salary.

7. **Employee Participation:** Employee's feels encouraged to notice their participation in managerial works. Thus, they offer their full cooperation in making successful policies.

8. **Employee Empowerment:** Employee empowerment refers to giving more freedom to the employees for taking decisions. When the employees' decision-making power increase, they consider that they are doing some important work in the organisation and this motivates them.

Difference between Monetary and Non-Monetary Incentives

Basis of Difference	Monetary Incentives	Non-Monetary Incentives
1. Measurement	These can be measured in terms of money.	These cannot be measured in terms of money.
2. Suitability	These are highly effective in case of workers.	These are effective in case of managers.

Basis of Difference	Monetary Incentives	Non-Monetary Incentives
3. Level of Satisfaction	These help in satisfying lower level needs (food, clothing and shelter).	These help in satisfying higher level needs (self-esteem and self-actualisation).
4. Visibility	Monetary incentives are visible as they are measurable in terms of money.	Non-monetary incentives may not be visible as they are not measurable in terms of money.

5.4 Leadership

5.4.1 Introduction

Leadership is a process by which an executive can direct, guide and influence the behaviour and work of others by accomplishing certain goals in a given circumstance. Leadership is the capability of a manager to persuade the subordinates to work confidently.

Leadership is the potential to influence the behaviour of others. It is also defined as the capacity to influence a group towards the realisation of a goal. Leaders need to develop future visions, and encourage the organisational members to achieve the visions.

Leadership is defined as "the process of social influence in which one person can enlist the aid and support of others in the accomplishment of a common task". A definition more inclusive of followers comes from **Alan Keith** of Genentech who said "Leadership is ultimately about creating a way for people to contribute to making something extraordinary happen". Leadership is one of the most important features of the organisational context. However, defining the concept of leadership has been challenging.

5.4.2 Meaning and Definitions of Leadership

Robbins defines leadership as the ability to influence a group towards the achievement of goals.

Paul Hersey and **Kenneth Blanchard** define leadership as the process of influencing group activities towards the accomplishment of goals in a given situation.

Although many definitions are mentioned, most of them depend on the theoretical orientation. In addition of influencing people, leadership has been defined in terms of group processes, persuasion power, goal achievement, communication, role differentiation, initiation of structure and combination of two or more.

Leadership is basically a continuous process of influencing behaviour. A leader breathes life into the group and motivates it towards goals. The lukewarm desires for achievement are transformed into a burning passion for accomplishment. Leadership is the ability (through whatever means) to influence the behaviour of others in a particular direction. Effective leadership is an essential ingredient of effective management.

Leadership is the process of influencing the activities of an individual or a group in efforts towards goal achievement in a given situation. Leadership is the influence – the art or process of influencing people so that they will strive willingly and enthusiastically towards the achievement of group goals. Leaders act to help a group to achieve objectives with the maximum application of its capabilities **(Harold Koontz, Cyril O' Donnel and Heinz Weihrich)**.

5.4.3 Importance of Leadership

Leadership is a significant function of management which helps in maximising efficiency and attaining organisational goals. The following points justify the significance of leadership in a concern.

1. **Initiates action:** A leader is an individual who begins his work by communicating the policies and plans to the subordinates from where the work actually starts.

2. **Motivation:** A leader plays the role of an incentive in the concern's working. He motivates the employees with financial and non-financial rewards and thus gets the work done from the subordinates.

3. **Providing guidance:** A leader has to not only manage but also guide the subordinates. Guidance here means teaching the subordinates the way they have to do their work effectively and efficiently.

4. **Creating confidence:** Confidence is a significant factor which can be attained through communicating the efforts to be put in the work, to the subordinates, explaining them clearly their role and giving them guidelines to attain the goals successfully. It is also significant to hear the employees' complaints and problems.

5. **Building morale:** Morale indicates an employee's willingness and co-operation towards their work and getting them into confidence and winning their trust. A leader can be a morale booster by attaining full co-operation so that the employees do their level best in achieving the goals.

6. **Builds work environment:** Management is getting its work done from the people. A well-organised work environment helps in a sound and stable growth. Thus, human relationships should be acknowledged by a leader. He should have personal contacts with the employees and should pay attention to their problems and solve them. He should treat the employees kindly.

7. **Co-ordination:** Co-ordination can be attained through integrating individual interests with organisational goals. This synchronisation can be attained through an appropriate and effective co-ordination which should be the main motive of a leader.

5.4.4 Characteristics of Leadership

1. **Leadership involves non-coercive influence:** The leadership process involves the power to control others, that is, how much a leader is able to change the deeds or attitude of numerous group members or subordinates. The influence can be

coercive where the leader works like a dictator, where the followers have no choice other than obeying him. However, influence can be non-coercive where the follower can opt to agree to or refuse the influence offered. In the leadership process, the degree of influence range from coercive to non-coercive influence methods. An effective leadership is the result of the few positive emotions between the leaders and their subordinates. The subordinates accept influence from the leaders because they respect or admire them.

2. **Leadership influence is goal directed:** All the definitions emphasise the exercise of influence for a reason, in a leadership process, to achieve group or organisational goals. Thus, they apply pressure on the follower's behaviour, which does not work in achieving the group's goals.

3. **Leadership requires followers:** Leadership process needs two parties, where one wants to influence and others want to be influenced. A leader cannot work in an empty space; he requires directing a group of followers towards achievement of a common goal. Sometimes, it is the other way where the followers influence the leaders because leaders cannot lead without the followers.

5.4.5 Functions of a Leader

A leader has to perform various functions and this depends upon the structure, type and gaols of the group. For example, the functions or the roles that a general of the army has to perform are quite different from the functions that a social, political or religious leader has to perform.

Following are the various functions that a leader has to perform –

1. **Policy Maker:** Planning out the group's objectives, goals and policies is an important function of a leader of any social group. He is supposed to lay down specific objectives and policies and thus inspire subordinates to work towards the attainment of the goals.

2. **Planner:** The leader also has to function as a planner wherein he decides the means and ways to be adopted for achieving the group's objectives. He draws up both short-term as well as long-term plans. Based on this, he prepares a step-by-step plan for achieving the group's objectives, contingencies and unexpected events.

3. **Executive:** Drawing plans and setting goals are of no use unless they are implemented. Under his executive function, a leader has to ensure that the plans are well executed, wherein he has to coordinate the activities of the group. Being an executive, a leader himself will not carry out activities or work but will assign it to other group members and thus ensure that they are properly implemented.

4. **External Group Representative:** The leader assumes the role of representative of the group in its external relations, wherein all the incoming and outgoing communications are channelled through him. Other group members deal with the leader as a representative of that particular group as he is the official spokesperson of that group.

5. **Controller of Internal Group Relationship:** The leader has to control the internal relations amongst the group members as all the communication in the group is channelled through him. He encourages team spirit, tries to establish good relations amongst group members and tries to develop the group in to a cohesive unit.

6. **Controller of Reward and Punishment:** The leader uses the power to give rewards and punishments to discipline, motivate and control group members. Members are rewarded for their contribution and working towards the attainment of the group goals and those who obstruct the group's progress are punished.

   Rewards are in various forms like cash rewards, promotion, and appreciation in public, increased status, etc. Punishment can also be in various forms like penalties, taking away responsibility assigned and scolding etc.

7. **Arbitrator and Mediator:** The leader acts as an arbitrator and mediator when there are differences or conflicts in the group as he has to resolve disputes in a fair and just manner. He tries to reduce tensions in the group, establish good inter-group relationships and harmony.

8. **Exemplar:** The leader serves as a role model to the group members. He must "walk the talk" and must set an example for others to follow by setting high standards. He practices beliefs, ideologies, values and norms laid down in the group.

9. **Father Figure:** At times, the leader has to play the emotional role of a father figure for the group members. He is a source of moral and psychological support to the followers. He helps the group members in their personal life and guides them in their work-related issues too. The group members vent out their feelings to him as he acts as a punching bag for their frustrations.

10. **Scapegoat:** The leader is solely accountable for the group performance; hence, he gets a lot of credit if the group performs well. Similarly, the leader is held responsible if the group fails to perform well even though the leader might have tried everything possible. Thus he plays the role of a scapegoat.

5.4.6 Leadership Styles

Leadership is a term that conjures up different images in different people. While to some it means charisma, to others it means power and authority. According to **George K. Terry,** "Leadership is the activity of influencing people to strive willingly for group objectives."

The term leadership style refers to a consistent behaviour pattern as perceived by people around a leader; every leader develops a pattern or style while handling his subordinates. Leadership style can also be said as the outcome of a person's philosophy, personality and experience; it also depends on the type of followers and the environment of an organisation.

1. **Autocratic Style:** An autocratic or authoritarian style of leadership implies absolute power over his subordinates. Being an autocratic leader he expects complete

obedience from his subordinates and the power of making a decision is centralised to the leader himself and he does not entertain any sort of suggestions and initiatives from his subordinates. This type of leadership is not encouraged by many companies as human resources cannot be retained.

2. **Democratic or Participative Leader:** Democratic or Participative style of Leadership stands in between the two extremes of the autocratic style and the laissez-fair style of leadership, in this style, the leader acts friendly to his subordinates and goes with any decision after having a mutual consent and discussion with them, the subordinates are encouraged to put forth their suggestions to the leader and the organisation which motivates the employee as he gets the confidence of the leader and is able to perform better in his work.

3. **Laissez-faire or Free Rein Leader: Lewin Lippitt** was the one who described the laissez-faire style of leadership style along with autocratic and democratic style of leadership. The laissez-faire leadership is sometimes otherwise known as "hands off" leadership; this French phrase means "leave it be"; the leader leaves his colleague to get on with their work usually with no directions but this type of leadership can be effective only if the leader provides proper monitoring over his subordinates.

5.4.7 Traits of Leadership

Leaders are mostly competent but few qualify as remarkable. Following are the qualities which a leader must possess, although they are not easy but the rewards can be truly phenomenal.

1. **Awareness:** There is a vast difference between employees and management, workers and bosses. Leaders have to understand this difference and accept it to inform their actions, image and communication. Their conduct sets them apart from the other group members – not in a manner which suggests them better than the rest, but in such a way that permits them to retain an objective perspective on everything that's happening in the organisation.

2. **Decisiveness:** All leaders have to take tough decisions as it goes with the job. They accept the fact that in various situations, timely and difficult decisions are to be made in the best interests of the entire organisations, which requires finality, authority and firmness that might not please everyone. Extraordinary leaders do not step back in such situations as they know when not to act unilaterally but instead foster collaborative decision-making.

3. **Empathy:** Extraordinary leaders address problems in private and praises in public with a genuine concern. The best leaders are always on the lookout for solutions to foster the long-term success of the organisation and thus guide employees through challenges. They look for constructive solutions and focus on moving forward, rather than making things personal when they encounter problems or blaming the individuals.

4. **Accountability:** Extraordinary leaders take responsibility of everybody's performance in the group, including their own. They keep a check on employees, follow up on all outstanding issues and monitor the effectiveness of company's procedures and policies. They praise the things that are going well and will identify the problems quickly, seek solutions and get things back on track.

5. **Confidence:** The best leaders are not only confident, but are contagious because of which employees are naturally drawn to them, seek their advise and feel more confident as a result. During challenging times, they don't give in easily as they know their opinions, ideas and strategies are well-informed and the result of much hard work. But when they are proved wrong, they take the responsibility and act quickly for improving the situations within their authority.

6. **Optimism:** The best leaders are a source of positive energy. They are intrinsically helpful, communicate easily and genuinely concerned for other people's welfare. They always know what to say to inspire and reassure and always seem to have a solution. They look for ways to gain consensus and get people to work together effectively and efficiently as a team and avoid personal criticism and pessimistic thinking.

7. **Honesty:** Good leaders treat others the way in which they like to be treated. They are highly ethical and believe that effort, honesty and reliability form the foundation of success. They embody these values so overtly that no employee can doubt their integrity for a minute. They share information openly with others and avoid spin control.

8. **Focus:** Great leaders plan well in advance and are supremely organised. They consider viable alternatives while making plans and strategies which are all targeted towards success, thinking through multiple scenarios and the possible impacts of their decisions. Once prepared, they establish processes, strategies and routines so that high performance is easily defined, tangible and monitored. They communicate their plans to the main players and have contingency plans in the event which requires last-minute changes for a new direction.

9. **Inspiration:** An extraordinary leader is someone who communicates concisely, clearly and motivates everyone in the group to give his best at all times. They create challenges to their people by setting high but attainable expectations and standards and then giving them the required tools, support, latitude and training to pursue those goals and become the best employees that they can possibly be.

5.4.8 Leaders vs. Managers

It is a generally accepted fact that leaders are not required to be managers and managers are not required to be leaders. However, the disagreement among researchers is sharp about how much overlap is present between the two roles within organisations. The differences have been pointed on many fronts.

Basis	Managers	Leaders
Basic values	Create and maintain stability, order, efficiency, changing only when forced to. 'Why disturb it if it is working fine?'	Flexibility, innovation, adaptation, seeking risk, 'Let's take the game to its next level/let's go for another game.'
Basic concern	Get the work done, make people perform better. Solve up-and-coming problems rationally and conventionally.	Assist people to see the meaning in goals and get them to agree upon what are the most significant and meaningful things, to get the work done.
Kind of people they are	'People who do the things right'.	'People who do the right things'.
Core process	Bring certainty and order through traditional management functions.	Create organisational change through vision, its communication, and inspiring subordinates.
Type of relationship with others	Hierarchical authority relationship with subordinates.	Multidirectional influential relationship involving the superiors, peers, associates and subordinates.
Basic culture	Aims at control so as to attain given organisational goals.	Thrive in disorder; arouse expectations, new thinking and new choices using imagination.
Basic goals	Are given from top out of need. Goals are deeply rooted in the organisational history and culture.	Arise out of dreams and desire. Goals are forward-looking and form an appropriate culture and history.

Source: Based on Yukl (2002, p. 5-6), Zaleznik (1992).

However, managerial success essentially involves leading, regardless of one's position in the organisation, thanks to the changes in the environment, pressure to deliver results and leaner organisations. What are the skills that will be useful for a leader regardless of his level in the hierarchy?

5.5 Theories of Leadership

There are various theories for leadership. They are as follows:

5.5.1 Trait Theory

Lincoln, Gandhi, Hitler, Ambedkar are all known as leaders. Early researchers believed that leaders were those who possessed some unique qualities and traits that distinguished them from their peers. These characteristics or traits were considered to be relatively stable over a period of time and enduring.

According to the trait approach, these leaders possessed important traits like intelligence, dominance, self-confidence, energy, and technical and work expertise. These were possessed by leaders in varying levels of consistency and also there were innumerable traits that came to be listed over the years. However, this is because researchers were unable to enumerate the specific list of traits possessed by leaders to make them different from managers or management.

In recent years, though, the researchers have found renewed interest where they have been able to list out some specific traits common to leaders today. They are listed as emotional intelligence, drive, motivation, honesty, integrity, cognitive ability, self-confidence, technical expertise and charisma. So, this approach with these variations continues to hold in modern times of leadership.

5.5.2 The Great Person Theory

If you study the stories of the great leaders of this modern age like Bill Gates, Warren Buffett, Narayana Murthy, and Azim Premji, you will see that all of them possess extraordinary traits and an intense ambition and drive to succeed. It is the kind of orientation in this approach, which is known as Great Person Theory. According to this orientation, great leaders possess key traits that set them apart from other human beings.

It also suggests that all great leaders share these characteristics, which are as follows –

1.   Leadership motivation and the desire to lead
2.   Flexibility
3.   Focus on morality

1.   Leadership motivation and the desire to lead

Such leaders are intensely motivated to lead. However even the motivation to lead can take a negative connotation like seeking power and the exertion of the same to be wielded by the leader. Such a power may be reflected by the leader to exert coercion and influence on the subordinates. The other kind of power is to seek influence and drive the subordinates and others and share expertise, ideas, innovation and drive to achieve shared goals and purposes. Such types of leaders seek networks, coalitions, and socialised power. They rely on motivation and cooperate with others, develop networks and generally work with subordinates rather than trying to dominate others. So, this type of leadership is far more adaptive for organisations rather than personalised leadership motivation.

2. Flexibility

Today the most effective leaders are the ones who are very flexible in their behaviour to situations and to their subordinates. They do not exhibit uniform behaviour but adapt to the situation and the needs of the subordinates and colleagues.

3. Focus on morality

Authentic leadership is concerned with the focus on ethics or morally acceptable behaviour. Such leaders accept focus on morality and ethics in all their dealings and relationships. Authentic leadership is concerned with highly moral individuals with a confident, hopeful, optimistic nature and who are aware of the contexts in which they operate. Their key role is in the development of the ethical and moral conduct and development of their peers and colleagues and not only themselves.

5.5.3 Fiedler's Leadership Contingency Theory

The Fiedler Contingency Model is a leadership theory of industrial and organisational psychology developed by Fred Fiedler, one of the leading scientists who helped his field move from the research of traits and personal characteristics of leaders to leadership styles and behaviours.

The Two Factors of Fiedler's Contingency Model

Many scholars assumed that there was one best style of leadership. Fiedler's contingency model postulates that the leader's effectiveness is based on situational contingency, which is a result of interaction of two factors –

1. Least preferred co-worker (LPC)
2. Situational favourableness

More than 400 studies have since investigated this relationship.

1. Least Preferred Co-worker (LPC)

The leadership style of the leader, thus, fixed and measured by what he calls the least preferred co-worker (LPC) scale, an instrument for measuring an individual's leadership orientation. The LPC scale asks a leader to think of all the people with whom they have ever worked and then describe the person, with whom they have worked least well, using a series of bipolar scales of 1 to 8, such as the following –

Unfriendly 1 2 3 4 5 6 7 8 Friendly

Uncooperative 1 2 3 4 5 6 7 8 Cooperative

Hostile 1 2 3 4 5 6 7 8 Supportive

...........1 2 3 4 5 6 7 8................

Guarded 1 2 3 4 5 6 7 8 Open

The responses to these scales (usually 18-25 in total) are summed and averaged; a high LPC score suggests that the leader has a human relations orientation, while a low LPC score indicates a task orientation.

Fiedler assumes that everybody's least preferred co-worker is in fact on average equally unpleasant. But, people who are indeed relationship-motivated tend to describe their least preferred co-workers in a more positive manner, for example, more pleasant and more efficient. Therefore, they receive higher LPC scores.

People who are task-motivated, on the other hand, tend to rate their least preferred co-workers in a more negative manner. Therefore, they receive lower LPC scores. So, the least preferred co-worker (LPC) scale is actually not about the least preferred worker at all; instead, it is about the person who takes the test; it is about that person's motivation type. This is so, because, individuals who rate their least preferred co-worker in relatively favourable light on these scales derive satisfaction out of interpersonal relationship, and those who rate the co-worker in a relatively unfavourable light get satisfaction out of successful task performance.

This method reveals an individual's emotional reaction to people with whom he or she cannot work. Critics point out that this is not always an accurate measurement of leadership effectiveness.

2. Situational favourableness

According to Fiedler, there is no ideal leader. Both low-LPC (task-oriented) and high-LPC (relationship-oriented) leaders can be effective if their leadership orientation fits the situation. The contingency theory allows for predicting the characteristics of the appropriate situations for effectiveness.

Three situational components determine the favourableness or situational control –

1. **Leader-Member Relations**, referring to the degree of mutual trust, respect and confidence between the leader and the subordinates.
2. **Task Structure**, referring to the extent to which group tasks are clear and structured.
3. **Leader Position Power**, referring to the power inherent in the leaders' positions itself.

When there is a good leader-member relation, a highly structured task, and high leader position power, the situation is considered a "favourable situation." Fiedler found that low-LPC leaders are more effective in extremely favourable or unfavourable situations, whereas high-LPC leaders perform best in situations with intermediate favourability.

Leader-Situational Match and Mismatch

Since personality is relatively stable, the contingency model suggests that improving effectiveness requires changing the situation to fit the leader. This is called "job engineering." The organisation or the leader may increase or decrease task structure and position power; also training and group development may improve leader-member relations. In his 1976 book 'Improving Leadership Effectiveness: The Leader Match Concept', Fiedler (with Martin Chemers and Linda Mahar) offers a self-paced leadership training programme designed to help leaders alter the favourableness of the situation, or situational control.

Examples of Fiedler's Contingency Model

• Task-oriented leadership would be advisable in natural disaster, like a flood or fire. In an uncertain situation the leader-member relations are usually poor, the task is unstructured, and the position power is weak. The one who emerges as a leader to direct the group's activity usually does not know any of his or her subordinates personally. The task-oriented leader who gets things accomplished proves to be the most successful. If the leader is considerate (relationship-oriented), he or she may waste so much time in the disaster, which may lead things to get out of control and lives might get lost.

• Blue-collar workers generally want to know exactly what they are supposed to do. Therefore, their work environment is usually highly structured. The leader's position power is strong if management backs his or her decision.

Finally, even though the leader may not be relationship-oriented, leader-member relations may be extremely strong if he or she is able to gain promotions and salary increases for subordinates. Under these situations the task-oriented style of leadership is preferred over the (considerate) relationship-oriented style.

• The considerate (relationship-oriented) style of leadership can be appropriate in an environment where the situation is moderately favourable or certain. For example, when

(1) Leader-member relations are good,

(2) The task is unstructured, and

(3) Position power is weak.

Situations like this exist with research scientists, who do not like superiors to structure the task for them. They prefer to follow their own creative leads in order to solve problems. In a situation like this a considerate style of leadership is preferred over the task-oriented

Summary of Fiedler's Contingency Model

To Fiedler, stress is a key determinant of leader effectiveness (Fiedler and Garcia 1987; Fiedler et al. 1994), and a distinction is made between stress related to the leader's superior attitude, and stress related to subordinates or the situation itself. In stressful situations, leaders dwell on the stressful relations with others and cannot focus their intellectual abilities on the job.

Thus, intelligence is more effective and used more often in stress-free situations. Fiedler has found that experience impairs performance in low-stress conditions but contributes to performance under high-stress conditions. As with other situational factors, for stressful situations Fiedler recommends altering or engineering the leadership situation to capitalise on the leader's strengths.

Despite all the criticism, Fiedler's contingency theory is an important theory because it established a brand new perspective for the study of leadership. Many approaches after Fiedler's theory have adopted the contingency perspective.

Fred Fiedler's situational contingency theory holds that group effectiveness depends on an appropriate match between a leader's style (essentially a trait measure) and the demands of the situation. Fiedler considers situational control, the extent to which a leader can determine what his or her group is going to do, to be the primary contingency factor in determining the effectiveness of leader behaviour.

5.5.4 Four Framework Approach

In the Four-Framework approach, Bolman and Deal suggest that leaders display leadership behaviour in one of four types of framework.

Types of frameworks

- (i)   Structural
- (ii) Human Resources
- (iii) Political
- (iv) Symbolic

We also need to understand ourselves, as each of us tends to have a preferred approach. We need to be conscious of these at all times and be aware of the limitations of just favouring one approach.

- **(i)   Structural Framework:** In an effective leadership situation, the leader is a social architect whose leadership style is analytical and creative. Structural leaders focus on structure, strategy, environment, implementation, experimentation, and adaptation.

- **(ii) Human Resource Framework:** In an effective leadership situation, the leader is a catalyst whose leadership style is supporting, advocating, and empowering. Human resource leaders believe in people and communicate that belief; they are visible and accessible; they empower, increase participation, support, share information, and move decision-making down into the organisation.

- **(iii) Political Framework:** In an effective leadership situation, the leader is an advocate whose leadership style is coalition and building. Political leaders clarify what they want and what they can get; they assess the distribution of power and interests; they build linkages to other stakeholders, use persuasion first, and then use negotiation and coercion only if necessary.

- **(iv) Symbolic Framework:** In an effective leadership situation, the leader is a prophet, whose leadership style is an inspiration. Symbolic leaders view organisations as a stage or theatre to play certain roles and give impressions; these leaders use symbols to capture attention; they try to frame experience by providing plausible interpretations of experiences; they discover and communicate a vision.

5.5.5 Path-Goal Theory

Path-goal theory is developed by Robert House, which extracts the elements from the Ohio State University leadership research on initiating structure and consideration and the expectancy theory of motivation. It explains that it is the leader's job to provide followers with the support and information of other resources that are necessary for achieving the goals. The term "path-goal" implies that effective leaders clarify followers' path to their work goals and make the journey easier by reducing roadblocks.

As per the path-goal theory, whether a leader must be supportive or directive or demonstrate some other behaviour depends on a complex analysis of the situation. It helps in predicting the following –

- Directive leadership tends to yield greater satisfaction when tasks are stressful or ambiguous than when they are highly structured and well laid out.
- Supportive leadership results in high satisfaction and performance when employees are performing structured tasks.
- Directive leadership is perceived as redundant by employees with considerable experience or high ability.

It is not easy for testing the path-goal theory. An evidence review suggests missed support saying, "These results suggest that either effective leadership does not rest in the removal of roadblocks and pitfalls to employee path instrumentalities path-goal theories propose or that the nature of these hindrances is not in accord with the proposition of the theories". Others say that adequate tests are yet to be conducted for the theory. Thus, the jury is still out because path-goal theory is so complex to test that it may remain the same for some time.

It is observed that the worker's conscientiousness was related to higher performance levels only when supervisors set goals, defines roles, responsibilities and priorities. Another observation is that goal-focused leadership can lead to higher levels of emotional exhaustion for subordinates who are low in emotional stability and conscientiousness. These observations explain that leaders who set goals help the conscientious followers to achieve higher performance and may cause stress for workers who are low in conscientiousness.

5.5.6 Charismatic Theory

The charismatic school is known to focus on specific leader on specific leader behaviours that inspires higher levels of action amongst followers. While the charismatic and transformational leaders succeed in taking the goals, values and aspirations of the subordinates to higher levels, charisma is meant to be understood as a necessary but not sufficient condition for transformational leadership.

Charismatic leaders are known to arouse strong identifications and emotions with the leader, while their followers perceive the charismatic leader as one who possesses superhuman qualities and accepts unconditionally, the leader's directives and mission for actions. It is believed that charisma is generated by inspirational motivation and idealised influence dimensions the first two dimensions of transformational leadership combined with the leader's personal ability. To be specific, observable behaviours, the charismatic leaders engage in the following categories as mentioned below –

- Vision and its articulation is about consistently having new and exciting goals and ideas about possibilities in the future and communicating them to others effectively.

- Environmental sensitivity, especially about understanding the barriers, constraints and limitations present within the environment and in others, as well as recognising opportunities.

  Surprising or even unconventional behaviour or means for achieving organisational goals.

- Personal willingness and risk to engage in acts of self-sacrifice organisational goals.

- Personal concern and sensitivity for the member's needs and developing mutual respect and linking.

- Questioning the status quo.

Charismatic behaviour can have a more positive and stronger influence on the satisfaction, performance and adjustment of followers than the impact of considerate and directive behaviours. In fact, charismatic leaders energise their followers to such extraordinary levels that they can profoundly be different from the followers of non-charismatic leaders. This is because, probably, only charismatic leaders engage their followers at an emotional level, whereas the non-charismatic leaders are limited to the rational influence. Under this magnetic aspect, the charismatic leaders change the follower's self-concept and motivate them for transcending their own self-interests for the team's sake or the organisation or the larger policy.

Charismatic leaders are transformational leaders and are similar to each other and –

- Elevate their follower's needs from lower to higher levels in the Maslow hierarchy.

- Raise the followers to higher levels of morality, to 'more principled levels of judgement.

- Successfully motivate followers to transcend their own self-interests for the sake of the team, the organisation or the larger policy.

The transformational and charismatic leadership styles have a major difference between them, which is that the transformational leaders empower and elevate the followers whereas the charismatic leaders sometimes keep the followers dependent and weak, thus creating personal loyalty rather than commitment to ideals. This might be the reason why the changes initiated by charismatic leaders are often not sustained and the groups, systems and organisations slide back to the previous state after the charismatic leaders take an exit. Finally, the personal commitment and the motivational processes generated by the charismatic leaders can lead to dangerous values and blind fanaticism just like it may lead to heroic self-sacrifice in the service of a beneficial cause.

5.5.7 Ohio State Leadership Quadrants

In the year 1945, Ohio State has initiated the most comprehensive and extensive research programme. It aims at identifying independent dimensions of the leader's behaviour. Starting with over a thousand dimensions, the leader's behaviour description was narrowed down to two dimensions, initiating the structure and considering that substantially accounted for most of the leadership behaviour described by the subordinates. Initiating structures refers to the extent to which a leader is likely to structure and define his role and those of subordinates in the search for goal attainment. It is inclusive of behaviour which attempts to organise goals and work relationship. The leader characterised as high in initiating structure could be described in terms such as expect workers to maintain definite standards of performance, assign group members to particular tasks and emphasise the meeting of deadlines. Consideration is described as the extent to which a person is likely to have job relationship which are characterised by respect, mutual trust for subordinate's regard and ideas for their feelings. A leader who is high in consideration could be described as the one who helps the subordinates with his personal problems in a friendly and approachable manner and treats all the subordinates as equal.

In this context, the Ohio staff has developed the LBDQ, which is an instrument designed to describe the holy leaders carrying out their activities. Respondents judged the frequency with which the leaders engaged in each behavioural form by checking one of the five descriptions of 30 items, wherein fifteen pertaining to consideration and fifteen pertaining to initiating structure. A Leader Opinion Questionnaire (LOQ) about self-perceptions was also developed, that leaders had about their won leadership style. Both the dimensions, that is the consideration and the initiating structure were considered separate mind distinct.

Following are the four quadrants, which were developed to show various combinations of the two dimensions –

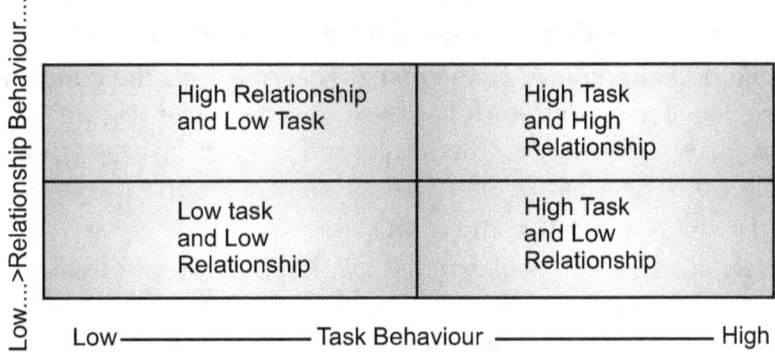

Fig. 5.3: Basic Leader Behaviour Styles

In the above conducted studies, it is observed that the leaders high in initiating structure and consideration tend to achieve high subordinate performance and satisfaction more frequently than those who rated low on either or both. Major example for this is absenteeism, greater rates of grievances and turnover levels of job satisfactions for workers performing routine tasks. On the other hand, it was also observed that high consideration was negatively related to performance ratings of the leader by his superior. Thus, it can be concluded that the Ohio State studies suggested that the high-style generally resulted in positive outcomes, however, enough exceptions were found for indicating that situational factors needed to be integrated into the theory.

Along with the two-dimensional approach, Blake and Mouton popularised the concepts of task and relationship dimensions in their managerial grid. Various types of leaders that were based on the managerial grid were: task, country club, impoverished, middle-of-the-road team. In essence, managerial grid gave popular terminology to five points within the four quadrants of the Ohio state studies.

5.5.8 Blake and Mouton's Managerial (Leadership) Grid

Managerial Grid is known to be the best model of managerial behaviour, which appeared first in the early '60s and has been revised and refined several times (Blake & McCanse, 1991; Blake & Mouton, 1964, 1978, 1985). This model has been used extensively for the organisational training and development. Later, the Managerial Grid was renamed the Leadership Grid, and was designed to explain how leaders help the organisations to reach their purposes through two factors: concern for production and concern for people.

Concern for production defines how a leader is concerned with achieving the organisational tasks. This involves a wide range of activities like new product development, attention to policy decisions, workload, process issues, and sales volume to name a few. Concern for production can refer to whatever the organisation is seeking to accomplish and not limited to an organisation's manufactured product or service (Blake and Mouton, 1964).

Concern for people defines how a leader attends to the organisation's people who are trying to achieve its goals. This includes promoting the personal worth of followers, building organisational commitment and trust, maintaining a fair salary structure, providing good working conditions and promoting good social relations (Blake and Mouton, 1964).

The leadership grid also known as the managerial grid joins the concern for production and concern for people in a model which has two interesting axes (Figure 5.4). The horizontal axes represent the leader's concern for the results and the vertical axes represent the leader's concern for people. Both the axes are drawn as a 9-point scale on which a score of 1 refers to minimum concern and 9 refers to maximum concern.

Various leadership styles can be illustrated by plotting scores from each of the axes. The leadership grid portrays five major leadership styles, that is, authority-compliance (9, 1), country-club management (1, 9), impoverished management (1, 1), middle-of-the-road management (5, 5), and team management (9, 9).

1.   Authority-Compliance (9, 1)

The 9, 1 style of leadership places heavy emphasis on job requirements and task and less emphasis on people, except to the extent that people are tools for getting their jobs done. Communicating is not emphasised with the subordinates except for the purpose of giving instructions about the task. This style is results driven and people are regarded as tools till the end. The 9, 1 leader is usually seen demanding, controlling, overpowering and hard-driving.

2.   Country-Club Management (1, 9)

The 1, 9 style of leadership refers to a low concern for task accomplishment linked with a high concern for interpersonal relationships. De-emphasising production, 1, 9 leaders stress the feelings and attitudes of people, making sure the social and personal needs of the followers are met. They try creating a positive climate by eagerly helping, being agreeable, uncontroversial and comforting.

3. Impoverished Management (1, 1)

The 1, 1 style refers to a leader who is not concerned with both the task as well as the interpersonal relationships. This type of leader goes through the motions of being a leader, however, acts withdrawn and uninvolved. This leader usually has little contact with the followers and could be described as noncommittal, indifferent, and apathetic and resigned.

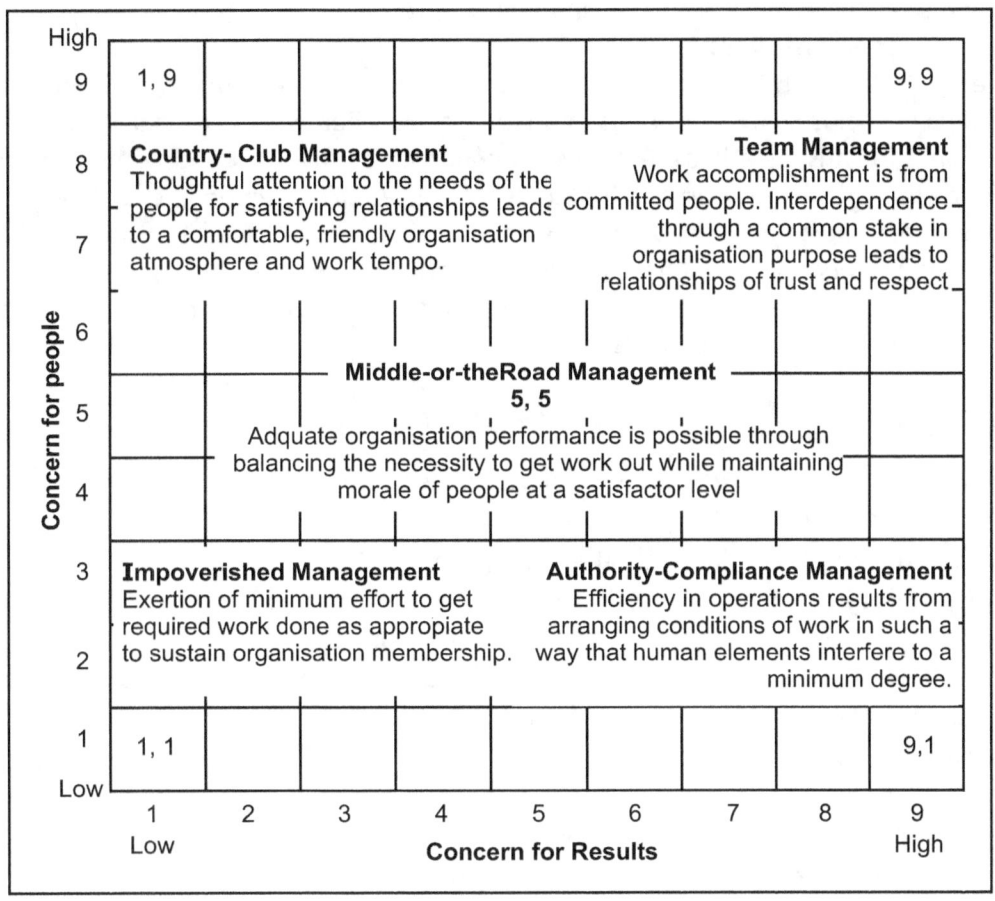

Fig. 5.4: The Leadership Grid

Source: The Leadership Grid figure, Paternalism figure, and Opportunism figure from Leadership Dilemmas—Grid Solutions, by Robert R. Blake and Anne Adams McCanse.

(Formerly the Managerial Grid by Robert R. Blake and Jane S. Mouton.) Houston: Gulf Publishing Company (Grid figure: p. 29, Paternalism figure: p. 30, Opportunism figure: p. 31). Copyright 1991 by Scientific Methods, Inc. Reproduced by permission of the owners.

4. Middle-of-the-Road Management (5, 5)

The 5, 5 style describes leaders who are compromisers and have an intermediate concern for the task as well as for the people who do the task. They strike a balance between taking people into account and still emphasising the requirements related to work. Their style of compromising gives up some of the push for production and some of the attention to the needs of the employees. To arrive at equilibrium, the 5, 5 leader emphasises moderate levels of production and interpersonal relationships and avoids conflicts. This leadership style is usually described as the one who is expedient, prefers soft-pedals disagreement, middle ground and swallows convictions in the interest of "progress".

5. Team Management (9, 9)

The 9, 9 leadership style refers to strong emphasis on tasks and interpersonal relationships. It helps in promoting a high degree of teamwork and participation in the organisation and satisfies a basic employee's needs to be involved and committed to their work. Following are a few phrases that could be used to describe the 9, 9 leader; acts determined, stimulates participation, makes priorities clear, gets issues into the open, follows through, enjoys working and behaves open-minded. Moreover, Blake and colleagues have identified two more behaviours that incorporate multiple aspects of grid which is an addition to the five major styles described above.

Points to Remember

- **Motive** is an emotion, desire, physiological need, or similar impulse that acts as an incitement to action.
- **Motivation** is an inner drive to behave or act in a certain manner.
- **Equity theory** looks at an individual's perceived fairness of an employment situation and finds that perceived inequalities can lead to changes in behaviour.
- **Leadership** is the process of influencing the activities of an individual or a group in efforts towards goal achievement in a given situation.
- **Leadership Styles**
  1. Autocratic Style
  2. Democratic or Participative Leader
  3. Laissez-Faire or Free Rein Leader
- An **autocratic or authoritarian style** of leadership implies absolute power over his subordinates.
- In **democratic or participative style** of leadership the leader acts friendly to his subordinates and goes with any decision after having a mutual consent and discussion with them.
- In the **laissez-faire leadership** the leader leaves his colleagues to get on with their work usually with no directions but this type of leadership can be effective only if the leader provides proper monitoring over his subordinates.

- **Theories of Leadership**
  1. Trait Theory
  2. Great Person Theory
  3. Contingency Leadership Approach
  4. Four-Framework Approach

- According to the **trait approach**, leaders like Gandhi, Hitler, and Ambedkar possessed important traits like intelligence, dominance, self-confidence, energy, and technical and work expertise.

- In the **four-framework approach**, Bolman and Deal suggest that leaders display leadership behaviour in one of four types of framework, that is, structural, human resources, political and symbolic.

Questions for Discussion

1. Explain Maslow's motivation theory.
2. List the types of motivation.
3. Summarise the effects of motivation on work behaviour.
4. Define leadership and its importance.
5. Elaborate on the various leadership styles.
6. How would you distinguish between leaders and managers?
7. Explain the Fiedler contingency leadership theory.

Chapter **6**...

Change Management and Organisational Development

Contents ...

Learning Objectives ...

 ➢ To describe the various forces of change
 ➢ To understand the term stability and change respectively
 ➢ To describe the process of change
 ➢ To demonstrate the resistance to change
 ➢ To illustrate the different objectives of organisational development
 ➢ To illustrate the various ways of managing stress

6.1 Organisational Change

6.1.1 Introduction

There is nothing permanent except change. It has become an unavoidable fact of life; a basic part of historical evolution. Change is unavoidable in a progressive culture. Change in truth is accelerating in our society. Revolutions are occurring in political, scientific, technological and institutional areas. Organisations cannot fully protect themselves from this environmental instability. Change is made by internal and external forces. Meeting this challenge of change is the main duty of the management. An organisation that lacks adaptability to change has no future. Adaptability to change is an essential quality of good management. Modern managers have the duty to develop management practices that best meet the new challenges and make use of the opportunities for the growth of the organisation.

The topic of managing change is one that is closest in explaining the totality of a manager's job. Almost everything a manager does is in some way related with implementing change.

• Hiring a new employee – Changing the work group.

• Buying a new piece of furniture – Changing work methods equipment.

• Rearranging work station – Changing work flows.

All require information of how to manage change effectively.

Organisational change refers to an alteration of the organisation's structure, processes or goods. Flexibility needs the organisations to be open to change in all areas, including the structure of the organisation itself. In an organisation that is flexible, employees cannot believe that their roles fit the terms of a job description. They frequently have to change the tasks that they carry out and learn new skills. The most flexible organisations have a culture that (a) values change, and (b) managers who understand how to implement changes effectively.

6.1.2 Why Organisational Change?

In today's fast-moving world any business that is looking for the speed of change too slow will probably be deeply disappointed. In fact, businesses should embrace change.

Change is significant for any organisation because, without change, companies would likely lose their competitive edge and fail to meet the requirements of what most hope to be a growing base of loyal clients.

1. **Technology**

Without change, entrepreneurs would still be dictating correspondence to secretaries, editing their words and sending them back to the drawing board, wasting the time of people that are involved. Change that results from accepting new technology is common in most companies and while it can be disruptive at first, finally the change tends to increase productivity and service technology also has changed the way we talk. No longer do business people dial a rotary phone, get a busy signal, and try until they get through. No longer do business people have to painstakingly contact people, personally, to find about other people who might be helpful resources; they can search for experts online through search engines plus through social media sites. Today's growing communication technology represents changes that enable organisations to learn more, more quickly, than ever before.

2. **Customer Needs**

Customers who were happy with traditional ovens are sometimes impatient with the microwave today. As the world develops, customer requirements change and grow, creating new demand for new kinds of products and services and opening up new areas of opportunity for firms to meet those requirements.

3. **The Economy**

The economy can impact organisations in both positive and negative ways and both can be demanding. A strong economy and increasing demand for products and services will mean that the firms should think about expanding and that might involve adding extra staff and new facilities. These changes provide opportunities for staff, but also represent new challenges. A weak economy can create even more issues as firms find themselves making difficult decisions that can affect employees' salaries and benefits and even threaten their jobs. The ability to manage both ends of the spectrum is important for organisations that want to maintain a strong brand and strong relations with customers as well as employees.

4. **Growth Opportunities**

Training can be given through traditional classroom settings or, increasingly, through online learning opportunities. Essentially, organisations need to do a good job of assessing employees' capabilities and then take steps to fill the gaps between the present skills and the skills needed to respond to growth.

6.1.3 Forms of Change

Change has become the norm in most organisations. Adaptation, flexibility and responsiveness are the terms used to describe the organisations that will succeed in two basic forms of change in organisations which will be successful in meeting the competitive challenges that companies face. There are two basic forms of change in organisations – planned change and unplanned change.

(1) **Planned Change:** Planned change is the change that results from a deliberate decision to modify the organisation. It is an intentional, goal-oriented activity. The goals of planned change are –

- First, it seeks to improve the ability of the organisation to adapt to changes in its environment,

- Second, it seeks to change the behaviour of its employees.

(2) **Unplanned Change:** Not all change is planned. Unplanned change is imposed on the organisation and is often unpredicted. Responsiveness to unplanned change needs tremendous flexibility and adaptability on the part of organisations. Examples of unplanned changes are changes in government regulations and changes in the economy.

The Role of Change Agents: Change in organisations is unavoidable, but change is a process that can be administered. The person or group that assumes the task of introducing and managing a change in a company is called as a change agent. Change agents can be of two types –

(i) **Internal change agents:** Change agents can be internal, such as managers or employees who are chosen to supervise the change process.

Internal change agents' law has certain advantages in managing the change process.

- They are familiar with the history of the organisations, its political system, and its culture.

- Internal change agents are very cautious about managing change because they must live with the results of their change efforts.

There are also disadvantages of wing internal change agents.

- They may be connected to certain groups within the organisation and may easily be blamed of favouritism.

- Internal change agents might be very close to the situation to have an objective view of what requires to be done.

(ii) **External change agents:** Change agents can also be external, such as external consultants. They bring an outsider's objective view to the organisation.

External change agents have certain advantages.

- They might be favoured by employees because of their impartiality.

- They have more authority in directing changes if employees notice that the change agents are honest, possess significant skills, and have a track record that establishes credibility.

There are also disadvantages of using external change agents.

- External change agents encounter particular problems, including their limited knowledge of the organisation's history.

- They may be viewed with suspicion by organisation members.

6.1.4 Forces of Organisational Change

There are both external and internal forces that result in pressure for change.

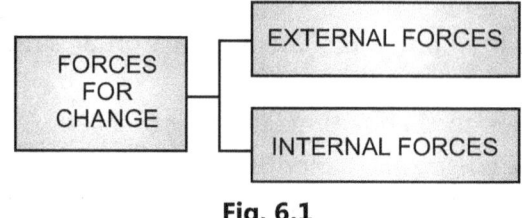

Fig. 6.1

A. External Forces

The major external forces for change are –

1. **Nature of the workforce:** About every organisation must adjust to a multicultural surrounding, demographic changes, immigration and outsourcing.

2. **Technology:** Technology is constantly changing jobs and organisation, for example, faster, cheaper and more mobile computers and handheld devices.

3. **Economic shocks:** Increase and decrease of global housing market, financial sector collapse and global recession.

4. **Competition:** Competition is changing constantly. Competitors are as likely to come from across the ocean as from across town, for example, a rise in government regulation of commerce.

5. **Social trends:** Social trends do not remain stagnant. Firms should constantly adjust the product and marketing strategies to be sensitive to changing social trends. The State Bank of India did the same when it started a zero-balance bank account program for villagers.

B. Internal Forces

1. **Declining effectiveness:** Declining effectiveness is a pressure to change. A firm that experiences its third periodical loss within a fiscal year is without doubt encouraged to do something about it. Some firms react by establishing layoffs and massive cost-cutting programs, whereas others look at the bigger picture, they see the loss as an indicative of an underlying problem, and try to find the reason of the problem.

2. **A crisis situation:** A crisis situation may also stimulate change in an organisation. A strike in the company may force the management to change the wage structure. The resignation of an important decision-maker is one disaster that causes the firm to rethink the composition of its management team and its role in the organisation.

   A much publicised crisis that led to change with Exxon was the oil spill accident with Exxon's Valdez oil tanker. The accident brought about many changes in Exxon's environmental policies.

3. **Changes:** Changes in employee expectations also can set off a change in organisations. A firm that employs a group of young newcomers may have a

different set of expectations from those expressed by older employees. The personnel are more educated than ever before. Although this has its advantages, employees that are well educated demand more of employers. Today's workers are also concerned with career and family balance issues, such as dependent care. The several sources of personnel diversity hold potential for a host of varying expectations among employees.

The work environment at an organisation can also stimulate a change. Personnel who appear tired, unmotivated, and unhappy need to be addressed. This symptom is common in organisations that have experienced layoffs. Employees who have escaped a layoff may feel sad for those who have lost their jobs and may find it difficult to continue to be productive. They may be scared that they will be laid off as well, and many employees lose confidence in their jobs.

6.1.5 Planned Change

A new and scientific way of observing change is 'the planned alteration in the existing organisational system'. Planned organisational change is 'the deliberate effort put by an organisation to influence the *status quo* itself. Planned changes are prepared by the organisation with the purpose of attaining something that might otherwise be unachievable, or accomplishable with great difficulty. Through planned changes organisations reach new boundaries and progress more quickly towards a given set of goals and objectives.

Planned change has two significant goals. Firstly, it seeks to improve the capacity of the organisation to adjust to the changes that are made in its environment. Secondly, it seeks to change employee behaviour. To live in the competitive world, the organisation must respond to changes in a clever way. It must also teach employees new ways of doing things by changing their behaviour.

Features of Planned Change

- It is deliberately, systematically and intentionally undertaken.
- It occurs in all organisations at differing speeds and degrees of importance.
- It happens in all parts of an organisation.
- It challenges the status quo and sets the organisation on a new course.
- It can have positive as well as negative effects. When observed positively, employees accept and carry out changes earnestly. If employees look at it in a hostile way, they tend to go against it vehemently.
- Planned change concentrates on the organisation's technology, products, markets, processes, people etc.
- Planned changes are difficult to create; it is costly and time consuming.

Planned Change Process

Change takes places in stages, till the change is accepted in the organisation. Rarely the change or new concept is accepted in one shot. Changing system/practice/procedure is a cumbersome process. Planning is prepared by an expert group and implementation is made by a different group. The hazards of failure can be decreased if the concerned people are involved in planning, assessment and by good communication, among all the people who will ultimately be touched by the new practice.

Organisational change is a difficult and dynamic process which happens gradually and requires good planning. The steps taken for it are as follows.

Most change management models deliver a series of steps and checkpoints along the change journey that help in managing and monitoring the progress towards a defined and agreed goal. The simplest of these concepts is Lewin's Three-Step Model which suggests that the objective is to

1. Unfreeze the existing position,
2. Change,
3. Refreeze the new position.

1. Unfreezing

The manager as a change agent has to assume the responsibility to disintegrate the shell of satisfaction and self-righteousness among his subordinates. He has to recognise the background factors that contribute and resist change. He should explain to the subordinates the problems with the current situation, the need for change, the pace and volume of proposed change, the direction and the implications of such change. The manager should also clear all the doubts of the subordinates about the proposed change. This is important to prepare the employees to develop a positive attitude about change.

Unfreezing calls loosen the emotional connection with the old work techniques and practices. It helps in unlearning old things and learn new ones. The people are compelled to forget about their old working habits, techniques, routines, etc., for learning new types of behaviour. The forces which drive change should be made strong and the forces which discourage change should be made weak. Rewards may be given to those who accept the change. The employees who resist change should be convinced to accept the change.

2. Change

Once the subordinates become open to change, the manager should introduce the proposed change systematically with the complete co-operation of subordinates. They should be guided and helped to learn new techniques that are implicit in the proposed change. To attain this, two mechanisms are used. It should remain as stable and permanent feature of the system until there is a need for another change. The new roles, associations and behavioural patterns should assume the characteristics of habits. If this is not completed, the people may go back to the old patterns after some time. Change becomes stable only if adequate reinforcements are provided for the desired behaviour. The people should get a genuine feeling that the benefits produced by the change are useful.

Actual change takes place at this phase. New value systems, behaviours, or structures substitute the old ones. This is the action-oriented stage. This can be a time of uncertainty, disorientation, and despair mixed with hope and discovery.

3. Refreeze

At this phase the change becomes permanent. The newly acquired values, beliefs, and structures get refrozen. A new status quo is established at this phase. Refreezing is significant because without it there is nothing.

Unfreezing	Changing (Moving)	Refreezing

1. Recognising the need for change (diagnosis)
2. Increasing the driving forces of change
3. Decreasing resisting forces of change (overcoming)
	1. Making changes in all components
	2. People
	   (a) Individual components
	   (b) Group components
	3. Task components
	4. Structural components
	5. Technology components
		1. Reinforcing the newly learned behaviour (reward)
		2. Finding "FITS" between organisational components that are supportive of new behaviour
		3. Maintaining "FITS" between organisational components so as to find a moving equilibrium

6.1.6 Resistance to Change

In today's economy, change is all-pervasive in organisations. It occurs constantly, at quick speed. Because change has become a daily part of organisational dynamics, employees who oppose change can actually cripple an organisation. Resistance is an unavoidable reaction to any major change. People naturally get scared if they feel their security or status is threatened. **Folger** and **Skarlicki** claim that "organisational change can generate scepticism and resistance in employees, making it difficult or impossible to execute organisational improvements".

If the management does not know, accept and put efforts to work with resistance, it can weaken even the most well-intentioned and well-conceived change efforts. **Coetsee** states "any management's ability to achieve maximum benefits from change depends in part of how effectively they create and maintain a climate that minimises resistant behaviour and encourages acceptance and support".

It is difficult for organisations to stay away from change, as new concepts promote growth for them and their members. Change happens for many reasons such as new staff roles; rise or reduction in funding; acquisition of new technology; new missions, vision or goals; and to reach new members or customers. Changes can create new opportunities, but are often met with criticism from the people within the group that resist change.

Managers usually face the problem of resistance to change because –

(i)   New habits are required.

(ii)   Of homeostasis.

(iii)   People require a steady state of their fulfilment.

(iv)   Fear of change disrupts their working.

(v)   All changes have some cost.

Factors in Resistance to Change

Factors affecting resistance to change can be identified in persons as well as in a group.

(A) Individual Resistance: It can be recognised in the following three ways –

1. Economic Factors

People usually think that they will be badly affected by the change in terms of their need satisfaction which is –

   (a)   Skill advancement: Because of advancement of technology and methods which the old people cannot deal with, they fear that they will be replaced or they will get degraded in the organisation.

   (b)   Economic loss: Those employees who cannot adapt with the new changes fear their economic loss.

   (c)   Incentives scheme: Incentives like bonus etc. will be lost because of change as they need new skills.

2. Psychological Factors

These are based on employees' attitudes, emotions and sentiments which are –

   (a)   Hurt ego: A change may hurt the ego of an individual as it will expose his weakness.

   (b)   Work pattern: People do not want to upset their work pattern and existing stability of their life.

   (c)   Less of tolerance: People are less tolerant towards changes as it upsets their routine work of life.

   (d)   No trust in change: People usually do not trust the change agent (the management).

   (e)   Unknown result: People feel that the results of change are not certain and can give a bad result.

3. Social Factors

People require social need satisfaction through mutual communication. For this they form their own social groups at their workplace. They usually assist the change as these needs are affected by it which is because of –

   (i)   Maintaining existing social interaction: People desire to maintain already existing social communication as they are used to it, hence resistance to change.

   (ii) Change by upper social class: People think that the change is done by the upper social class for their own benefit and thus create interference in their own work, hence, they resist change.

(B) Group Resistance

People may notice the change in person but they communicate it in the form of group, hence the group itself becomes a source of resistance. It can be –

   (i) According to group dynamics. Group dynamics decides the behaviour of the group member towards accepting or rejecting the change. If they are from the similar group it will then become more effective.

   (ii) The influential members of the group try to fulfil their own requirements by a uniform response for a change as is much prevailed in the labour unions.

Organisational Resistance

Organisations also resist change because of –

   (a) Elaborating past victories by a particular way of working hence become too stiff to change and thus are left far behind the newer organisations.

   (b) Stability of the established system which has particular fixed rules like authority, relationship and providing reward and punishment system, etc.

   (c) Limitation of resources for new technology.

   (d) Agreement with other organisations who do not like changes.

Someone has said rightly that there are three types of companies –

   (i) Those that make things happen.

   (ii) Those who observe things happen.

   (iii) Those who wonder what happened.

Thus, it shows the difference between changes that are initiated by firms and changes that are resisted by firms. **Miles and Snow** have classified them into the following four categories. They are –

1. Defenders

   (i) Concentrate on small market products and keep it.

   (ii) Emphasise on

   (a) Cost effectiveness.

   (b) Central control and

   (c) Intensive planning.

   (iii) Less emphasis on environmental scanning.

2. Prospectors

   (i) Search and plan new market products regularly.

   (ii) Use broad environmental scanning.

   (iii) Emphasise on decentralised control.

   (iv) Keep some sources for utilising in future.

3. **Analysers**

These lie in between the above two and at times act as defenders and occasionally as prospectors.

4. **Reactors**

The specific environment of such organisations is changing but they fail to adjust hence they have to accept one of them for their continued existence.

6.1.7 Managing Resistance to Change

John Kotter and Leonard Schlesinger offered six ways of overcoming resistance to change, which highly relies on the situation. More than one of these methods may be used in any given situation.

1. **Education and Communication:** If the logic and advantages of the change are described early to the team members, resistance can be decreased. This can be attained through one-to-one discussions, memos, group presentations, or reports. This tactic assumes that the source of resistance lies in misinformed or poor communication. If the team members receive complete details and have their misunderstandings cleared up, their resistance will diminish. Once people accept the idea, they will implement the change. The only problem is that this is a time-consuming process, if too many people are to be communicated with.

2. **Participation and Involvement:** Resistance to change can be decreased or removed by those who are involved to take part in the decision of the change through meetings and induction. It is difficult for people to resist a change decision in which they took part; once people get an opportunity to contribute ideas and become a part of the change process, they will be less inclined to see it fail. On the other hand, working in committees or task forces is a time-consuming activity, and hence it takes a long time to bring about a change.

3. **Facilitation and Support:** Easing the change process and providing support for those held up in it is another way that managers could handle resistance. Retraining programs, giving free time after a difficult period, and offering emotional support and understanding may also help. This emotional support can be given through empathic listening, offering training and other kinds of help. Such facilitation and emotional support helps a person to efficiently deal with their adjustment problems. This process consumes a lot of time and there is no warranty that it will always work.

4. **Negotiation and Agreement:** It is sometimes necessary for a team leader to negotiate with potential resistance or exchange something that is important to decrease the resistance. For example, if the resistance is from people who have power in the team, a specific reward package can be negotiated that will meet their individual requirements, though in some cases this may be an easy way to gain acceptance. It is likely that this could be a costly way of effecting changes as well. Also, if the use of this strategy comes to public knowledge, others might also want to try to negotiate before they accept the change.

5. **Manipulation and Co-optation:** The team leader seeks to bribe the important members who are resisting by giving them a significant role in the change decision. The team leader's advice is sought after, not to reach a better decision but to get their endorsement. Some of the co-opting methods include selectively sharing information and deliberately structuring particular kinds of events that would win support. This can be a fast, easy and cheap strategy to gain support. However, the purpose will be defeated if people feel they are being manipulated.

6. **Explicit and Implicit Coercion:** The team leaders can force the members to accept the changes by threatening them with loss or transfers of jobs, lack of promotion, etc. Such methods, though not unusual, is more difficult to gain support for future change efforts. This strategy can be particularly applied when changes have to be enforced quickly or when changes are of a temporary nature. Though speedy and effective in the short run, it may make people angry and resort to all types of bad behaviours in the long run.

6.2 Organisational Development

6.2.1 Introduction

The term 'Organisational Development' is a systematic planned approach to improve enterprise effectiveness. Organisational development refers to a series of strategies, systems and procedures for carrying out planned organisational change as a measure to meet the changed circumstances in which modern organisations survive, or actively familiarise themselves to their environment. The concept of organisational development was developed in the 1950s and 1960s. It was made famous by theorists and academicians like **Blake and Mouton, Shepard, Beckhard and Koontz**.

Organisational development is based on scientific awareness of human behaviour and organisation dynamics. It seeks to use behavioural data to change the principles, attitudes, values, strategies, structures and practices, etc. to assess the organisation to form an internal environment of openness, trust, mutual confidence and collaboration and to help the members of the organisation to communicate more efficiently in pursuing organisational goals. Thus, the organisation can better adjust to competitive actions, technological advances, and the fast pace of other changes in the environment. Organisational development assists the managers in identifying that organisations are systems with dynamic interpersonal relations that hold them together.

The understanding principle of organisational development is the attempt to change groups, units and complete organisations so that they would support and not substitute, change efforts. Thus, it develops organisation, allowing it to become more responsive, more effective, and more capable of organisational leaning and self-renewal.

6.2.2 Meaning and Definitions of Organisational Development

Organisational development is a field of theory, research and practice dedicated to expanding the effectiveness and knowledge of people for accomplishing more successful organisational performance and change.

Organisational development is a process of continuous diagnosis, action planning, implementation and evaluation with the aim of transferring skills and knowledge to organisations for improving their capacity to solve problems and manage the future change.

"Organisational development represents a response to change, a complex educational strategy purporting to change the beliefs, attitudes, values and organisational structures with a view to effectively adapt to new technologies, markets and challenges and the unsteady rate to change itself".

– Bennis

"Organisational development is an educational strategy which focuses on the whole culture of the organisation in order to bring about planned change".   **– Keith Davis**

"Organisational development is a planned, organisation wide and managed from the top efforts aiming to increase an organisation's effectiveness and health through planned interventions in the organisational processes, employing behavioural science knowledge".

– R. Beckhard

"Organisational development is a long-range effort to enhance an organisation's problem-solving capabilities, and its ability to cope with change in its external environment with the aid of change agents".   **– French and Bell**

"Organisational development as a systematic method of introducing change, based on a structural model for thinking and moving in a programmatic sequence of steps from individual learning to organisational application, concentrating upon the silent and frequently negative qualities of culture which dictate actions contradicting the business logic; stressing, confronting and resolving conflict as prerequisites to avoid problem solving; and using techniques of organisational study and self learning to achieve the required change".

– Blake and Mouton

After analysing the definitions, organisational development presents that it is the process of bringing change in the entire aspects of the organisation. Organisational development must be managed from the top. The desired organisational outcomes of the organisational development efforts include increase effectiveness, problem solving, adequacy and adaptability. For human resource development, organisational development attempts to provide opportunities to be "human" and to increase awareness, participation, and influence. The main goal is to integrate individual and organisational objectives.

6.2.3 Characteristics of Organisational Development

Organisational development (OD) can be defined as a method for bringing change in the complete aspect of the organisation, rather than concentrating on individuals, so that change is easily absorbed. According to **Warren G. Bennis**, the chief characteristics of organisational development are the following –

1. **Planned Change:** The chief feature of the OD is to apply the changes in a planned way. It clearly means that OD is not a process under which the changes are introduced all of a sudden but is a process which involves an intensive study of the

plan and then the change is introduced slowly or by phases. Under the OD, a plan is carefully mapped out to create co-ordination between the different parts of organisation system and the dynamic environment.

2. **Organisational Level Changes:** Under OD the complete organisation is looked upon in its entirety. It is an accepted fact that if changes in a particular department are made it will have an effect on the other departments as well. It is impossible to introduce changes in one specific department and leave out the remaining departments. Therefore, under OD changes are introduced keeping in mind the entire organisation.

3. **Long-Term Change:** In OD not only the short-term effect changes but also long-term effect changes are introduced. These changes maintain the efficiency, effectiveness and satisfaction of the members of the organisation for a long time. In order to attain this goal, no plan can be prepared overnight. It takes a long time to prepare and execute such a plan. This period can range between a few months and, in some circumstances, a few years.

4. **Dynamic Process:** It is very obvious that OD is not a process that can be finished in one go. It takes a great deal of time in planning and implementing it. It is quite possible that during this phase there may be some change in the objectives of the organisation or changes may take place in some other factors. These changes shall automatically necessitate changes in the process of the OD. Thus, it can be said that the OD is not a process that does not need a re-look. Changes have to be made to make it effective when required.

5. **Change Agent:** A great deal of efforts has to be put in for the collection of statistics and their analysis in order to make preparations for the organisational development. This work cannot be performed by some regular member of the organisation. It needs a specialist. They are called from outside the organisation. They are called Change Agents/Catalysts. Under the process of the OD the members are not told to do the work by themselves, instead they are supplied with prepared plans. Their only job is to extend their co-operation in implementing the plans.

6. **Emphasis on Intervention and Action Research:** Under OD the organisation system is interfered with. Interference with the organisation is not just a useless tinkering or some meddlesome unprofessional exercise but it is a planned activity. Before any planned activity becomes functional, a lot of research work goes into its preparation. Research needs survey, collection of data and analysis. It is only on the basis of this that interference is determined—what is to be done, and how it is to be done.

7. **Managed by Top Level:** The entire process of OD right from the thought down to the level of implementation and the feedback is dealt by the top-level managers. This is a job that is to be completed on a large scale; the interest of all the departments is kept in mind. That is why the whole process is finished with the

assistance of top-level managers and the specialists. In case there is any requirement, information can be gathered from the middle-level or lower-level managers. But they are not involved directly in this process. The top-level managers are committed to their work and they complete this process successfully.

8. **Problem-Oriented:** Every organisation has several problems and there are many ways to solve them. The purpose of OD is to improve the problem-solving methodology that is available in the organisation. Thus, it can be said that OD is a problem-oriented process.

9. **Action-Oriented:** OD is an action-oriented ideology. It means that the research which is undertaken in this process is not meant to be kept only in the files but is to be implemented. The problems that require solutions get treated with the help of this research. The OD not only tries to understand the problems but actually removes them and thereby assists in developing the organisation.

10. **Group-Oriented:** In the process of OD group activities are given more importance than the individual activities. Every effort is made to increase the group effectiveness; predominantly the group discussion is adequately encouraged. At the same time, the group members are motivated to have better mutual relationship.

11. **Focus on Better Performance:** The OD is an ideology that emphasises on better work performance. Usually it is considered to be a solution only for the sick industrial units. However, it is in fact an incorrect thought. Improvement is needed for all the units whether they happen to be sick or healthy. Thus, it is said that OD is not connected to any particular type of units but is needed by any such unit which immediately needs improvement and improvement is required by every unit.

13. **Better Adjustment Possible:** OD is the ideology which increases the prospects of better co-ordination. It means accepting the dynamic environment together and moving ahead effectively. It is, really, very important to mingle with the dynamic environment and progress quickly towards success. Those establishments who fail to do so fall behind and their future is certain. Therefore, OD provides a unique strength to the organisation and makes it able to face any problem successfully.

14. **Related with Management:** OD is the result of the thinking on the part of the managers. It is only the managers who feel its requirement, prepare it with the help of the experts, apply it and get feedback. Hence, it can be said that OD is connected to the management. In other words, without management OD will not exist.

15. **Goal Setting and Planning:** Since OD is concerned with the complete organisation, the change agent defines the goals of the group and will see to it that together they all work to attain them.

16. **Normative Re-educative Strategy:** Organisational development is based on the principle that *"norms form the basis for behaviour and change is a re-educative process of replacing old by new ones"*.

Organisational development is based on well-established principles concerning the (i) individual and (ii) group behaviours in the organisation and hence it is very easy for the OD practitioners to introduce the changes that are needed by educating them.

6.2.4 Objectives of Organisational Development

The programme of organisational development is designed and executed in accordance with the requirements of an individual organisation. But the goal of these programmes is to increase organisational effectiveness by developing new organisational culture and competencies. More specifically the programmes of organisational development are pursued with the following objectives.

The aim of organisational development technology is to develop new ways of handling organisational problems. The main focus is on improving productivity, morale and satisfaction of employees in an organisation. It is not difficult to list the other significant objectives of OD.

The chief objectives of the organisational development are the following –

1. **To Change the Organisation Culture:** The primary objective of OD is to create a change in the culture of the organisation. There is a need to make comprehensive changes in the organisation so as to allow it to face the modern dynamic environment. This is, however, not possible without creating changes in the culture of the organisation.

2. **To Increase the Organisation Effectiveness:** The second major objective of OD is to improve the effectiveness of the organisation. Effectiveness is very much related to the attainment of goals. An organisation that succeeds in attaining all its goals is called an effective organisation. OD renders an organisation sufficiently capable to attain all its goals efficiently and easily.

3. **To Increase Sense of Belongingness:** OD is needed to increase the sense of belongingness among the members of the organisation. In this, an atmosphere is created which communicates a sense of pride to the people that are working in it. As a result, they develop a sense of belongingness to the organisation.

4. **To Create the Climate of Openness:** It is important to have an open environment in the organisation. The employees can communicate themselves freely only by living in an open atmosphere. OD takes a special care of this feature so that the employees are provided an environment in which they can communicate openly. This gives them extra confidence which results in co-operation.

5. **To Increase Participation:** The need of OD is to improve the employees' participation in the decision-making. This is the requirement that the employees should take part in making decisions in the organisation. But it is not the case and this is hardly ever observed. This object can be attained through the medium of OD. Under OD, efforts are made to increase the sense of belongingness to the organisation among the employees. The moment this sense of belongingness

becomes a part of the employees' attitude, they begin to take interest in the decisions.

6. **To Increase the Sense of Humanity:** The goal of OD is to increase the sense of humanity among the people. In order to make complete use of people's capability, they are required to be treated kindly. The primary condition for implementing OD is that the manpower should not be treated only as a source of production but they should be treated as human beings.

7. **To Reduce the Dysfunctional Conflicts:** Dysfunctional conflicts give negative results. It is important for every organisation to not allow dysfunctional conflicts to breed. In case, these dysfunctional conflicts raise their head, they should be solved instantly. OD advocates checking such conflicts.

8. **To Increase Enthusiasm:** OD aims to increase people's enthusiasm. In this, an atmosphere is created which motivates the people to face challenges of huge dimensions happily. The managers also begin to set challenging but attainable goals for themselves.

9. **To Enhance Adjustment Capacity:** The objective of OD is to improve the capacity of adjustment of the organisation. The factors that rule the environment continuously go through changes. Such a dynamic atmosphere requires absolute adjustment that alone can guarantee moving along nicely. OD provides such strength to the organisation that it can face any change without difficulty.

10. **To Enhance Satisfaction:** The objective of OD is to improve the satisfaction level among the members of the organisation. OD creates an atmosphere that is characterised by an absolute sense of satisfaction and a complete healthy outlook. Any person working in such an environment will be completely satisfied.

In brief, it can be said that the purpose of OD is to increase the effectiveness of the organisation and increasing the satisfaction of all the related parties.

6.3 Work Stress

6.3.1 Introduction

Our present life is full of stress where rapid changes are happening in the environment. Urbanisation, industrialisation, unemployment, poverty, career planning, etc. are causing stress in life. In organisational life planning, participation, communication, transaction and reputation have become important issues with its dissatisfaction attached. Stress is a part of life and it cannot be avoided. And stress is multiplied with increase in size and number of activities. Hence, the modern manager should know the causes of stress and apply strategies for decreasing it.

Stress is a difficult concept that does not lend itself to a simple definition. It can best be understood in terms of the internal and external conditions that are required for its arousal and the symptoms by which it is recognised. Its identifiable symptoms are both psychological and physiological. Stress carries a negative connotation for some individuals, as though it is something that can be avoided. This is unfortunate, because stress is a great asset in managing lawful emergencies and attaining peak performance.

Everyone experiences stress in differing degrees and types. In truth, in today's time, stress has become an essential part of everybody's life. One is capable of managing stress more effectively if one knows what stress actually is.

6.3.2 Meaning and Definitions of Stress

Stress can be understood as the body's response to a hostile situation, which makes a person angry and even frustrates him. Stress can be experienced not only at work but also at home. As we all know our bodies intuitively respond to any changes in the surrounding environment.

Hence, stress implies that something unusual happening in the environment increases stress. It can either be caused naturally or it is man-made. A problem need not necessarily cause stress. If one is not able to solve the problem then that becomes stressful. It has also been scientifically proved that those who are often exposed to stressful situations suffer more from nervous breakdowns as well as physical and mental anguish.

For an outsider, stress is an occurrence that will make a person lose himself mentally, physically and psychologically. It is often seen as a conclusion of a breakdown where all the systems of an individual become less motivated to continue.

According to **J. C. Quick and J. D. Quick**, "*Stress, or the stress response, is the unconscious preparation to fight or flee a person experiences when faced with any demand*". According to **A. Mikhail**, "*Stress refers to a psychological and physiological state that results when certain features of an individual's environment challenge that person, creating an actual or perceived imbalance between demand and capability to adjust that results in a non-specific response*".

Some useful definitions of stress which have been developed are as given below –

"*Stress arises when individuals perceive that they cannot adequately cope with the demands being made on them or with threats to their well being*".   **– R. S. Lazarus**

Stress, is defined as "*A perceptual phenomenon arising from a comparison between the demand on the person and his or her ability to cope. An imbalance in this mechanism, when coping is important, gives rise to the experience of stress and to the stress response*".   **– T. Cox**

"*Stress results from an imbalance between demands and resources*".

                                     – Lazarus and Folkman

"*Stress is the psychological, physiological and behavioural response by an individual when they perceive a lack of equilibrium between the demands placed upon them and their ability to meet those demands, which, over a period of time, leads to ill health*".   **– Palmer**

A simple definition that can be used is "*Stress occurs when pressure exceeds your perceived ability to cope*".   **– Palmer**

6.3.3 Nature of Stress

Following are the characteristics of change –

1. **It is the result of environmental factors:** Stress is caused due to various environmental factors. It means the total sum of all the factors that surrounds us from all the sides and thus affects us, like technical changes, economic condition, organisational policies, social help, etc. For example, a person holding some superior position will always be under stress.

2. **It may be positive or negative:** Stress can have positive as well as negative effects. The positive effect is that it helps us to do something which will in turn increase our efficiency and thus we can make some progress, whereas, it's negative effect leads to anger, sadness, disbelief, etc.

3. **It may be temporary or long-run:** The nature of stress can be a prolonged one or temporary. There are ample situations in life where one gets rid of stress very quickly and easily. On the other hand, there are situations in life which prolongs the stress and thus it leads to dangerous diseases.

4. **It represents a very significant cost to organisations:** Stress and efficiency are negatively correlated. If the employees are stressed out over something, then their efficiency will get reduced automatically, as a result of which the costs goes up and vice-versa. Stress is an important part of any organisation's costs. The organisations which want to control their costs shall have to control the stress costs even before handling their other costs like labour, material, etc.

5. **It may result in multiple deviations:** Stress leads to various deviations in an individual, like, physical, psychological and behavioural. Physical deviation leads to heart diseases and high blood pressure. Psychological deviations lead to depression. Similarly, behavioural deviation leads to aggression and absenteeism.

6. **It is individualistic:** Stress has different effects on different individuals. Some people can face stress very bravely and have a greater degree of toleration. They are encouraged by it and do not get afraid of it and thus start putting in more work. On the other hand, some people have very little resistance and get nervous by stress. They start trembling even to face daily issues causing stress.

6.3.4 Sources of Stress/Work Stressors

There may be a number of conditions in which people may feel stress. Conditions that have a tendency to cause stress are called stressors. Although even a single stressor, like the death of near one, may cause major stress, usually stressors unite to press a person in several ways until stress develops. The different stressors can be grouped into four categories – individuals, groups, organisational, and extra-organisational. Within each group, there may be numerous stressors. Though, stressors have been classified into these categories, all ultimately get down to the individual level and put stress on individuals.

The antecedents of stress or the so-called "stressors" impacting on employees are shown hereunder. These causes come from both (i) outside and (ii) inside the organisation. These come from the (i) groups and (ii) employees themselves.

Fig. 6.2: Sources of Stress

A. Individual Stressors

There are a lot of stressors at the level of an individual, which might be produced in the context of organisational life or his personal life. There are many such events, which may work as stressors. These are life and careers changes, personality type, and role characteristics.

1. **Life and Career Changes:** Stress is generated by many changes in life and career. Research studies show that generally, every change generates stress. Individuals in newer places experience such state of transition of stress. Young adults between 20 and 30 years of age have made more reports of stress than the older people. Stress has been found more amongst urban population than rural, and greater in higher educational categories.

2. **Personality Type:** Personality characteristics have also become a source of stress. People who have a higher work ethic almost burn themselves out. They (also known as workaholics) are always in a rush and are always seen to be walking fast, eating fast, talking fast, doing two or more things at a time, constantly feeling pressure of time, measuring success in terms of quantity, being more aggressive and competitive, and feeling boredom during leisure period. These people experience more stress.

3. **Role Characteristics:** There may be role stress either due to role conflict of role ambiguity. Role conflict occurs because there is disagreement between two or more roles. When people become members of many systems like family, club, voluntary organisation, work organisation, etc., they are expected to complete certain

obligations to each system and to fix them into defined places in that system. In several situations, the different roles may have demands that conflict and people experience stress, as they are not capable of fulfilling the conflicting role needs.

B. Group Stressors

Group interaction has an effect on human behaviour. Therefore, there may be some factors in group processes which act as stressors. Following are the major group stressors.

1. **Lack of Group Cohesiveness:** Group cohesiveness is significant for satisfying a person's in-group interaction. When they are not given a chance for this cohesiveness it becomes very stressing for them as they get negative reaction from group members.

2. **Lack of Social Support:** When individuals get social support from members of the group, they are able to satisfy their social needs and they are better off. When this social support does not come, it becomes stressing for them.

3. **Conflict:** Any conflict arising out of group communication may be stressful for the people, be it interpersonal conflict, among the group members or inter-group conflict.

C. Organisational Stressors

An organisation is composed of individuals and groups and, therefore, individual and group stressors exist in organisational context. On the other hand, there are macro level dimensions of organisational functioning, which operate as stressors. The major organisational stressors are as follows –

1. **Organisational Policies:** Organisational policies provide guidelines for taking action. Unfavourable and ambiguous policies may influence the functioning of the individuals badly and they may experience stress. Thus, unfair and arbitrary performance assessment, unrealistic job description, frequent reallocation affectivities, rotating work shifts, ambiguous procedures, inflexible rules, inequality of incentives, etc., work as stressors.

2. **Organisation Structure:** Organisation structure provides formal relationships among people in an organisation. Any defect in organisation structure like lack of opportunity of participation in decision-making, lack of opportunity for advancement, high degree of specialisation, excessive interdependence of different departments, line and staff conflict, etc. work as stressors as relations among people and groups do not work efficiently.

3. **Organisational Processes:** Organisational processes also have an effect on individual behaviour at work. Faulty organisational processes like poor communication, poor and insufficient feedback of work performance, unclear and conflicting, unfair rules, unfair control systems, insufficient information flow cause stress for people in the organisation.

4. **Physical Conditions:** Organisational physical conditions have an effect on work performance. Thus, poor physical conditions like crowding and lack of privacy, excessive noise, excessive heat or cold, pressure of toxic chemicals and radiation, air pollution, safety hazards, poor lighting, etc., create stress for people.

D. Extra-Organisational Stressors

Most analysis of job stress disregards the significance of outside forces and events that have a huge impact on employees. Taking an open system viewpoint of an organisation, it is clear that job stress is not just restricted to things that happen inside the organisation during working hours. Researchers recognise extra-organisational stressors such as (i) societal, (ii) family, (iii) economic, (iv) financial, and (v) residential conditions, etc.

An individual's family has a big effect on personality development. A brief crisis in the family such as (i) the illness of a family member or (ii) long strained relations with the spouse can act as an important stressor for the employee.

Sociological variables such as (i) race, (ii) sex, and (iii) class can also become stressors. Sociologists have noted, over the years, that "have-nots" may have more stressors than the "haves". In a recent research it was found that women who work in organisations that are dominated by males are under continuous stress than men. The same is true of the local community or regions that one comes from.

6.3.5 Consequences of Stress

Stress has various consequences. As we have noted earlier, it is positive which results in more enthusiasm, energy and motivation. It can also be negative which results in producing individual consequences, organisational consequences and burn out.

It must be noted that most of the factors that are listed above are interrelated. If the category for a consequence seems somewhat arbitrary, be aware that each consequence is categorised according to the area of its primary influence. For example, an alcoholic abuse is shown as an individual consequence; however, it also effects the organisation the person works for. An employee who drinks on the job may perform poorly and create a hazard for others.

A. Individual Consequences

The outcomes are the individual consequences of stress that mainly affect the individual. Even the organisation may suffer, either directly or indirectly; however, it is mainly the individual who pays the real price. Stress may reduce psychological, behavioural and medical consequences.

1. **Behavioural Consequences:** The behavioural consequences of stress may harm the individual under stress or others. For example, smoking is one such behaviour, wherein, people who smoke will tend to smoke more during stress although the relationship is less well-documented. Other examples are alcohol and drug abuse, violence, accident proneness and appetite disorders.

2. **Psychological Consequences:** The psychological consequences of stress relates to a person's people experience. For example, too much stress at work causes depression and individuals find themselves sleeping too much or too little. It may also lead to sexual difficulties and family problems.

3. **Medical Consequences:** The medical consequences of stress affect a person's physical well-being. For example, heart diseases, strokes, backaches, headaches, ulcers, stomach-related disorders, intestinal-related disorders, skin conditions and many.

B. Organisational Consequences

Any of the individual consequences that we have discussed above, can also affect the organisation. Other stress results may have more direct consequences for organisations which include withdrawal, decline in performance and negative changes in attitudes.

1. **Performance:** One of the most clear organisational consequences of over stress is a decline in performance. For managers, this may mean disruptions in relationships or faulty decision-making as a person becomes irritable and hard to get along with. For operating workers, this means poor quality work or drop in productivity levels.

2. **Withdrawal:** Stress also leads to withdrawal behaviour. Absenteeism and quitting are the two most significant forms of withdrawal behaviour for an organisation. People usually fall sick or consider leaving the current organisation for good, if they are having a hard time coping with stress in their jobs. Stress may also produce other more subtle forms of withdrawal, for example, an employee may withdraw psychologically by stopping to care about the job and the organisation. Similarly, a manager may start taking longer lunch breaks or missing deadlines. As noted earlier, employee violence is a potential individual consequence of stress, which also has obvious organisational implications as well, especially if the violence is directed at the organisation in general or an employee.

3. **Attitudes:** Attitudes are another direct organisational consequence which is related to employee stress. As we have noted above, morale, job satisfaction and organisational commitment can be all proper, along with the motivation to perform at high levels. Thus, people may be more prone to complain about unimportant things and will do enough work to get by and so forth.

C. Burnout

Another consequence of stress is burnout which has clear implications for both people and organisations. It is a general feeling of exhaustion which develops too much pressure on a person and has too few sources of satisfaction.

Burnout generally develops in the following process. First prime candidates for burnout under certain conditions are people with high aspirations and strong motivation for getting things done. They especially get vulnerable when an organisation limits or suppresses their initiative while constantly demanding that they serve the organisations both ends.

In such cases, an individual is likely to get too involved with his job. In simpler words, a person may keep trying for fulfil his own agenda while simultaneously trying to fulfil the organisation's goals. Fatigue, prolonged stress, helplessness and frustration are the most likely effects of this situation under the burden of overwhelming demands. A person literally exhausts his motivation and aspirations which leads to psychological withdrawal and self-confidence and ultimately burn out. At this stage, a person will start dreading to go to work every day, may put in longer hours to work but may generally display physical and mental exhaustion and accomplish less than before.

6.3.6 Coping Strategies for Stress

Now, the significant question is how to end stress? Stress can be overcome with the help of stress management, but how to manage stress is still another important question. Management of stress is possible with the help of the following methods –

1. Individual Coping Strategies
2. Organisation Coping Strategies

We shall now study in detail both these techniques of stress management.

1. Individual Coping Strategies

It should be clearly understood that it is really possible to get rid of stress. If a person desires, he can change the stressful situation. He can gather courage to face it. In order to get rid of stress, following efforts can be made on the personal level.

(i) **Meditation:** Meditation is a significant way of coming out of stress. Meditation means taking your mind away from the thoughts that disturb you and focussing your mind on some other point. Meditation requires you to sit in some quiet corner of your room with eyes closed. Some 'mantra' is constantly spoken. By doing so the useless thoughts that appear in your mind get removed; this gives you peace, physically and mentally. When such a peace is achieved, stress gets removed.

(ii) **Yoga:** Yoga is becoming famous the last many years. This is a great stress buster. Baba Ram Dev has demonstrated the hidden power of yoga to people. Under yoga some 'asanas' are performed. These 'asanas' bring flexibility to our bones and muscles. Because of it, our nervous system gets activated and our body gets a balanced blood supply. Like this, we attain physical and mental peace. Under such a condition, stress is removed.

(iii) **Exercise:** Apart from meditation and yoga, light exercises also help in decreasing stress. Light exercises consist of walking, jogging, hopping, cycling, swimming, etc.

(iv) **Balanced Diet:** A balanced diet provides us physical and mental strength. Because of it, we face stress with strength. Our food should consist of fruits, vegetables, pulses, bread, milk, etc. in sufficient quantity. Taking too much food or little food than necessary is damaging; hence, we can save ourselves by taking a balanced diet.

(v) **Time Management:** Generally we see that only those people who are stressed fail to complete their job in time. Its cause is absence of time management. Therefore, we can avoid stress by time management. Following things should be remembered regarding time management.

- What is to be done tomorrow should be decided on the eve of today.
- Each day's priorities should be determined.
- Doing only a single job at a time.
- One should try to complete the job quickly after the job is assigned to you.

(vi) Sufficient Sleep: Sleep is equally important for a person like other things. Sufficient amount of sleep refreshes our body and mind and stress cannot trouble us.

(vii) Be Aware of Limits: Some people remain under stress just because all the people are not satisfied with them. Everybody should stay away from doing any evil to others. As far as possible we should be good to others. But even with your best efforts if you fail to make someone happy, do not bother yourself. There is a limit to please everybody. It is better that we understand this truth, the earlier the better. By doing so, you can easily avoid stress.

(viii) Social Support: Generally, it has been seen that no individual is happy all the time. Difficulties do come in life. In such a condition, it is natural for a person to feel stressed. This stress can be removed with the help of social support. Social support means support from the family, neighbours, friends, relatives, colleagues, etc. Everyone needs people so that he can share his difficulties with them. If he gets this support, he will surely come out of the stressful situation. That is why it is very important for every person to maintain his relation with different parts of society so that he can ask for help, when he requires it. Apart from it, seeking God's help gives us mental strength and we can easily get rid of stress.

(ix) Realistic Goals: Generally, people set very high goals for themselves which is sometimes difficult to attain. When their goals are not accomplished, they come under stress. Therefore, we should set goals which are practical and which we are able to achieve. If at times we find that the goals set by us seem to be unachievable, we should be wise enough to modify our goals to make them achievable. Setting goals that are achievable will keep us safe from stress.

(x) Massage: Massage helps our muscles to relax which gives us a sound sleep which in turn refreshes our body. Consequently, stress also gets relieved.

2. Organisation Coping Strategies

There are several factors connected to the organisation which put the employees under stress. Chief among them are the policies, rules, procedures, organisational structure, authorities, responsibilities, etc. When all these factors oppose the wishes of the employees, stress is the natural result. Therefore, apart from implementing individual related methods to get rid of stress, efforts should also be taken at the organisational level to help the employees to be free from stress. Following are the major efforts taken at the organisational level to help the employees to ease out their stress.

(i) **Job Enrichment:** Job enrichment aims at enhancing the significance of work. In other words, such a job which (a) has an extensive field of authority, responsibility and challenge, (b) requires high level of knowledge and experience, (c) opportunities for individual development, (d) freedom of taking decision. The employees feel respected on getting such a job and their interest in the job increases. In this manner, the stress of the employees can be removed by way of job enrichment.

(ii) **Imparting Training:** Every employee wishes to be competent in his work. Keeping this in mind efforts should be made for their training. As a result, they will gain competence in their job and they will get recognition in the organisation. This will keep them happy and stress will not affect them.

(iii) **Participation in Management:** Generally, it has been observed that the employees do not know their role in the organisation. As a result of this, they remain under stress. The reason is that they have no role in taking decisions in the organisation. If the employees are made a part of the process of decision-making concerning their job, then it will be beneficial to them. First, the employees will feel privileged, second, they will come to know about their role in the organisation and ultimately, they will apply the decision whole-heartedly and will not go against them. By being a part of the decision-making process, they will come to realise the organisation's expectations out of them. Their efficiency will rise and they will remain happy and will be capable of facing stress boldly.

(iv) **Open Communication:** Open communication is a channel of getting free from stress. Under this procedure, all the employees listen to others' opinions with an open mind and they will put forward their own views frankly. This procedure leads to a free exchange of orders, suggestions, complaints, etc. Such a situation removes all types of ambiguities and employees remain stress-free.

(v) **Proper Selection:** Improper selection increases the level of stress. If the employees are not assigned work in accordance with their taste and ability, it will have an effect on their efficiency. They will feel stressed. Therefore, while choosing the employees the requirements of the job should always be remembered. Every job should get an experienced man. This will guarantee employees' satisfaction and keep stress away.

(vi) **Effective Reward System:** If the work of the employees is recognised and they are suitably rewarded for their efforts, they will not have to face the problem of stress. Thus, those employees who perform skilfully should always be rewarded. This will improve their efficiency and stress will be removed.

(vii) **Career Advancement Opportunity:** When the employees feel that they are not getting a chance to develop their career, they get stressed. They get a feeling that their capabilities are not completely utilised. They become indifferent towards their job. In such a condition if they are given career advancement opportunities, they can rise above their stress. Every employee wants to get a promotion. This requires competence and an employee can be competent only when he has the opportunities for training and development. Thus, by providing these facilities the way to their promotion can be made smooth. This will bring happiness to them and make them stress-free.

(viii) Employees' Welfare Scheme: There are several employees' welfare schemes which can be applied to ease the pressure from the employees. The reason these welfare schemes were made was because they wanted to help them leave their evil habits. For example, special lectures by experts can be arranged on subjects that talk about the evils of drinking, smoking, deceit, shirking, etc. With the help of the experts they can be familiarised with their rights and duties. Besides that, arrangement can be made in the firm concerning meditation, yoga, etc. By doing so, the employees will get a feeling that the firm is taking interest in their welfare. This will boost their confidence. They will be more competent and stress-free.

(ix) Suitable Policies: In order to run the organisation smoothly, policies are formed. If these policies oppose the expectation of the employees, it creates stress for them. Therefore, the policies have to be suitable to avoid any stress for the employees. The policies should be formed so that it is accepted by both the parties. If, however, some policy has to be prepared and which is not welcome by the employees, it should always be completed only with their consultation. This will surely help in easing out the stress of the employees.

(x) Easy Processes: Many processes are at work in every organisation, for example, decision-making, communication, controlling, etc. If these processes are unclear and difficult, no work will be completed in time and the employees will automatically become stressful. Therefore, all the process in the organisation should be clear and easy. By doing so, everybody will be capable of understanding them and observe them. Consequently, his efficiency will increase and his stress will be removed.

6.3.7 Stress and Task Performance

Management has one major concern which is the negative impact that stress has on job performance. People working under high stress tend to withdraw from contact with the stressor in the form of absenteeism and turnover and may also result in sabotage in extreme cases. At times, workers create mechanical failures in order to take a break from the strain of monotonous work. Any factor that causes negative effects on our psychological and physical well-being is also expected to affect our work behaviour. Exposure to enduring and strong stress influences important aspects of our behaviour at the job thus affecting productivity.

It is a rather complex relationship that appears between stress and performance. It is affected by the nature of specific stressor involved, the difficult of the task being performed and a wide range of personal and situational factors. But, in general, productivity is considered at peak with moderate stress levels. Performance is noted to be poor at low and high stress levels. At low stress levels, an individual may not be energised sufficiently and may not be involved whole-heartedly in his work thus resulting in low productivity. As the stress levels increase from moderate and lower levels, the performance also increases in order to reach the peak level. An optimum stress level exists for any task. If the stress continues to be increasing from this level, an individual becomes too frustrated and agitated thus resulting in performance deterioration.

It is believed that the relationship between stress and performance is curvilinear which follows an inverted u-shaped curve as shown earlier and reproduced here, but the validity of the clear-cut relationship is being questioned. Various behavioural scientists believe that performance actually decreases when stress increases from low levels to moderate levels, even though the decrease rate in performance is less than the decrease rate when stress increases from moderate to high levels.

Stress also impairs the ability to make effective decisions. People under stress are unable to concentrate and are in state of irritation. They are more likely to postpone or avoid making decisions and become impatient. They are more likely to forget some important pieces of available information and are less likely to seek new information. Thus, the quality of decisions they make is low and the cost of wrong decision-making can be very high.

Points to Remember

- **Organisational change** refers to a modification of the organisational structure, processes or goods.
- **Change** is important in organisations to allow employees to learn new skills, explore new opportunities and exercise their creativity in ways that ultimately benefit the organisation through new ideas and increased commitment. Preparing employees to deal with these changes involves an analysis of the tools and training required to help them learn new skills.
- **Reaction change** involves a reflexive behaviour whereas proactive change involves purposive change.
- **Organisational change** is a complex and dynamic process which occurs gradually and which requires a good planning.
- **Organisational development** is based on scientific awareness of human behaviour and organisational dynamics. It seeks to use behavioural knowledge to change beliefs, attitudes, values, etc.
- **Stress** implies that something undesirable happening in the environment gives a rise to a stress response. It can be caused by natural factor or manmade factor.
- Conditions that tend to cause stress are called **stressors**.

Questions for Discussion

1. Enumerate the forces of organisational change.
2. Contrast between proactive and reaction change.
3. Define the process of change.
4. Define organisational development.
5. Enumerate the objectives of organisational development.
6. Explain stress and work stressors.